*WOLF AT THE DOOR*

Cover Design and Interior Format

# WOLF

## AT THE

# DOOR

### DOORS OF THE HEART BOOK 2

# P.F. SPENCER

*To Dale Dyer and Linda Galloway Fitch,*
*new friends, with my thanks,*
*and in loving memory of my grandmother,*
*Zenna Beaver Hurley*

# PROLOGUE

*North Georgia, Summer, 1837*

THE FOREST WAS SILENT. SLOWLY, softly, Jacob crept toward the small, secluded clearing. It was noon, time for him to unpack the bread and cheese his mother had given him that morning, but he had another urge, and it was more powerful than the ache in his empty stomach.

He had seen them in the clearing every day for a week, two Cherokee girls. The elder looked to be about his age, the younger probably her little sister. They were always busy with some task, gathering mushrooms, herbs, or berries, before stopping to eat a midday meal. Today, they were sewing something. It looked, from his distance, like pieces for a quilt.

The older girl was beautiful. Her unbound black hair fell down her slim back almost to her waist. Jacob thought her face was as lovely as a flower, though he had not yet decided *which* flower. He knew only one thing for certain. He wanted to be near her for the rest of his life.

Jacob was sixteen. He longed to bury his hands

in her hair, to tilt up her face to capture her lips with his own, to hold her in his arms, and to protect her always. He had never felt this way before.

He knew how to hunt for food, how to clear the land for crops, and how to build a cabin suitable for a family. He and his father had done all that after they claimed their farmland in the recent land lottery. But now, he was at a loss. He had no notion of how to approach her. Frightening her was the last thing he wanted to do.

He wished he knew her name. He called her Belle in his imagination, but her Cherokee name would be quite different. Though he had mastered only a few words in the Cherokee language so far, he knew that much. His father often traded with the Indians, while Jacob listened and learned.

Lately, there was worrisome news. The Congress in Washington had passed a bill giving white settlers the right to seize Cherokee lands for their own use. There was a rumor that if the Cherokee refused to sell their land to the new settlers, American soldiers would be sent to drive the Indians away. A small band of Cherokee had already traveled to Oklahoma Territory to settle in land that had been set aside as their new country, but most had stayed in their ancestral home places, here in the eastern mountains and forests.

Jacob was unsure how he felt about that. Yes, the land rightfully belonged to the Cherokee, but they should be willing to sell it to the white settlers. The Indians who sold their land would have to leave, of course. He hoped his Belle and her family could find a way to stay.

He knew where her village was located. He even had seen her father when he followed Belle and her sister home one day. The man looked fierce. Jacob had backed away quietly, and then, as soon as it was safe, he had run all the way home.

❦

"I see you. Come here."

Jacob almost dropped his hunting gun. She was looking straight at him. He was crouched behind a tree, but it had failed to hide him.

"I see you. Come here!" she repeated, more loudly this time.

He stood slowly, and cautiously approached the clearing.

"Why have you come here to spy on us? We have seen you here each day this week."

Jacob lost the ability to speak. He choked, cleared his throat, and tried again. "To see you. Wait, you speak English?"

"We attend the Mission school. Why are you spying on us?"

He hesitated, and then decided he might as well tell her the truth. "You are beautiful. I wanted to get to know you, but I didn't know how. I didn't know you could speak English."

"Of course. We speak Cherokee when we are alone, but even my little sister speaks English. But, I do not understand. Why did you want to meet us?"

"I was out hunting a few days ago, and I saw you. I wanted to get to know you, that's all. I thought we might like each other."

"My sister, too?"

"Yes."

"Well then, come and sit with us. It is time to break our fast."

A dusky, rose-colored flush flooded her cheeks. Now, Jacob believed, she was even more beautiful than before.

❦

Over the next days, turning to weeks and then months, they met as often as possible, and Jacob learned her name. Translated from the Cherokee into English, it was Rose. Her namesake was the wild white rose he had seen blooming in the forest. It fit her perfectly.

They each had chores to do, tasks that were sometimes hard, even dangerous. Even so, they tried never to miss their rendezvous. Soon, the little sister sat apart from them, so they could talk privately together. As their friendship blossomed, so did the love in their hearts.

And finally, Jacob achieved a part of his heart's desire. Each day, for a brief time, whether in the heat of summer or in winter's chill, he could hold Rose in his arms, kiss her beloved lips, and bury his hands in her thick, beautiful hair. She loved him too, and Jacob knew he was tasting heaven.

❦

It could never last. When Jacob's father discovered them one day the following summer, he was outraged. How, he thundered to Jacob, could he "take up" with a "savage"? Those "filthy

Indians" were going to be gone soon, and good riddance. The soldiers were coming at last.

And they did. U.S. Army soldiers brutally chased and captured Cherokee individuals and families, burning their homes and businesses, destroying their farms and villages. The soldiers drove their captives into stockades, where they held them with little food or shelter until more Cherokee could be caught.

Over the following months, stretching to two years, the soldiers forced group after group of Cherokee to travel more than twelve hundred miles westward to Oklahoma Territory. Many were sent on foot, and others in wagons, on horseback, or by river boat. The Cherokee were allowed only to bring as much as they could carry.

Once on the trail, the soldiers pushed the people relentlessly over rugged terrain, in blistering sun, soaking rainstorms, wind, sleet, and snow. Horses and people died, wagons broke down, and boats sank.

Many of the once proud and strong Cherokee people, especially the old and the very young, perished of starvation, exposure to the elements, exhaustion, and diseases that included whooping cough, typhus, dysentery, and cholera.

Of the approximately fifteen thousand Cherokee who were forced to travel along what came to be called the Trail of Tears, more than four thousand died.

❧

Jacob was frantic when the soldiers came. He

raced to Rose's village, only to discover that he was too late. It had been burned. The ground was littered with broken and blackened tools, weapons, and pottery. If there were survivors, they were gone. The village was deserted.

Jacob was devastated. He wandered in the mountain forests for three days, desperately searching for Rose and her family. Unable to imagine living without her, he ignored his body's demands for water, food, or sleep.

At last, at dusk on the third day of Jacob's desperate search, Rose's little sister, who had been out hunting for berries, found him as she was hurrying back to her hiding place. Her family were among several hundred Cherokee who refused to leave their homeland, finding refuge in remote mountain hideaways.

Carefully, she took his hand and led him there. When Jacob finally saw Rose, he collapsed at her feet. She and her family nursed him, and kept him with them until the soldiers at last were ordered to stop their pursuit of rebellious Cherokee, and leave the area.

By that time, Rose's family had accepted Jacob and consented to their marriage. Jacob was a valuable asset for them. He could trade with the white settlers, find jobs that paid good wages in goods or currency, and most importantly, bring the latest news back to Rose's family.

Though he often saw one or both of his parents in town, they refused to acknowledge him. They were angry, and ashamed of him, and they instructed Jacob's younger sisters and brothers to shun him also. Jacob was saddened by their attitude, but he was happy with Rose and their growing family. He loved them too much to ever think of leaving them.

He and Rose worked hard and they saved every spare penny Jacob earned. Finally, they were able to buy a small farm of their own.

The spark of love that first ignited in that quiet forest clearing in the summer of 1837, lived on through their children, their grandchildren, and down through the generations until the present day.

# CHAPTER 1

☽

*Fannin County, North Georgia*
*Six Generations Later*

I CHECKED THE CLOCK ON MY rental car's dashboard. The last thing I wanted was to be late.

The sun glinted off the rear window of the car I was following. Blinded for a moment, I blinked hard and the road reappeared, climbing steadily through the mountains. The driver ahead was taking his time, and I was beginning to be anxious.

I took a deep breath and tried to relax and enjoy the scenery. Around almost every bend there was another view of the lush green valley below. Though it was a cool day for late April, I lowered the car's windows a few inches. The spicy scent of pine trees filled the car, and over the engine's soft growl, I imagined I could hear birds calling in the forest that cloaked the mountains on either side of the road. There were a few dogwood trees in bloom, and deep within the forest, I caught glimpses of large shrubs, bright with orange and yellow blossoms. I wondered what they were.

The GPS chirped, pulling my attention back to business. *"Turn left in point two miles, and your destination will be on the left."* I checked the clock again. Relieved, I saw that I was going to be on time after all.

I was rarely nervous when meeting new people, but though the man I was to meet today had been highly recommended to me, I was uneasy.

His name was Thomas R. D. Wolf and, in the photo on his website, his professional smile seemed appropriately predatory. His teeth were blindingly white against his bronze skin and his long, straight black hair fell well below his shirt collar. His face was lean, with prominent cheekbones, a large hooked nose, sparkling brown eyes set off by arched black eyebrows, and a strong chin. He was not classically handsome, but there was something compelling about his face in that photo, and a bit disturbing.

I hoped this journey to see him, the main reason I had come to Georgia this week, was not a mistake.

I continued up the narrow road, turned into a gravel driveway, and parked near a rambling, two-story log home. Next to the driveway, attached to the fence that held his mailbox, was a small sign: Thomas R. D. Wolf, Real Estate.

The log home looked rustic, but it, and its surrounding property, were fastidiously neat, with freshly mown grass and orderly split rail fences. I could see a large, red-painted barn set back and to the right of the house, and I guessed there were other outbuildings just out of sight.

A gravel path led from the driveway to the

house, and pots of colorful pansies were set on either side of the front steps. Two white-painted rocking chairs, with red and gold plaid cushions, sat on the deep porch. There were wide picture windows, as well as narrow sidelight windows on either side of the red-painted front door.

A large coal-black horse, in a corral a short distance away, was eyeing me and dancing restlessly. In the pasture beyond, two other horses grazed peacefully, ignoring me completely.

The door opened, and a man stepped out. He stopped in the shadow of the porch roof.

I got out of the car and swallowed hard. Squaring my shoulders, I strode up the gravel path to his porch. My bravado slipped when I tripped on the first step, and almost fell.

The man, Thomas Wolf, presumably, had stood immobile as I approached, but now he moved quickly. He caught me by my upper arms, and pulled back slightly as though surprised. Then, he grinned the predatory grin I had seen in his website photo. Did he think my almost falling on his steps was funny?

"Well, hello. I'm Tom Wolf, and you must be Suzanna Smith. You need to watch that first step." Laughing softly, he escorted me up the remaining steps, keeping one hand under my elbow.

My cheeks burning, I struggled to regain my composure. "Yes, Mr. Wolf, I am Suzanna Smith. I believe you were expecting me?"

Of course, he was expecting me. Was I losing my mind? My arms were tingling where he had caught me, and so was my elbow, as though he had given me a small jolt of electricity.

Safely on the porch, I thrust out my right hand to shake his. As he took it, I felt the strange electricity again. I glanced up at him, wondering if he felt it too. If so, he was hiding his reaction. He was still grinning that wolfish grin.

I looked away, but not before I noticed the way the skin crinkled at the outer corners of his dark brown eyes, and that he was at least six inches taller than my five-feet-nine. He was lean, though he filled out his jeans and tucked white Oxford shirt extremely well. His rolled-up shirt sleeves displayed muscled forearms and large, well-shaped hands. His website photo had lied. He was much better looking in person.

His black hair was amazing: straight and thick, shining with health, and even longer than in his photo. Brushed back from his forehead and tucked behind his ears, it reached almost to the middle of his back. Millions of women would love to have hair like his. I longed to touch it.

"Just call me Tom," he drawled. His voice was deep and probably unintentionally sensual. I shivered. I was going to have trouble with his voice, and his thick, almost musical, Southern accent. I hoped I could avoid swooning at his feet.

"Cold?" Of course, he had seen me shiver. "Come on inside where it's warmer. These late April days can be chilly."

I nodded. He let go of my arm to open the front door, and ushered me in.

As I stepped into the foyer, my first impression was that the house was as rustic inside as out, but my first impression was wrong. A few steps farther, and I gasped. The house was more spacious than it looked from the outside, but that was not what surprised me. I turned around slowly to take it all in.

I was standing in an open-plan great room. The walls were painted the color of buttery cream, the flooring was polished oak.

Opposite the front entryway, a huge, grey stone fireplace took up most of the back wall. Over it, two large paintings depicted on the left, native warriors dancing in a circle, and on the right, two native women cooking over an open fire. I was not a trained connoisseur of art, but I thought they were both magnificent. It looked as if they had been painted by different artists, and I wondered if they were Cherokee.

Facing the fireplace was a massive couch, covered in rich, dark chocolate leather, and flanked on either side by two matching easy chairs. A glass-topped, wrought iron cocktail table sat in front of the couch with a colorful woolen rug on the floor beneath it.

Wrought iron and glass end tables between the couch and each easy chair held different but complimentary Tiffany-style lamps. A woolen blanket in a red and gold plaid adorned the back of the couch, and interesting, country-style accessories were placed around the room for maximum effect.

To the right, against the wall, there was a wide, floor-to-ceiling bookcase filled with books, geological specimens, and other natural objects, including a bird's nest. Hanging next to the bookcase was a dressed deer hide and, next to that, there was a hallway and stairs to the second floor, leading, I guessed, to bedrooms and baths. To the right of the hallway, there was a handsome oak desk with a matching file cabinet and swivel chair, obviously Tom's office area. The desktop was arranged neatly with stacked file folders, a laptop computer, and another Tiffany-style lamp.

On the front wall to the left of the foyer, under a large picture window, there were two wrought iron chairs upholstered in chocolate leather for Tom's clients. On the other side of the foyer, under a similar window, there was a wrought iron bench, covered in matching leather, but more deeply padded.

Along the side wall opposite Tom's office area, there was an enormous glass-topped wrought iron dining table with a huge Tiffany-style hanging lamp centered over it. The table was surrounded by a dozen wrought iron armchairs, their seats and backs upholstered in dark red and gold plaid wool.

To the right of the table, a large granite-topped island with a built-in wet bar separated the dining area from the kitchen. Four wrought iron stools were pulled up to the island, their padded seats covered in dark red wool.

The kitchen was fitted with what looked like professional-grade stainless steel appliances, granite countertops, and country-style oak cabinets. A flat screen TV was attached to the wall above one of the countertops and was visible from the island.

At the back of the kitchen, there was a sliding glass door. I could see a few feet of red brick paving through the glass, probably a patio and a walkway to the barn.

This was country chic at its finest. Tom seemed especially taken with Tiffany-style lamps. I had not yet seen the rest of his home, but the entire great room was drop-dead gorgeous. Who, I wondered, had decorated this room? If not for the fact that this was Tom's domain, and of course, that it was more than eight hundred miles from my job in Manhattan, I would have been thrilled to move in. I was especially envious of the kitchen. My tiny New York City condo was severely limited in that department.

❦

"Come by the fire and have a seat," said my host, indicating the couch. "You'll soon warm up. Okay if I call you Suzanna?"

I nodded, glancing up at him. "Most people call me Suzi."

His stare was both intense and appraising, and I felt my cheeks warming again.

"Nah. I'm goin' to call you Suzanna."

I shrugged my shoulders and moved to the fireplace. I stood staring into the flames for a few minutes, warming my hands and trying to get my bearings. Now that Tom had directed my attention back on himself and not on his stunning home, I was feeling oddly crowded and more than a little off balance. I had never met anyone like him before. His presence seemed to fill this large, beautiful room to bursting, leaving me feeling slightly breathless.

When, at last, I turned around, he gestured toward my jacket. "Are you warm enough now to take that off? If so, I'll hang it on a peg in the foyer."

He waited, and when I was slow to respond, he spread his hands, and with elaborate patience said, "Okay?"

I nodded again, and began to unbutton the light jacket I had put on that morning. I had assumed I would be taking it off as the day warmed, but the temperature had remained a little too chilly for that. I moved a few steps closer to him and handed it over.

He stood holding it, letting it dangle from one long bronze finger, while he looked me over slowly from head to toe. He seemed not to miss anything I was wearing, and I was certain he was mentally undressing me. He chuckled again. "You'll need to get used to wearin' warmer clothes up here this time of year. And, it's a lot colder at night."

"I'm not going to be here at night!" I crossed my arms over my breasts and clutched my upper arms defensively. What was he assuming?

"Oh, excuse me," he drawled. "I didn't mean to offend you."

I nodded curtly, and sat down in the closest armchair. Oddly enough, I realized that I was not offended, exactly. I was proud of my body. I always had been athletic. I visited a Manhattan gym regularly, and I liked to walk. I preferred to get around the city on foot whenever I had time to do so.

Tom returned from the foyer and sat on the couch near my chair. "So, what can I do for you?" He leaned toward me, still grinning that grin.

"As I mentioned in my email, you were

recommended to me by Daniel Hardy, a genealogist I consulted in New York. According to him you're a realtor and an amateur genealogist, as well as a student of local history." I hesitated a little. "He also said you're Cherokee."

"That's right. Is that important?"

"It might be. I want to trace my grandmother's people. She claimed to be part Cherokee, and was born here in Fannin County. I don't have much information about her parents, and I'm hoping to find out more about them, and go back further, if possible.

"I intend to take a ten-week leave of absence from my job this summer, from early June through the beginning of September, and I'll need to find a place to rent for that time. Mr. Hardy told me you probably could help me with both. I want to get to know this area a bit, and if you can help me trace my grandmother's line back several generations, I'm planning to write her story."

"Are you a writer?"

"Not really. I work in public relations, and that involves quite a bit of writing. But, this would be for me and my brother and our children, so they can know a little about who we are and where we came from."

"Oh? You have children?"

"No, but I hope to one day. My brother and his wife have two boys."

"I see."

I doubted that. "I'll explain. Last year I spent a few days in Wilkes County, Georgia, researching my grandfather Kelly's side of the family. It was a great experience, and I met so many helpful people. I was surprised to learn that both my great-grandfather and great-grandmother Kelly are buried here in Fannin County, in the Methodist cemetery in Epworth. So, you see, all roads led to Fannin County."

"Really? That's interestin'. That cemetery's not far from here. I'll take you there when you come back this summer."

"Thanks. We'll see. Right now, I'm kind of pressed for time. I'm on a one-week vacation from my job in Manhattan. This is a scouting trip, really. I flew into Atlanta and spent the first few days visiting friends and touring the city. I drove up here to Blue Ridge this morning, and just had time enough to check into my hotel and grab some lunch before driving up here. I have to fly back home the day after tomorrow."

"Okay. I should be able to find you somethin' to rent before you need to leave. But, in the meantime, why don't you tell me a little bit more about yourself and your grandmother."

"Okay, well… my last name is kind of unusual. Not, of course, because Smith is an unusual name, but because of an odd circumstance. Smith was my Grandmother Rose's maiden name which, for reasons unknown to me, she kept after her marriage to my grandfather, John Kelly. My mother also kept Smith as her surname when she married my father, James Walker, and when I was born, she bequeathed it to me. I thought I might have a hard time combing through all the Georgia Smiths to find *our* family of Smiths. I'll need help."

Tom nodded, probably hoping I would hurry up and get to the point.

"Grandma was the eldest of seven sisters, and as I mentioned before, she claimed to be part Cherokee. She seemed to have mixed emotions about that, proud, but also slightly ashamed. Her attitude toward her heritage has always puzzled me."

Tom looked closely at me, and gave me a slow nod. "Sure, Suzanna. I'll be happy to help you," he drawled. I was having trouble both with his voice and his slow, sexy accent. They were making me, alternatively, both shivery and much too warm.

"But for now, tell me what you have in mind for a rental. Do you want a condo in town, or somethin' more rustic here in the mountains? I'm guessin' you'll want somethin' completely furnished."

"Yes, I don't want to have to buy or rent furniture for such a short time. But, as to condo or cabin, I don't know yet. Can you show me examples of both? My budget isn't very large, but it's somewhere in the mid-range for this area. I've done a little homework."

"That's good. No surprises, then. And it's good you've come now. The best seasonal rentals are goin' fast as we get closer to summer."

He thought for a minute, and then nodded. "I can show you five different condos and at least four cabins. None of 'em is very big, but they have all the essentials. They're fully furnished with heat, hot and cold runnin' water, workin' appliances, pots and pans, dishes and utensils, bed linens, and towels. You'd have to stock soaps, bathroom tissue and other paper goods, and whatever lotions and whatnot you use." He was grinning again by the end of that statement.

"Of course," I said. He probably had no real intention of insulting me, but there was something about the way he spoke, and the way he looked at me, frankly assessing, that set my teeth on edge.

He made me uncertain whether I wanted to do business with him. But realistically, I had little choice. There was no one else in the area who was both a licensed realtor and an expert in local history. That he was also Cherokee was a huge bonus. It would be great if he was able to help me learn about my possible Cherokee ancestors.

I sighed. I would have to try to get along with him.

"Look," he said. "Have dinner with me tonight, and I'll bring some brochures to show you. If you like the looks of 'em, I'll take you around to see 'em tomorrow. Okay?"

"Dinner? Where?" I had not expected that.

"I'll pick you up at your hotel and take you to Billy's BBQ. Billy Jr.'s a high school friend of mine. He served as an Army Sergeant in Afghanistan and was wounded. He got a medical discharge and as soon as he healed enough to get around again, he headed back up here to help his dad run the family restaurant. The décor is pretty basic, but you can't get better barbeque east of Texas. Or, you could stay here and I could cook dinner for you."

"Stay here?" I croaked, trying to clear my throat. I glanced at my watch. "It's not even two-thirty yet!"

"Dusk still falls pretty early now, and it gets colder, as I mentioned before. I usually try to serve dinner between four-thirty and six, dependin' on the season, so my guests can get home before it's pitch dark. There aren't any street lights on these mountain roads. Much later than six o'clock, and people sleep over. I have five bedrooms."

I stood, poised to leave. "It won't be necessary to cook for me. I really don't understand why you won't show me the brochures now, and take me to one or two places this afternoon?"

He stood too, still smiling. His height was intimidating, and he was standing much too close for comfort. I shivered again and my stomach did a flip-flop.

"Because," he said, "I want to have dinner with you, and spend some time goin' over the brochures this evenin'. I have chores to do this afternoon before dark, but tomorrow we can get an early start. I can show you just the condos and cabins you've chosen to see, or all of 'em if you want. Once we nail down the right rental, we can start workin' on your family's history. You only have one full day left, right?"

I nodded.

"So, we need to get goin' as soon as possible tonight."

I sighed. He was right about needing to get going soon. "Okay. If you'll tell me where this restaurant is, I'll meet you there."

"Oh, I don't think so. It's kind of out of the way. I'll come get you at six-thirty."

He grinned that grin again, with predictable results to my insides. I was sure my face was turning pink, but this time it was partly in anger. I took a deep breath and tried to relax. Realistically,

I would be much better off not looking for a hard-to-find restaurant in the dark.

"Okay. I'll be ready by six-thirty."

We moved to the door and he helped me into my jacket. "I hope you have somethin' warmer than this to wear tonight." He kept one warm hand on my shoulder while he opened the door with the other.

"Yes, I have a coat with me."

"Good. You'll need it." He moved his hand to my elbow and escorted me down the porch steps and out to my car. He waited there until I was in the driver's seat and had my seatbelt fastened before he stepped away.

"See you at six-thirty," he called.

He stood watching me back out of his driveway, and then headed for his corral as I drove away.

I was still feeling the effects of the final jolt of electricity between us when he squeezed my hand in parting.

# CHAPTER 2

❦

BACK IN MY HOTEL ROOM in the town
of Blue Ridge, Fannin County's largest
municipality, I surveyed my scanty wardrobe. I
wished I could pick something to wear tonight
from my closet in Manhattan. For this trip, I had
packed only as much as would fit in an airline-sized
carry-on suitcase.

There was a pair of blue jeans I liked to wear
with brown loafers while traveling. I decided they
would be okay for a barbeque restaurant. The
jeans fit well, and looked presentable. I also had
a soft woolen turtleneck sweater in my favorite
shade of cinnamon brown. It looked terrific with
my dark red hair, and my thick cardigan sweater,
which was striped with dark blue, beige, and more
cinnamon, was a perfect match for the turtleneck.
I would bring my coat for later, in case it really
got that cold.

At least, I would be able to dress more casually
here than in Manhattan. I could leave most of my
business clothing and evening wear in storage.

With that subject covered, I decided to go for
a walk in the town's business district, only a few

blocks away from my hotel. I sat down on the bed to change into walking shoes and yawned. The bed looked so inviting. It must be the mountain air, I thought, as I lay back with my hands behind my head… and fell asleep.

☾

I sat up with a start, wondering what had awakened me. I checked the bedside clock. It was five-thirty already!

Panicked, I stripped off my clothes, and headed for the bathroom. I would have barely enough time to shower, dress, fix my hair, and apply a little makeup. I wanted to be ready before Tom arrived to pick me up.

Forty minutes later, I stepped into the lobby. Tom was there already, leaning over the counter to flirt with the receptionist, a pretty, petite blonde.

She looked up over his shoulder, frowned at me, and said something to him that I was too far away to hear. He straightened, murmured an answer to her, and turned around.

He looked me over carefully and, I guessed, approvingly, because he was grinning the wolfish grin I was beginning to expect. Expecting it, though, did nothing to stop my physical reaction to it. My face was warm. I knew I was blushing again.

"Well! Hi, Suzanna," he said. "I didn't think you'd be ready this early. We'll have to take the long road to Billy's. Our reservation is for seven o'clock. But, that gives us time to get to know each other better. Come on. My car's just outside."

When I glanced back at the receptionist, she was still scowling at me, her pretty face distorted by an expression that bordered on fury. I wondered why she seemed so angry. Mentally, shaking my head, I took the arm Tom offered me.

He behaved like a perfect gentleman. He held the lobby door open for me, guided me to his white, two-door convertible sports car with his hand under my elbow, and opened the car door. Taking my coat, he laid it gently on the back seat, and pushed the passenger seatback upright again so I could get in.

He waited for me to settle myself and fasten my seatbelt before closing the door and going around to the driver's side. He got in, and looked me over again. "Comfortable?"

I nodded, and glanced around the interior of the car. It was an unfamiliar, to me, make and model, sleek and spotless. The dark gray leather seats were soft and smooth, and the dashboard looked like it belonged in an airplane cockpit. The engine purred and whined as he skillfully shifted gears. Obviously, the real estate business in Fannin County was booming.

He must have read my mind, because the next thing he said was, "Don't get the wrong idea. I'm not filthy rich. I just like nice things, and as I live alone with no dependents, I can put most of my income into investments that make money. I've saved, even scrimped, to get where I am today."

"Really?" I was skeptical.

"Really," he replied, nodding his head. "My best friend in college became a whiz kid on Wall Street. He gives me advice from time to time, and it usually pans out. I've been lucky so far. Also, I don't let everythin' ride on one investment."

"That's smart." I was impressed. His immaculate and beautifully decorated home, and now this car, seemed much too expensive to belong to a local real estate agent. This was not Manhattan, after all, or even a large town. The total population of Fannin County was fewer than twenty-five thousand souls, and it was clearly not the most prosperous county in Georgia. I was certain his yearly income would be too small to support what I had seen so far.

"But enough about me," he drawled. "Tell me about what you do in Manhattan."

"I'm a public relations executive and special events manager at a large public relations firm. We handle accounts for both corporate clients and not-for-profit foundations. I can't tell you about individual accounts or name our clients, but it's one of the most prestigious PR companies in the city."

"Have you worked there long?"

"About five years. I majored in Communications in college, and worked for several years in smaller companies before I moved up to the job I'm in now. I put in long hours to earn my pay. Maybe you'd be willing to share your Wall Street whiz kid's expertise some time. I could use some good advice to enhance my income."

As Tom negotiated a tight turn, I noticed that it was already dark. Now, I could see what he meant about the dangers of driving at night in these mountains. One needed to know the roads very well. We had been steadily climbing and I judged we were already at a higher elevation than at Tom's house.

"Where did you go to school?" Tom glanced over at me. "My alma mater is a local campus of our state university. Nothin' fancy."

"I went to Williams College in Massachusetts. It's located in the Berkshire Mountains. The Berkshires are tall hills, really, and tame by western standards, but the area is beautiful. I did a lot of cross country skiing while I was there."

"Wow. I'm impressed. Isn't that a hard school to get into?"

"I was lucky. I got good grades in high school, and I guess they liked my resume. I had done quite a bit of community service and took several AP courses. Everything added up, and I had a good interview. The woman who conducted it was nice, and put me at ease right away. I know that doesn't always happen."

"I think you're bein' too modest. You sound like a brain. Did you get teased a lot? Anybody call you a nerd?"

"No! Of course not! I didn't go to school with kids like that." I laughed self-consciously.

In the dashboard's glow, I could see Tom's face well enough to notice the skeptical look he gave me, one expressive eyebrow raised. Though the light was dim, I could see that his eyes were smiling, the crinkles around them deepening attractively. I laughed again, more softly this time. I was somewhat relieved. He was easier to talk with than I had anticipated.

"Oh, okay." I shrugged. "Pretty much everyone was a nerd at my school. Of course, I've been called that, and worse, but I've never cared. I set my goals early and studied hard to achieve them."

This time, in the low dashboard light, I saw him eye me appreciatively and nod. I seemed to have won some points with him.

A moment later, he said, "We're almost there. I hope you're hungry. The portions are big, and it's not exactly health food."

"Don't worry. My lunch is a distant memory. I should be able to cope."

He swung the car around the last curve and pulled into a large, gravel parking lot. I thought it looked like it was full, but Tom found a space that was too narrow for the huge pick-up trucks and SUVs already parked. There was plenty of room for his sleek sports car.

He came around to open the car door for me and help me out. His touch, as usual, sent tingles up and down my arm. I shivered, and wondered if I would ever get used to that odd sensation between us. Not that I expected to see much of him this summer. Once our business was finished, he would be busy with other clients. At least, I was not blushing this time.

He saw me shiver, of course, and reached for my coat.

"It's okay. I'm not cold. I'm just not accustomed to the climate here."

He looked unconvinced, but closed the car door and led me into the restaurant. The proprietor, Billy, Sr., came bustling up to seat us.

"Hey, Tom. You're a little early, but your table's ready for you. Sit down, and I'll bring you a beer. What will the little lady drink?"

Little lady? I was unsure whether to take offense at that, but Tom read my mind, or maybe it was my face.

"Don't mind Billy. Every woman who comes in here is little to him. See the size of him?"

I looked up at Billy. He was even taller than Tom, and three times as wide. I saw Tom's point.

I took a deep breath and said, "For now, just a glass of water will do, thank you."

Billy looked shocked, but nodded. "Comin' right up. Do you want lemon with that?"

"Yes, please."

Billy waddled away and Tom led me to "his" table.

As we sat down, he said, "Billy always says this is my table. It started a few years ago when I helped him secure a business loan and he's felt obligated ever since. I keep tellin' him there's no need, but he keeps doin' it. I must say though, this place has become so popular, especially in tourist season, it's good to know I don't have to wait for a table."

"There's a tourist season in Fannin County?" My tone was teasing, but though the county's website listed tourist attractions, mostly outdoor activities, I had trouble believing in a *real* tourist season.

"Of course. We're not all hicks. People, sometimes rich people, come for fishin', water sports, hikin', and campin'. Our tourist season runs from late spring through early fall, and then, there's huntin' season after that. We've got other attractions too. We actually do a very nice tourist business."

"Sorry. I didn't mean to offend you. It's just that

it looks so… 'un-touristy' here, if I can use that word." I looked around for a menu.

"Well, we do try to keep up the folksy traditions people expect of us. There aren't any Wal-Marts here, but no Saks Fifth Avenues either, and we don't have any big fancy hotels or office buildin's. But the folks around here are not *all* like the characters in that old movie 'Deliverance.' We have some very well-educated people livin' here. Not everyone wears overalls, and some of us even have all our own teeth!"

He was laughing by the time he ended that speech, not really offended by my teasing. If I lived here this summer, I would find out for myself whether he was exaggerating or not.

A young, apron-clad waiter hurried up to deliver our drinks. Tom thanked him, and told him we would have "the usual."

The waiter nodded and grinned at me before heading toward the kitchen. I stared at Tom, surprised and shocked at his nerve. How dare he order for me without my even seeing a menu!

"Wait! I haven't even seen the menu. How do you know what I want?" I was annoyed but, I realized, I was more surprised than angry.

Tom was off-hand about it. "Oh, Billy doesn't have a menu. He just barbecues whatever meat he has on hand and the vegetables come from his own garden or from local farmers. It all depends on what's in season. Tonight, we'll probably get pork ribs, with boiled new potatoes, early peas, and cornbread. You'll see. Billy knows his way around a barbeque kitchen. His cornbread is somethin' special. And wait 'til you taste his sauce.

You'll just have to trust me."

I must have looked dubious and still a bit annoyed. "Please don't be upset," he said. "I apologize. I should have told you about the no-menu part in advance." He was grinning again. I was sure he was aware of how that grin would affect most women. Much to my annoyance, it certainly had an effect on me!

As soon as I thought I could control my voice, I said, "Okay. Okay. Don't worry. I'll get over it, especially if the food is good."

"Oh, it's good all right," he assured me. "You'll see."

I took a steadying breath and looked around. We were in a large room with a weathered look, as though it might once have been part of a barn. The high ceiling was crisscrossed with heavy dark beams that looked hand hewn, and the walls were wainscoted, painted dark green below and creamy white above. There were sturdy wooden booths and tables, both with padded seats upholstered in a forest-green, leather-like material.

Each table was covered with a green and white checked fabric tablecloth, and set with matching napkins and a small vase of daffodils, elegant touches I would not have expected here. The lighting was discreetly dim, especially near the bar, which was in a far corner.

Every booth and table was taken, as well as all the green-upholstered stools at the bar, where other patrons were standing three deep. The place felt homey and smelled delectable. I could hardly wait for the food to arrive.

While I was inspecting the décor, Tom sat

watching me, occasionally sipping his beer.

I was beginning to feel more comfortable with his scrutiny. Would I still feel comfortable if he wanted to become friendlier? But wait a minute. He was a beautiful man who could probably have any woman he wanted. Even if I wanted him, there was no guarantee he would want me.

"While we're waitin', tell me a little about your background. Where did you grow up? Was it in Manhattan?"

"No. On Long Island. My Grandma Rose and Grandpa Kelly raised my brother, Ron, and me after our parents were killed in a car crash. They burned to death before they could be rescued."

I stopped, but I was not going to cry, not now, not in front of Tom. I looked down. Tom had reached out across the table and enfolded one of my hands in his. There was an expression of compassion on his face. I smiled shakily at him, and withdrew my hand.

"I was three years old and Ron was six. My grandparents lost their only child and their son-in-law in that crash, but Ron tells me they hid their grief from us, took us back to their big Long Island house, and poured all their love into raising us.

"Grandpa died when I was twelve, after a long illness. Grandma's stories about growing up on her parents' poor dirt farm in Fannin County kept Ron and me fascinated when Grandpa's health problems made it necessary for us to be quiet."

"Your grandmother's still alive?"

"No." I looked down at my hands, now in my lap. It was still hard to talk about her illness and death. "Three years ago, she lost her final battle with cancer. I'm still not over it."

"Of course. I understand." There was that compassion again. He really did look as though he understood. "What about your brother? Does he still live on Long Island?"

"No. We sold the house when Grandma got so sick. The proceeds paid for her care in a nursing home in Houston, near where Ron and his wife and my two young nephews live. Now that Grandma Rose is gone, I rarely see them. We're very close, though. We call or text each other every week and share our memories on social media."

Tom made a sympathetic noise.

Uncomfortable now, I took a sip of my water. Thankfully, the waiter appeared with our food just as I was putting my glass down and searching my mind for another topic of conversation. I wanted to be done with talking about illness and death.

The food looked wonderful and smelled even better. It was a welcome distraction, but I was shocked at the immense amount of food on my outsized plate.

"Oh, this is too much. There is no way I can eat all this!"

"Don't worry. Just eat as much as you can. That's all Billy asks of his customers. There are lots of us who can handle Billy's portions just fine. And if you can't, it won't go to waste. He feeds any leftovers that folks don't take home to his pigs."

I laughed skeptically, not sure if he was kidding.

"Don't laugh. He does. And what goes around comes around, to borrow an overused expression.

One day, probably soon, those pigs will be barbequed."

I gasped.

Tom shrugged. "That's just the way it is here, and in lots of other parts of the world, too. Don't let it get in the way of your appetite."

Billy Jr., a younger and thinner version of his dad, appeared at our table, and Tom introduced me.

"Well, now, Miss Suzanna," he said, with a small bow and friendly smile. "Welcome to Billy's BBQ. Dad's in the kitchen right now, but he'll come out to check on you in a little while. How do you like our mountains, and more importantly, how do you like our barbecue?" He loomed over us, smiling expectantly.

I put a bite of barbeque into my mouth and savored the complex flavors. It was delicious, the best I had ever tasted. And, just as Tom had predicted, there were boiled baby potatoes and early peas. In the center of the table, fluffy yellow cornbread and a small container of whipped butter were nestled in a green wicker basket lined with a white cloth napkin.

I chewed blissfully and swallowed. "Billy, it's delicious. I've never had better. Thank you. And the mountains are beautiful!"

"Thank *you*," he responded, his grin now spread from ear to ear. "I'll tell Dad. He'll be pleased." He looked around and nodded to other diners. "Well, enjoy yourselves. I've got to keep movin'." Turning away, he greeted the people at the next table.

I had sampled everything, by now, including

the cornbread. Tom watched me closely, nodding in satisfaction at my obvious delight. I thought maybe I could finish everything on my enormous plate after all.

By some sort of unspoken agreement, both of us turned our full attention now to the food. There was little conversation as we began to work our way through the abundance.

Eventually, I had to stop. I was sure there was no room for another bite. Even Tom was slowing down, though he had done better than I could. We looked at each other, and both of us grinned the grin of satisfied defeat.

"Wow, Tom! That was truly awesome."

Our waiter returned to take our plates and ask about coffee and dessert.

I shook my head. "Sorry, I just can't eat or drink another thing."

Tom said, "Okay, Johnny, you heard the lady. Just bring the check, please."

Johnny hurried off, while I reached for my pocketbook.

Tom held up one large hand. "Oh, no. This is *my* treat. You're goin' to earn me some serious money if you rent a place from me for the summer. So, this is the least I can do."

I was dubious. I hated to be in debt to anyone, and always split restaurant checks with my friends. Tom looked as though he would insist, however, and I decided not to make an issue of it. Not this time, at least.

"All right," I said. "Just this once though, okay?" The last thing I wanted to convey was a willingness to let him have his way with me, in anything, not just dinner checks.

⟡

Back in the car, we were mostly quiet on the way down the mountain. When we arrived back at my hotel, he parked near the door and helped me out of the car. Reaching into the back seat, he took out a briefcase and my coat. Then, with his other hand under my elbow, he escorted me into the lobby.

The blonde woman Tom was talking with when I came downstairs to meet him was gone, replaced with a young black man.

"Hey Frankie. How's it goin'?"

"Great, Tom. It's good to see you. How's Sheila?"

Sheila? Who was Sheila? Oh well, it was none of my business. But if that were true, why, suddenly, was I feeling so let down?

"She's fine. Workin' hard. We'll have to get together with you and your lady one of these days soon."

Frankie smiled and nodded. "Any time, Tom."

A small fireplace burned brightly in the lobby. Sleek furniture was grouped nearby, but for now, at least, we were the only people interested in sitting there. We warmed our hands at the fireplace before taking seats, with me in an easy chair and Tom on a couch. He was close enough to show me the brochures he had brought, and point out the features of each, but clearly, he was dissatisfied.

"Come on over here so I can show you these

folders without gettin' a crick in my neck."

I shook my head, but he persisted. "Oh, come on. I won't bite."

I was unsure of that, but I decided to do as he asked. It would be more comfortable for me too. With a small show of reluctance, I sat beside him.

He handed me information on a few more condos and cabins than he had mentioned earlier, each with a different combination of features, and patiently answered my questions. Most of the condos were in, or at least close, to the town of Blue Ridge, though one was in a village not far away. All the cabins were in the mountains that surrounded the town. The proximity to Blue Ridge, the county seat of Fannin County, was important to me, as there were essential amenities here: a supermarket, a once-a-week greenmarket, a laundromat, the public library, a bank, and county records offices, among other things. Most of the condos had laundry facilities on site, but none of the cabins did.

After discussing the pros and cons of each one, I decided to look at three condos and two cabins. Tom seemed to approve my choices, though I wondered why his approval was important to me. Of course, I would make up my own mind! Though I hated to admit it to myself, I was close to surrendering to his charm.

He put the rejected folders back into his briefcase. "Let's help ourselves to coffee. You've probably noticed there's always a pot goin'. And the owner's wife, Sherry Wilkins, bakes terrific cookies. I'm ready to have some. How about you?"

"I don't know if I can eat any cookies, but coffee

sounds good." We stood and moved to the counter in the courtesy breakfast room where there was a full coffee pot and a covered plate of cookies.

"Who are Frankie and his lady? Not that it's any of my business."

Tom finished pouring coffee into our cups and put the pot down before answering. "Frankie and I played on the same sports teams in high school and were good friends, though I was a couple of years ahead of him. He had a football scholarship to Georgia Tech, but he was badly injured in practice durin' his junior year and had to stop playin'. His scholarship ran out, of course, and he had to leave school."

I shook my head in sympathy.

He added milk to his coffee and asked me how I liked mine. He followed my instructions, handed me my cup, and continued. "I was able to lend him a little money to help him finish college. He's almost done payin' me back. He's a full-time accountant durin' the day, and works here part-time at night. His wife, Mandy, just gave birth to their first child a couple of months ago. I know it's difficult for 'em, so I keep in close touch. They're really nice people."

I was beginning to see what a good friend Tom could be. He had the resources to help people when they needed it, and did so. The money was not a hand-out, just a little financial aid toward an achievable goal. I had seen two instances of his generosity this evening.

I realized that I might have misjudged him. Apparently, he wasn't simply a handsome hunk ready to take advantage of his looks. There might be an actual thinking person with a good heart inside that gorgeous exterior.

"That's very kind of you," I said. The coffee was hot and delicious. I was trying to resist the cookies. They were chocolate chip, my favorite. After eating so much at dinner, I could hardly believe I wanted cookies now.

Tom gathered his coffee cup, some napkins, and the plate of cookies and headed back to our couch. "I'll need to go soon, but I want you to know how happy I am that Mr. Hardy recommended me to you. I met him only once, but we've corresponded by e-mail several times. He knows his business."

"He spoke highly of you, too. I hope you'll be able to help me find out more about my grandmother's family."

"We'll see. There are some excellent resources in the library here, and there are more on-line. We'll go as far back as we can. Your grandmother told you she was part Cherokee?"

"Yes, though she didn't seem to be very pleased about it. I didn't understand her attitude. I'm very proud to be part Cherokee, though I guess it's only a very tiny part. She told me her great-grandmother was full-blood, so you can see how far back we need to go. Do you think it's possible, especially since we don't even know her great-grandmother's name? That's six generations counting me, a very long time."

"Assumin' we're successful, tell me again what you plan to do with the information."

"I'm going to write the story of our family's history this summer, or at least to get started on it. I want to do this for myself, for my brother, and for our children. He has two boys, and though I don't have any children of my own yet, I hope to one day."

He gave me a long considering look, took one more cookie, and drained his cup. "I must go. I'll pick you up at nine o'clock sharp tomorrow mornin'. We should be done by noon and then we'll go back up to my place so we can finalize your rental, have some lunch, and talk about your family. Bring all the information you have now: names; birth, marriage, and death dates; deeds; wills; and anythin' else you have. Genealogy is like a puzzle. The more pieces we have to start with, the better the chances of completin' the picture."

"Yes, I can see that," I said, nodding. "I'll bring everything I have."

He picked up his briefcase, and carried the cookie plate back to the breakfast room. I followed with our cups, and walked with him to the door.

He said goodnight to Frankie and turned to me. "I look forward to seein' you tomorrow. I hope you'll find a rental you really like."

"Me too!" I held out my hand to shake his, but he surprised me by taking it and brushing it gently with his lips.

I gasped, and wrenched my hand away. "What are you doing?"

This was not playing fair. He must know how susceptible most women would be to hand-kissing. They would find it, and him, irresistible! How dare he trade on that?

I turned around and stalked away toward the elevator, pausing only briefly to collect my pocketbook and coat.

❧

By the time I reached my room, I was beginning to calm down somewhat. I decided I might have overreacted a bit, but I was still shocked that he had tried that kind of move on me.

I also had to acknowledge that I was angrier with myself than with him. Before I came to my senses, I had been charmed. But we were supposed to be conducting business.

He had certainly awakened my interest, though. Beyond the electricity of his touch, I had reacted physically to his mere presence, not to mention his voice, his drawl, and his teasing remarks. His hand on my elbow had given me an electric jolt every time.

But surely my reaction was nothing more than loneliness and raging hormones. He probably tried these maneuvers on every reasonably attractive woman he encountered.

I wondered again about the mysterious Sheila. She could be his wife (though he said he lived alone and had no dependents, so... ex-wife?), his sister, his girlfriend, his aunt, his mother... The list was longer than I wanted to contemplate. I knew nothing of his personal life. And that was just fine, right?

I checked the time. Ellen Grant, my former college roommate and best friend, was briefly at home in upstate New York before jetting off to Africa to oversee the beginning of construction on her latest project, a large, full-service hospital in Nairobi. I was conscious of how precious her time was at home with her husband, Jon. So, our deal was simple. If she was busy, she would call me back as soon as she was free.

When we entered Williams College as freshmen, Ellen and I had been randomly paired as roommates. She was already in our dorm room when I arrived, just beginning to unpack and put her things away. We looked at each other that day, did a double take, and burst out laughing. We were the same size, and wore the same kinds of clothes. As we found out later, we had similar interests, and were both smart enough to do well at Williams. But the thing was, she and I looked so much alike, people often assumed we were twins.

Neither of us had a sister of our own. Almost immediately, we became to each other the sisters we had always longed for. Our green eyes, flame-colored hair, and outgoing personalities made us instant campus celebrities.

To my surprise, she picked up on the second ring.

"Hey, Suzi. How're things in Fannin County? Have you met your man yet?"

"Hey, yourself. Yes, I have. And he's as dangerous as I thought he'd be. He's gorgeous, has a sexy voice, and he's just as charming as I feared. I'm trying very hard not to fall for him. He took me to dinner tonight..."

"Dinner? How did that happen?"

I filled her in on the details of our meeting today, his surprising invitation to dinner, and our arrangements for tomorrow. Then I changed the subject.

"Ell, I've had the strangest feeling all day, ever since I saw a 'Welcome to Fannin County' sign on my way to Blue Ridge. I passed it almost before I realized it, and my eyes suddenly filled with tears. I found a place to pull over, grabbed my cell phone, and ran back to take pictures of the sign. I'm going to send them, and all the rest of my Fannin County photos, to Ron."

"Aw, Suzi!"

"Yeah..." I paused for a few seconds. "Grandma Rose told me so much about growing up in Fannin County, and now that I'm finally here, I've been feeling her presence and love all around me ever since I arrived. I always feel it, of course, but it's so much stronger here."

"Suzi, remember, I loved your Grandma Rose too. She was really something. It's no wonder you're feeling her presence so strongly. You know she would have gone to Fannin County with you years ago if she hadn't become so ill."

"I know. Another odd thing happened when I went down to the hotel lobby to ask about a place to eat lunch. The woman behind the desk recommended a nearby café, and asked if I had relatives in Blue Ridge. When I mentioned that the hamlet of Dial was my grandmother's birthplace, she was surprised. '*I* live in Dial,' she said.

"But, just then the phone rang and our conversation was cut short. I decided to go to lunch and ask her some questions about Dial later. My priority, after lunch, of course, was to keep my appointment with Tom, and once our business was concluded, I could use the rest of my time to explore as much of the countryside as possible before I fly home. So, anyway, I left the rental car in the hotel's lot and walked the few blocks to the café."

"How was your lunch?"

"It was simple, but delicious! I had a cup of cream of tomato soup flavored with a touch of basil, and half a thick grilled cheese sandwich on the most delicious sourdough bread. The weather was chilly today, so the hot food was perfect. The waiter was friendly and, since there weren't that many people in the restaurant, he found a few minutes to chat with me. But, you didn't ask the right question."

"Okay, I'll play. What's the right question?"

"What makes this café different from all other cafés? But wait, you don't have to ask, because I'm going to tell you. It's absolutely unique! It's in a historic bank building, complete with an open vault stocked with bank memorabilia on the one hand, and upscale giftware on the other: exotic teas, designer note paper, handmade pottery, and a bunch of other interesting items. It was really nice, and very attractive. You know I love history, right? Well, history surrounds you when you eat there!"

"Sounds nice. What did you buy me?"

"What? Anyway, when I finished eating and paid the check, I walked back to the hotel to get my rental car. I wanted to see if I could talk to the woman from Dial again, but I missed her! The man on duty told me she had gone for the day and wouldn't be returning to work until after I've flown back to New York. When I asked him if he knew how to get to Dial, he suggested I visit Blue Ridge's Chamber of Commerce office. So, I did.

"So far, everyone I've met here has been really friendly and helpful. The woman in the Chamber's office gave me an official Georgia state map and several local ones. Then, I asked her if she knew Tom Wolf."

"Did she?"

"She said she'd never met him personally, but that he has a very good professional reputation, and the ladies around there seem to find him quite fascinating on a personal level."

"Really!"

"Yes! Now that I've met him, I'm not surprised the local ladies find him fascinating! I wanted to ask her more questions about him, but I was afraid I'd be late. I had a two o'clock appointment with him at his home, where he apparently does all his business. It's about five miles from the town of Blue Ridge, up on one of the surrounding mountains."

"So, tell! What's he like?"

"Okay, but then I want to hear more about your hospital project."

After we finally hung up, I texted Ron to let him know I had arrived safely in Fannin County, sent him my "Welcome to Fannin County" sign photos, and promised to call him as soon as I returned to Manhattan.

I turned out the lights and lay awake, thinking about Grandma Rose and how lucky Ron and I were to have had her constant love and support as we grew up. When I finally drifted off to sleep, I dreamed we were still with her on Long Island.

# CHAPTER 3

❦

WHEN MY ALARM BUZZED NEXT morning at seven, I had a hard time persuading myself that I needed to leave the bed. The sun was up and shining though, so I dragged myself into the bathroom. Tom was coming to pick me up at nine, and I wanted to shower, dress, and eat some breakfast before he arrived.

The shower helped wake me, but coffee was what I really needed. I dressed quickly in layers, I was learning, and headed for the courtesy breakfast room. Fortified with caffeine, I helped myself to a ripe banana, a bowl of sweetened instant oatmeal and half a glazed donut. I told myself I needed all that sugar for energy.

I picked up a copy of the local weekly newspaper from a stack on the front counter and returned to my seat. I flipped through the paper as I ate, and found a column about fly fishing in the sports pages.

I had just finished my second cup of coffee when Tom arrived. He raised an eyebrow when he saw what I was reading.

"Well, I guess I'll have to make sure you have

a dock behind your rental if you're plannin' on goin' fishin'." His tone was challenging, and he was grinning that grin again.

"I can fish," I retorted. "My Grandpa used to take me out in his boat on Long Island Sound when I was little."

"Fishin' here is nuthin' like that. We're talkin' freshwater fishin', castin' with flies. It's different."

"Of course! I know that. I just wanted you to know I can handle a rod and reel, *and* bait my own hook. It's been a long time though. I'll need to learn about flies. Grandpa and I used chum as bait."

"There are quite a few expert fishers around here. You'll be able to learn all you need to know about freshwater fishin'."

While he was talking, he was preparing a cup of coffee to go. "Do you want me to fix one for you while I'm at it?"

"Sure. Thanks. I can use all the caffeine I can get."

After a minute he said, "Here you go, then." He handed me a Styrofoam cup, filled to the brim with regular coffee just the way I liked it, the lid carefully folded back so I could drink it without spilling it.

I stood, and watched him look me over. Apparently, he approved of my outfit, because he nodded once and grinned again. Predictably, my stomach lurched, and my cheeks warmed.

"Did you bring your family papers?"

"Yes, they're in an envelope here in my briefcase." I patted the portfolio I carried over my shoulder.

"Good. I was wonderin' why you were tryin' to wear that suitcase."

"It's a woman's briefcase!"

"Really? You could've fooled me."

He was smirking. What an infuriating man, I fumed, as I led the way toward the lobby entrance.

We stopped briefly at the front desk so Tom could flirt again with the pretty blonde woman behind the counter. She was the same one he was talking with when he came to take me to dinner last night. Maybe they had a thing going. I watched in silence while Tom beguiled her. He must be hard to resist when he turned on all that charm full blast.

When he said his final good-bye and turned back to me, I was surprised, again, at her expression. Like last night, she was staring at me. And, also like last night, her pretty face was twisted with rage. What was up with her?

Oblivious, Tom opened the door, put his hand under my elbow, and escorted me out to his car. Just as he had last evening, he helped me into the passenger seat and waited until I had buckled my seat belt before closing the door and getting in on the driver's side. Apparently, someone had at least *tried* to teach him some manners. I wondered who. My arm was tingling.

❦

"I thought we'd begin with the condos," Tom said. "One is a little further away, but the other two are right here in the middle of town." He pulled a length of black leather cord from his jacket pocket and tied his gorgeous hair in a low ponytail. I watched in awe, wanting to yank the cord off and run my hands through its magnificence. With difficulty, I restrained myself.

He started the car and pulled away from the hotel's front entrance. We turned onto Main Street, and went only two blocks before he parked the car.

"We could have walked," I said.

"Well, yeah, but then we'd have to walk back. The other condo on Main Street is four blocks from the hotel." He was laughing.

I shook my head. His laugh was contagious, but I was not in a mood to join him. Gas cost much less here than in New York, but that was no reason to waste it.

☾

I ruled out the first condo Tom showed me because it was in a building set half a block back from the street. At night, I would have to walk down a dark, narrow sidewalk to get to the front entrance. There was a parking lot behind the building and a back entry, but I thought I would probably be doing most of my errands on foot. The front entrance probably would be fine during the day, but I wanted to feel safe when I returned home after dark. I assumed I would be returning alone after dark.

We walked the two blocks to the second condo, his hand under my elbow as usual, and giving me the usual buzz. The building's entrance was directly on Main Street, and the condo was at the front, on the third floor. It was nice enough, but there was a bar and grill on the ground floor, and according to Tom, it was popular. I thought it might be too noisy in the condo at night, especially on the weekends.

We drove to the third condo, which was toward the other side of town. It was very modern, sleekly decorated in sophisticated grays and whites, with black leather furniture. The bathroom was luxurious and there was a small gym in the basement. That was an amenity the other condos lacked. I liked it, but it was not very cozy, and the monthly rent was daunting. It was at the very top of my price range.

Back in the car, Tom said, "So, what do you think?"

"I'd like to see the cabins before I make up my mind. Okay?"

"Sure. My time is yours."

We drove in silence for a few minutes. I was glad Tom felt no need to act as a tour guide. When I came back in the summer, I wanted to spend time meeting people and finding my way around on my own. This was my grandmother's birthplace, after all. I believed I could claim a bit of belonging here even though I was a stranger now.

*✧*

I wanted to ignore it, but I was increasingly aware that Tom was watching me. He was trying to look as though he were studying the scenery, but I could feel his eyes on me. Finally, he looked at me directly.

"Both of the cabins I'm goin' to show you are more rustic than the condos we've visited today. And, you'll have to drive into town every time you want to wash your clothes or buy some milk. Are you okay with that?"

"I think so. They're not too far away, according to the brochures you gave me. And, one of the cabins has a creek in the back. I'd have the chance to do some fishing, right?"

"There are plenty of places to fish. Aren't you afraid of snakes, or bears?"

He laughed when he saw the expression of horror on my face. "And don't forget the mosquitos. They're so big, we call 'em our state bird!"

I found my voice and croaked "Are you trying to frighten me?"

"No." He shook his head, no longer laughing. "I just need you to realize that this is backwoods Georgia, not Manhattan. It'll be a big change for you. Maybe too big a change?"

"You know nothing about me!" My voice quivered with outrage. "You think just because I live in the city I have no backwoods skills. You're wrong."

"So, tell me!"

"I swim in the ocean off Long Island on summer weekends, and I hike in the Catskill Mountains of upstate New York as often as I can. I've done some rock climbing, and I ski both downhill and cross-country. I can build a campfire, clean fish and cook them, and I can paddle a canoe or kayak. I make sure to pack everything I think I'll need for each outing. I let someone know where I'll be, if I'm going alone, and I keep my cell phone handy. I've been in a couple of tight spots, but I didn't panic. I'm not a novice."

"I'm impressed. Maybe you'll do after all."

"Huh! Nice of you to give me the benefit of your doubts!"

"Okay, okay, I'm sorry."

I looked at him suspiciously. Did he mean that? I was far from prepared to believe it.

"Look, I really am sorry. It's just that if you decide on one of the cabins, I'll feel responsible for your safety."

"Whoa! I'm responsible for my safety. You're not involved!"

He hesitated a second before saying, softly, "What if I'd like to be?"

"What are you talking about?"

"We're here," Tom said, with evident relief, as he pulled into a gravel driveway and stopped the car.

"What?" I was so angry, I had failed to notice our arrival.

"We'll have to continue this discussion later." Tom got out of the car and came around to open my door.

"We will not! There's nothing to discuss!" I ignored his helping hand, and struggled out of the low car. Getting out without his help was awkward. It felt like I had been sitting on the floor. Of course, my own stubbornness served only to make me angrier. Tossing my hair in a classic gesture of female irritation, I stalked up the gravel walk to the front door. Tom wisely trailed behind, jingling his keys.

The cabin was a disappointment, especially in

contrast to the luxurious condo I had toured only a few minutes earlier. Everything I would need was included, but the décor was… well, there was *no* décor. Instead of a fireplace, there was a rusty woodstove, and the furniture looked as if it had been pulled down from several different attics. Nothing matched, not that that was a deal-breaker for me, but the "great room" lacked even a tiny bit of appeal. The kitchen, bathroom, and bedroom were basic 1950s, and the view out the back door was uninspiring, despite a small, rocky stream. Living here, even for a few months, was *not* an option.

"Tom, this is not what I had in mind. The brochure lied! Is the other cabin like this one?" There was no point in seeing it unless it was substantially nicer.

"It's still a cabin, but it's a lot nicer. You'll see." He jingled his keys again. "Come on, let's go."

Tom reversed out of the rutted drive and drove back toward town. A few minutes later, he turned the car onto a shady lane that curved gently upward. Soon, he turned again, this time onto a well-graded gravel driveway. The cabin was set back from the road among sheltering trees. In the summer, the front of the cabin would be shaded at least for part of the day, but now the trees were merely in bud. Much less clumsy this time, I climbed out of the car without waiting for Tom to open my door.

The outside of the cabin looked even better in person than in the photo in the brochure. There was a deep porch, with a pale, greenish-blue-painted front door, flanked on one side by two rocking chairs, sitting side by side, and on the other, by a swing hanging from the porch ceiling, all of which were painted in the same greenish-blue. The swing was just wide enough for two people to sit together.

I waited impatiently for Tom to unlock the door.

When he did, and I stepped inside, I knew immediately that this was where I wanted to live this summer. The rental fees might be even higher than the fancy condo in town, but that hardly mattered. I would find a way to pay for it.

The great room contained a large stone fireplace, a comfortable sofa upholstered in a soft teal color that converted into a queen-sized bed, two coordinating easy chairs, a glass-topped wrought iron cocktail table and a side table of similar design. A low, black-painted bookcase held a flat-screen TV, with decorative objects and books of all kinds filling the shelves. Overhead, there was a black ceiling fan with oak paddles and decorative lights, and a wrought iron floor lamp stood beside the couch.

The spotless kitchen area contained modern appliances, sleek oak cabinets, and granite countertops in a tan-brown-black pattern. A square, black-painted table, topped with the same granite, and four black chairs were partially hidden from the living area by a wrought iron screen.

Down a short hallway, the bedroom held a double bed with a carved oak headboard, and a matching nine-drawer dresser and mirror. A smaller version of the ceiling fan in the great room hung above the bed, and there was a braided rug in multiple shades of blue, teal, and pale green that closely matched a larger one in front of the fireplace.

The bath was basic, but very clean. The floor and walls were tiled in white and shades of blue and teal, and the shower curtain was clear plastic, dotted with yellow-centered white daisies.

All the walls were painted in the palest blue-green, and the floors were of polished oak. Paintings and prints of mountain scenery hung in each room, and crisp, pale blue-green cotton, sprinkled liberally with daisies, curtained every window. It was obvious to me that this cabin was owned by a woman who loved her cozy mountain home, daisies, and many shades of blue.

"I guess the owner really likes blue. I do too. Some people find it depressing, but I've never thought so."

"Good. She does like blue, but there's another reason for using it. Here in the South, we have some beliefs and traditions borrowed from African slaves. One of those is that *haint* blue, like her pretty curtains, will chase away ghosts and evil spirits that might harm you. You'll probably notice other houses with doors, porch roofs, and shutters painted in similar shades of blue."

"Really? So... a haint is something that might haunt you?"

"Yep, possibly an evil spirit lookin' for revenge!"

"Well, I guess I don't have to worry about that here."

"Right. Let's go on out back."

When I stepped through the back door onto the wooden deck, I drew in my breath with surprise.

The view down the mountain was magnificent. I turned to Tom, who had followed me outside, but there was no need to say anything.

"This is the one. I can see that by the look on your face. The owner, Mrs. Margaret Buckley, lives here all year 'round, but this spring and summer she'll be visitin' her daughter in California to help take care of her first grandchild. The baby's not due 'til late June, but Margaret will be leavin' here in about three weeks. She's already put some of her personal items in storage, and she'll have cleared out the rest before you return."

"Oh, that's great." I was already mentally stocking the kitchen and putting my clothes into the closet. "Is it okay to look in the kitchen cabinets and drawers, and under the sink in the bathroom? I'll also need to peek into the bedroom closet."

"Sure, go ahead. I'll wait on the front porch."

Alone inside, I twirled around in glee. This was just what I had envisioned. The view, the comfortable furnishings... it had everything I wanted.

It took only a few minutes to look around, and then I joined Tom on the porch. He was sitting in the swing, gently swaying back and forth, but he stood when he saw me.

"It's perfect," I said, carefully straightening one of the rockers as if I already lived here. "I love it. But, how much is the monthly rental?"

"Margaret's just lookin' for somebody to stay here while she's gone. She dreaded leavin' it empty for such a long time. She wants whoever stays here just to pay for the normal expenses: utilities, phone service, cable, internet access, etc. Did you notice the flat screen TV in the great room? It's new. We probably don't get all the channels you do in the city, but we get enough for most of us."

"I'm sure it will be fine. I don't watch much TV. But," I hesitated, "that's really all she wants?"

Tom nodded.

"I can't believe it! Does she want me to give her a check up front to cover possible damage? She doesn't know me at all. Why would she trust me?"

"Ah, but she knows me," Tom said with an unexpectedly sweet smile, not his usual wolfish grin. "She knows I wouldn't let just anybody move in here."

"But you don't know me either," I pointed out.

"I know more about you than you think. I did a thorough background check on you before you came."

"You did what?" I was shocked, and outraged. "How dare you?"

Tom was unperturbed. "That's just the way it is these days. I have to protect myself *and* my clients, both owners and renters. Margaret means a lot to me, so this 'rental' is personal."

I took a breath. "Oh, I didn't think about that. I don't understand your relationship with Mrs. Buckley, but I guess it's really none of my business. I'm just glad to be able to stay here this summer."

Tom nodded, and gestured toward his car. "Come on. I'll take you back to my place so we can get the formal paperwork out of the way and

eat lunch. Then, I'll see if I can help you with
your family's history."

# CHAPTER 4

☾

WE PULLED INTO TOM'S DRIVEWAY only
minutes later. Once again, he came around
to my side of the car and opened my door. Hand
firmly under my elbow, he guided me out of the
car and into his house. He immediately went to the
fireplace and began building a fire. As soon as it
was burning brightly, I took off my jacket and hung
it next to his in the foyer. Meanwhile, Tom was
brewing coffee. It smelled wonderful.

"Sit down near the fire, and I'll get the papers
you need to sign."

He went to his desk, and picked up the top-most
folder. I had been watching him move around
the great room, going about his hosting and real
estate duties. He was wearing a black, skin tight,
long-sleeved T-shirt today, sleeves pushed up over
his elbows, with form-fitting black jeans. The
rippling muscles in his shoulders, arms, and thighs
were on enticing display. His body was beautiful,
strong, and supple.

He came toward me now, and sat down beside
me on the huge couch. Blinking, I sat up straighter
and tried to focus on the rental agreement he was

about to hand me.

I reached for the pen he held.

"Wait! I haven't told you yet about Margaret's other request. It's very important to her. You need to hear me out before you sign these."

I frowned. I had wondered if there was a catch. And, here it was. "What is it?"

"There's a small herb and vegetable garden near the back door. You probably didn't even notice it, because nuthin' much is growin' there yet, except some early peas. She wants whoever lives there this summer to weed, water, and harvest the herbs. There are also some vegetable and flower seed packets for her tenant to sow, if ..."

"Wait just a minute!" I held up a hand to stop him. "I don't know anything about herbs, and I buy my vegetables and flowers at the market."

Tom shook his head and smiled. "You really don't have to worry about plantin' the seeds, but you might find it fun just to see what would happen."

"I know what would happen! I'd kill whatever it was. I have a black thumb!"

"Really! I don't believe you. But, as I said, you don't have to plant any seeds if you don't want to."

I was only slightly relieved.

"However, you do have to agree to weed and water the herbs."

I frowned again and shook my head. Now he held up *his* hand. "Margaret keeps a herb diary in the kitchen. It has pictures of every herb in the garden, an explanation of what kind of care each one needs, and a sort of runnin' log describin' how things are goin'. She needs you to agree to keep that up. Okay?"

I was still frowning and feeling apprehensive.

"Don't worry. You can do it. If you need help or guidance, you can always call me."

"You know about herbs?" My voice reflected my doubts.

"Yep. I've helped Margaret in that garden every summer since I was eight years old."

I reached for the papers and signed them before I had time to recover my senses.

☾

He made photocopies of the agreement I had signed and gave me a set for my files. He kept one for himself and another for the green-thumbed Margaret.

"Come on over to the island and sit on a stool while I warm up our lunch."

He reached into his refrigerator and took out a covered dish. "Want some coffee while we wait for the food?" Without waiting for my answer, he popped the dish into the microwave and poured coffee for both of us.

He added sugar and a generous dollop of milk to mine and handed it to me. I held the cup in both hands to warm them, marveling again that he remembered exactly how I liked my coffee.

I sipped the delicious brew while he took rolls, butter, and a green salad from the fridge, and set out salad bowls, plates, napkins, and silverware. When the microwave beeped, he took out the covered dish and put the rolls in to warm. I had never encountered a man who knew his way around a kitchen, let alone someone as organized and tidy as Tom. I was so surprised, shocked was a better word, that I forgot my manners entirely.

"Oh, I'm so sorry. I should have offered to help."

"No need. It's a big kitchen, and I know where everythin' is." He served salad into our bowls, and came around to join me on an adjacent stool. "I don't know about you, but I'm ready to eat!"

"Yes, thanks. Me too." I picked up my napkin, buttered a roll and poured a little dressing onto my salad. I chewed and swallowed. "Umm. This dressing is delicious. What brand is it?"

"No brand. It's just herbs from Margaret's garden in a little olive oil and a big splash of red wine vinegar."

"Did you bake the rolls, too?" I was beginning to wonder if he was some sort of celebrity chef I'd never seen before. Maybe I should watch the Food Channel more often.

"Yep. They're from Margaret's recipe for herb rolls. I've tweaked it a little. I like more garlic than she does."

"They're amazing! I can't wait to see what's in that covered dish."

"It's a chicken stew…"

"Don't tell me. Margaret showed you how to make it, right?"

"Yep. She did." He removed our empty salad bowls, and uncovered the dish. The aroma was more than tantalizing.

He served me first, and waited while I tasted my first forkful. I sighed in surprised pleasure.

He smiled his sweet, unexpectedly gentle smile, and piled stew onto his own plate. "I'm glad you like it."

"I think 'like it' is too tame a phrase for how *much* I like it. You really need to stop feeding me. I'm in your debt."

"No debt. It's all included in my real estate service! And, I like you. So, no debt." He was looking at me intently. I felt my cheeks grow hot, much to my embarrassment.

He laughed softly.

When we finished, Tom said, "Let's go back over to the fire. I'm goin' to pour us some more coffee and get out Margaret's cookies for dessert. I want to see the information you've brought about your family, and we might as well get comfortable while I look it over. If I can't help you, I'll tell you so up front."

I nodded, and rose. He hardly could be fairer than that. I had been afraid he might try to drag out his investigation to make his fee larger, but on no more than one day's acquaintance, I was inclined to trust him. I decided that I must be crazy.

"Can I help you clear that away?" I gestured toward the remains of our excellent lunch.

"That's all right. It'll only take a couple of minutes and, besides, I know where everythin' is," he reminded me.

I stood warming my hands at the fire while Tom stacked our dishes into his dishwasher and put the rest of the stew back into the fridge. There was enough left for Tom's dinner tonight, or maybe his lunch tomorrow. I would be gone by then, driving back to Atlanta to catch my flight to New York.

He put a tray of mugs and cookies on the huge coffee table and patted the seat beside him on the couch.

For the third time today, my coffee was perfect, exactly the way I liked it. No man I had ever known before had bothered to ask how I liked my coffee.

The chocolate chip cookies were even better than the ones we had shared last evening at my hotel. Those had tasted homemade, but these were in a whole different class. They were much more than simply delicious. And they had been baked especially for Tom by the mysterious Margaret.

"All right!" I exclaimed as soon as I swallowed the first delectable bite. "Who is Margaret? I'm dying of curiosity."

He pulled the leather tie off his gorgeous hair. Again, I ached to run my fingers through it, and even leaned slightly toward him before coming to my senses. Unfortunately, he was completely unaware of my need. He shook it out, and tucked it behind his ears. Even his ears were attractive, perfectly proportioned to his face, without sticking out. I dragged my eyes away and contemplated a cookie as he began to speak.

"She's the closest thing to a mother I had growin' up. My own mom died when I was two and my dad left soon after. We eventually learned he'd been killed in a knife fight a few months after he disappeared. My older brother, Mike, and I were livin' with our granddad and I was growin' up pretty wild. Then, one day, when I was seven, Margaret caught me stealin' apples from the tree you'll be able to see from the window over her kitchen sink." He paused, smiling his sweet smile in memory of the incident.

"She was a local schoolteacher. The kids I knew had told me she was strict, and I wanted nuthin' to do with her. I tried to run away, but she caught me. By the time she stopped yellin', my ears were ringin'. She wanted to know how come she hadn't seen me in school. I told her I could read, write, and do sums. I didn't need to go to school. She just laughed.

"That evenin', she came to see my granddad. He told Mike and me to go into the other room and sit on our pallets until he called us. Boy, I was scared! I knew I'd catch hell from him, but I didn't know exactly how he'd punish me.

"After he did some yellin', things got real quiet. I was just thinkin' about eavesdroppin' at the door, when Granddad called us back in. He said they had come to an agreement: We were to start school the very next day. If we played hooky even once, we'd be subjected to a punishment so horrible, we might die from it.

"Of course, he never really would have hurt us, but I was too scared to realize that. Mike, who was fourteen and big for his age, declared he was *never* goin' to school. That night he packed a few clothes into a knapsack and snuck out the back. It was years before we heard from him again.

"I showed up at school next day, and every day after that until school was finished for the year. By then, I was hooked. I loved school, and didn't want it to end. But even more than I loved school, I loved Margaret. Of course, I didn't call her Margaret then. She was Miz Buckley. For some reason, she seemed to love me as much as I loved her.

"She was widowed before I met her and now she's retired from teachin'. The daughter who's havin' the baby is the oldest of her three girls. Margaret keeps me in cookies and good advice. I'd do just about anythin' for her."

Here was yet another side of Tom. He kept surprising me. What happened to Mike, I wondered, but before I could ask, he picked up the envelope I had brought and pulled out the contents.

There were a few photos of my grandmother at different ages, photocopies of her birth, marriage and death certificates, and the page from a well-thumbed bible on which someone, maybe her mother or father, had recorded the date and time of her birth. There was also a photocopy of her parents' headstones that I had found on-line.

"This cemetery is only a few miles away. I'll take you there when you come back this summer. But, is this all you have?"

"As you can see, my grandmother, Rose Montgomery Smith, was born on a farm in the hamlet of Dial. From my research and the stories she told me as I was growing up, I know Dial was pretty small then, and I'm looking forward to going there when I come back. Maybe I can get some idea of what it may have been like when she was young."

I stopped, remembering her descriptions of the little hamlet. I had promised myself that I would shed no tears today in front of Tom, and somehow, I managed not to.

He gazed at me for a long moment, then nodded.

"I know I haven't given you much, but I do have a story she told me once when I was about ten years old."

I paused to gauge his reaction. Tom nodded again for me to continue.

"I'd invited my best friend to come over after school so we could do our homework together. Grandma overheard me tell her, proudly, that I was one-eighth Cherokee Indian. After my friend left, she sat me down and told me that I was wrong. *She* was the one who was one-eighth Cherokee.

"Grandma Rose was what people call a handsome woman. She wasn't classically beautiful, but she was striking. You can see that from her pictures, especially the ones in black and white. She had thick, straight black hair, high cheekbones, and she always seemed to have a special sparkle in her beautiful brown eyes. I don't think her skin was particularly dark, except in the summer, but it was darker than mine."

Tom picked up one of the photos that showed her as a young woman, and looked at it closely. He made a noncommittal noise. I took that as agreement.

"Anyway, she told me an interesting story about an incident that happened when she was fourteen or fifteen years old. One summer morning, she and three of her younger sisters had washed their hair and were out on the front porch brushing it dry in the sun. Their dad, my great-grandfather, was mending a fence in a nearby corral when a group of young Cherokee men on horseback rode into the yard with fur skins to trade. The leader of the group kept gazing at my grandmother while he spoke with her father. When she noticed that he was staring at her, she became self-conscious and a little alarmed. She hurried back inside the farmhouse, taking her sisters with her. After the men rode away, her father told her that the young Cherokee leader had apologized for upsetting her. He said he couldn't stop staring at her because she looked exactly like his sister."

Tom was surprised. "Like his sister?"

"That's what she told me."

"That *is* interestin'." He still held the photo in his hand. "I wonder if she had seen him before. Did they know each other?"

"I gathered from other conversations with her that the farm families and the Cherokee didn't mix socially. But she didn't say whether she knew him or had ever seen him before."

Tom gave me a considering look. He gathered my papers and photos together and returned them to the envelope. "How much do you know about the history of this area?"

"I've done a little research. I've always been interested in learning more about the Cherokee, and I've been appalled at what I've read about the Trail of Tears. The U.S. soldiers who rounded up the Cherokee, and people of other tribes, and marched them away to Oklahoma Territory, were terribly, and in my opinion, unnecessarily brutal."

Tom turned away from me and stared into the fire. He began to speak, softly at the beginning, but with more and more passion as he went on.

"These mountains, rivers, and valleys were our homeland. At first, when the white settlers started movin' in, we thought we could make treaties with 'em, that they would honor our traditional ways of livin' on the land, that we could share it. But, after the war that gave your government freedom from British domination, more and more settlers came.

"Meanwhile, we had set up our own government, patterned on yours, and many of us learned to speak English, dressed like white people, and converted to Christianity. We learned to farm in the English manner, and run our own businesses. We developed a Cherokee alphabet, somethin' no other American Indian tribe had done at that time. We attended Missionary schools and learned how to read our own language as well as English. We published a weekly newspaper, *The Cherokee Phoenix*, in both English and Cherokee, and within a few years, we achieved almost universal literacy.

"And, even though we had done all that, your government, and most of the white settlers, treated us like ignorant savages. They tricked and cheated us, and broke treaty after treaty. Then, gold was discovered in our mountains. The white stampede for gold and land became more and more violent.

"The great white thinkers in Washington had come up with this grand theory to justify their greed. They called it *Manifest Destiny*. The idea was that Americans, white Americans, not only had the right to all the land in North America, but that they had the duty to take it.

"Some Washington Senators were appalled at the idea and even spoke out against it in Congress. But, most white people agreed with it and used it to justify their actions. More and more trouble broke out between white settlers, the Cherokee, and the neighborin' Creek, Choctaw, and Chickasaw tribes. Massacres and terrible atrocities were committed by people on both sides, which only bred more fear and hatred. Some of that mistrust still exists today."

He paused. He was staring into the flames in the fireplace, but it was clear he was seeing very different pictures. He bowed his head and a curtain of black hair hid his face. Tom had done his best to keep his voice level, but I could see the effort it cost him. He was breathing hard and the knuckles of his clasped hands were pale.

I reached over and put my hand on his clenched ones. "I understand. If I could apologize for our government's treachery and the white settlers' greed, and that would be enough, I would do so, gladly. But that's not enough. It could never be enough."

His body flinched, as though he had forgotten anyone else was in the room.

"Oh! My God! I'm sorry." He pushed his hair off his face and shook his head in disbelief. "I don't usually go off like that. In fact, I don't *ever* talk about it. You must be so bored!"

"Not at all!" I paused for a moment to think. "Tom, look, we can't change history or bring back your dead ancestors, but we can honor them. I want very much to know if I can honor a Cherokee ancestor of my own. That's why I'm here. Do you think you can help me?" Tom looked down, noticing for the first time my hand on top of his. I gave his hands a squeeze and let them go.

He took a long, steadying breath, and let it out in a sigh. He turned his head and looked at me as though searching for the answer to a riddle. Finally, he nodded.

"I'll try. I can't promise anythin', really. But, I will try."

"Do you want to keep the envelope, or should I take it now and bring it back this summer?"

Tom shook his head. "As long as you don't mind, I'll keep it for now. When you come back this summer, I'll take you over to the library here. It's in the County Courthouse buildin' and they have a room dedicated to genealogical research. They also have free access to on-line genealogy sites, and there are all sorts of other reference materials in there as well. It's probably the best place to start. We'll see how that goes, and where it leads us next."

I stood. "Well, thanks so much for your time, the delicious lunch, and Margaret's cookies. I wish I could get the chance to meet her before I leave."

Tom rose too, and looked down into my eyes. He was standing very close. "Me too. I think you'd like each other."

"Where is she now?" I backed away slightly. He was too close. My heart was skipping whole beats.

"She has a sister, Gladys, who lives about forty miles from here. Because she'll be away for so long, she's over there now visitin' with Gladys. She won't be back for a few more days."

I started to move toward the front door and the safety of the outdoors. "Please thank her for me. I can't wait to move in!"

We put our jackets back on, and I waited on the porch while Tom locked the door to his house. He escorted me down the porch steps and back out to his car, keeping his hand, as usual, under my tingling elbow.

❦

He settled me inside his car and when he climbed in beside me and started the engine, he turned to me and said, "How about I drive you to Dial this afternoon? It's only a few miles from here, and we can visit what used to be the general store. What do you say?"

"Oh, Tom. That would be great! You don't mind?"

He smiled his sweet smile, and drawled, "Nah. I want you to have somethin' special to remember when you're back in New York."

"All right, then, let's go!" I was smiling, too. I already had some special memories, and many of them involved Tom.

He put the car in gear and as we drove down the mountain, I could hardly contain my excitement.

"Do you know anything about Dial? My research turned up only a few tidbits."

"Well, I don't know anyone who lives there now, and there's never been an actual town. It's just a scatterin' of houses, cabins, and farms. I hope you won't be disappointed. There used to be a U.S. Post Office, but it was decommissioned before either of us was born."

"Yeah, I read that it was open only for a little over sixty years. Is the building still standing?"

"Nah, it's gone now, but I know where it was. I can show you the spot."

We sighed, almost in unison.

"At least the general store is still there," Tom said, "though it's been transformed by the new owner. He bought it a few years ago and made it into a luncheonette, though you can still buy lots of other things there. You'll see. We'll stop there first. I don't know if any of the family he bought it from is still around, but their ancestors began doin' business on the site back in the mid-1830s. Dial was one of the first settlements in Fannin County, and in fact, the county wasn't formed until a couple of decades later, in the 1850s."

"Then, weren't most of your people still here when Dial was first settled?"

"Yep, but I think we've covered enough history for now, okay?"

I nodded and held my tongue. He was uncomfortable now with the subject of the Cherokee's conflicts with the region's white settlers.

Soon, we reached flatter land and I twisted around in my seat, trying to see everything at once.

A few minutes later, we turned into an asphalt parking lot, next to a small bridge. When Tom helped me out of the car, I could hear the muted rush and tumble of a river. There was birdsong too, coming from the trees that overhung the bridge and lined what I could see of the riverbanks.

"Here we are, Dial's general store and luncheonette." Tom gestured toward the free-standing building in front of us. It was long and low, with a wide porch decorated with signs advertising some of the luncheonette's menu items: sandwiches, burgers, cold drinks, etc.

I stood for a minute taking in the scenery. The store itself was set against tall trees, but across the road, there were lush green farm pastures that stretched far away, almost to the distant mountains. There was a soft breeze. It may have been my imagination, but it felt warmer here, not quite so chilly.

Tom waited until I was ready, and then took my arm. I smiled up at him as we walked toward the store's entrance. 'Established in 1834' read a sign on the façade. The building looked rustic from a distance, but when we got closer, I could see no trace of the original building. The outside must have been renovated several times through the years, and probably again when it had changed hands most recently.

Inside, the store was bright, colorful and modern. There were still a few patrons eating a late lunch in the small dining area, and a youngish couple was sitting at the counter. We joined them and bought bottled water. This time, Tom let me pay without too much of a struggle.

The owner was relatively new to the area and knew little of its history, but was friendly and talkative, as was the couple, who told us they owned a cabin a few miles away. They described a county-maintained, riverside picnic area that was not far away, and gave us directions to the scenic dirt road that led to it.

The store carried a selection of staple foods and a bit of everything else, from camping gear to costume jewelry made by the owner's wife. Among her designs, I found the perfect earrings to go with a colorful beaded necklace I had purchased in Atlanta. I paid for them and we said good-bye.

Before climbing back into the car, we walked over to the nearby river. We crossed to the middle of the bridge and leaned over the stone walls on each side to admire the view.

Apart from the birdsong, the only sounds were the hum of the very occasional passing car or pickup truck and the powerful music of the river as it flowed swiftly between its banks.

"Tom, is this the Toccoa River?"

He nodded.

Standing there, taking it all in, I felt a mix of sadness and exhilaration.

"I'm imagining my grandma as a young girl, walking to the Post Office to pick up her family's mail, or buying a piece of penny candy at the general store. She must have stood here sometimes, watching the river. Maybe she waited on the bridge for a friend to join her on the way to school, or fished with her father along the river's banks. I remember her telling me that he taught her how to fish."

Tom stood silently beside me. He was giving me the time I needed to form this special memory, but I was also conscious of his warm hand, still at my tingling elbow.

There was a picturesque farmhouse with a barn and other outbuildings on one side of the bridge, with neat fields surrounding it. On the other, there was a rambling house whose backyard reached down to the riverbank. A wooden two-seater swing, attached to a large tree limb, hung over the riverbank and swayed gently in the breeze.

While we stood there, a rowboat floated downstream carrying two young girls and an older teenaged boy. We watched as the girls cast fishing lines off either side of the boat, while the boy lazily moved his paddle to steer it away from the banks. He looked up before the boat swept under the bridge and waved at us.

Finally, I was ready to go. We walked back to the car and drove over the bridge. At the T-junction on the other side, we turned right and drove slowly along the road. Tom pointed out the spot where the Post Office once stood, but of course, there was nothing of it left to see. There were several houses further along the road. As Tom had remarked on the drive here, there was no actual town, only a collection of dwellings and fields.

"Looks like nobody's at home in any of these houses. They must all be at work. There are plenty of other people who live in Dial though, and some of them are probably at home. I guess they just don't happen to live on this road."

Since Tom still had some time before he had to be back to take care of his animals, we decided to look for the dirt road that led to the picnic area the couple in the general store had mentioned. We found the road with no difficulty, but as it narrowed, it became increasingly rough. Reluctantly, he turned back before something happened to his sportscar. It was not meant to be an all-terrain vehicle.

"I'll borrow a Jeep and take you there when you

come back this summer. Funny, I've never heard of it, but it sure sounds like it's worth the trip. We'll have to bring a picnic lunch."

I looked at him in surprise. I was expecting to see very little of him this summer, only meeting to discuss his genealogical findings. Again, I held my tongue.

We crossed the bridge once more, and returned to Blue Ridge on the same road. We passed a vineyard at one point, and a dairy farm a few miles later. They looked prosperous. I watched again as the scenery changed from flat farmland to dense forest that climbed the steep hillsides.

### ☾

When we reached Blue Ridge's business district, it was after three o'clock. We had been mostly silent on the drive back, but when we passed the scenic railway that ran through the middle of town, I remembered to ask Tom about it. The business district was split into two parallel streets, East Main and West Main, with the railroad tracks running between them. Boutiques, restaurants, and other stores lined the far sides of each street.

"Tom, when will the Scenic Railway begin running this season? I've always liked trains, especially historic ones. This steam engine looks like it's had lots of TLC, and the antique passenger cars do too. Where does it go?"

"We'll have to take a trip on it when you come back," he answered.

Again, I looked at him in surprise. He seemed not to notice.

"To answer your questions, it runs from late spring to the end of the year, and it goes north for about thirteen miles to McCaysville, on the Tennessee border. It stops over for a couple of hours so the passengers can step over the state border to Copperhill, Tennessee, and eat lunch and shop in either town. Then it comes back here. The round trip takes about four hours. It's fun. Dependin' on the weather, you can ride in an open or a closed car."

The trip did sound like fun, but I found it hard to believe I would be going on it with Tom. I was sure he had more important things to do than to take me on these promised sightseeing trips.

&

Before I knew it, we were back at my hotel. He stopped the car under the portico and came around to help me out. He stood next to me, too close.

"I need to get back home and finish my chores."

I nodded. "Thanks for everything." I was feeling very unhappy that he was about to drive away.

He seemed reluctant to go. "I hope you'll keep in touch. You have my email."

"Yes. I do."

"It was a pleasure showin' you 'round. I know you'll be happy in Margaret's place."

"Thank you. I'm pretty sure I will."

He sighed, then groaned in frustration and pulled me into an awkward embrace. Before I realized what he was going to do, he kissed my cheek, and then captured my mouth in a passionate kiss.

I should have protested. Told him he had some nerve! But I didn't. I kissed him back with equal passion.

And, after a long, very satisfactory moment, we both pulled back in shock.

I grabbed my briefcase out of the back seat and fled into the hotel.

I heard the screech of tires as he roared away.

# CHAPTER 5

❦

SOMEHOW, I MADE IT TO my room and even
managed to unlock my door without fainting,
bumping into walls, or dropping my keycard. My
lips were tingling, and so was the rest of me.

His arms were warm, strong. I wanted them
around me still. His lips... there were no words
to describe how all the brave defenses I had piled
up against him had simply melted away at his
kiss. I felt as if I had lost something. Something
important.

I dropped my briefcase on the bed and stripped
off my jacket. I was burning up, or freezing cold. I
had no idea which. I stumbled into the bathroom
and ran cold water. I washed my hands in it, and
splashed it on my face.

It had been a long time since I had felt such
intense desire. Now, while my body slowly began
to relax, I wished my mind would calm down,
too. My thoughts were in chaos.

Of course, his kiss meant nothing. There was
Sheila, remember? Who was Sheila? He had
mentioned her only once, in answer to Frankie's
question about her. I had seen no evidence of a

live-in female in Tom's home, but I had never visited a bathroom there, let alone seen a bedroom. Was she just a friend? Ex-wife? Ex-girlfriend? Sister? Aunt? Not mother, she was dead. I had run through the possibilities last night, but I had forgotten one of them. Maybe Sheila was the girl at the hotel's reception desk, the pretty blonde who kept making angry faces at me.

I was leaving tomorrow, flying back to my sane and normal life in Manhattan, back to work, back to my friends and colleagues. That was good. So, why was I feeling so let down?

I needed to pack, decide where to eat tonight, without Tom. I wanted to cry.

☾

As usual, when I was in distress, I picked up my phone to call Ellen.

To each other, we were family. We had been faithful friends since the day we became college roommates. During school holidays, I had often come with Ellen to visit her mother, Sharon Grant, in upstate New York. We had shared our hopes, fears, and dreams for the future with each other. We had studied together, double dated, hiked, and skied together. When we both interned in Manhattan in the summer between our junior and senior years at Williams College, we had shared a tiny Manhattan studio.

She was Maid of Honor at my wedding. I was Matron of Honor at hers. She had traveled with me to Texas when my grandmother was dying of cancer, and had held my hand during my divorce. I had grieved with her when her beloved father, the famous architect Dale Grant, died in a freak traffic accident. And, I had been almost as unhappy as she was when her widowed mother decided to move to Europe with her young son, Ellen's half-brother, Nicholas.

Ellen missed them both very much, but now she was head of her father's architectural firm, and quickly becoming as well-known as he had been for beautiful, innovative, sustainable, and structurally-sound designs. She traveled all over the world these days, meeting clients, overseeing projects, and finding new inspiration for her work. Her husband, Jon Taylor, was also an architect, and they lived in the beautiful house in upstate New York that her father, Dale, had built for his family.

I wondered whether she was still at home now, or if she had already left for Africa. If she could, she would answer my call, or call me back later when she was free.

My phone buzzed. I looked at it in surprise. It was Ellen! How did she know?

"Hi, Ell. Where are you?"

"I'm actually still home right now. I was supposed to have left today for Nairobi, but my trip has been delayed. There's trouble there, and our State Department has stopped travel to the area until it's safer. But enough about me. How's it going in Georgia? How did you get along with your good-looking Cherokee real estate man? Did he find you a place to rent this summer?"

"Yes! It's a cozy cabin with the most spectacular view down the mountain from the back deck. It belongs to a woman named Margaret who will be away this summer visiting her daughter and her soon-to-be-born grandchild. The daughter lives in California, and Margaret will be flying out there in a few weeks. She's not coming home until the baby is at least six months old, but I'll be back at work long before that."

"So, tell me about the cabin, and more about that hunky real-estate man!"

"I don't know what to think about him. One minute he makes me furious and the next he's a sweetheart. He's fierce about how the Cherokee were treated at white men's hands, but seems prepared to forgive me for being mostly white. Maybe he'll like me better if we can prove Grandma was right, and I'm part, though a very small part, Cherokee. There's a woman named Sheila though. I don't know whether she's his ex-wife, girlfriend, sister, cousin, or just a friend. Haven't met her yet."

"But you will, presumably, when you come back to Georgia, right?"

"Maybe."

"Okay, so tell me about the cabin. If I can get away this summer, I'll want to come and visit you!"

"Great! So… the cabin…"

When we finally said good-bye, I was exhausted. Somehow, despite my previous agitation, I'd managed calmly to tell Ellen all the important details about my visit here. All but one, anyway. I had left out the detail that troubled me most: Tom's kiss and what it meant for my relationship with him. Of course, I had no real relationship with

Tom, but there was something. He disturbed me in ways I had never felt before, not even with my ex-husband. Especially not with my ex-husband.

Ugh! Now that my memory had gone there, I was helpless to stop my sad tale from flashing through my head. I tried not to dwell on the reasons behind my brief marriage and quick divorce, but sometimes, like now when I was already feeling low, they crept in. My only excuse for what happened with him was that I was barely twenty-three when I met him, and naïve as only a young woman can be whose life, up until then, had been sheltered from bad guys and con artists.

# CHAPTER 6

I MET JAY, JEREMY DAVIDSON PORTER IV,
at a party at the Waldorf Astoria for one of
my previous firm's most prestigious clients. I was
a lowly public relations flack then, just two years
after graduation from Williams College. It was my
job that evening to make sure no one at the party
needed anything: someone to talk to, a button
replaced, a hem mended, a plate of food, a taxi, a
room if someone needed to sleep off too much
alcohol, and so on. That was me, the bright-eyed,
eager to advance my career, fix-it girl.

Jay was not the client, but he was an acquaintance
of the client. He introduced himself to me when
he came in, and almost immediately became
involved in conversations with others at the party.
He appeared not to need me for anything, and
though I felt his eyes on me several times, I was
too busy to wonder why.

At the end of the evening, when I was leaving
the hotel and hoping to find a taxi, he was waiting
for me, leaning casually against the side of a
newsstand.

"I thought you'd never come out. They

obviously work you too hard. Don't know if you remember me from earlier this evening. I'm Jay Porter."

I nodded. I was tired and my feet were aching.

"Look, I know you must be tired, but do you think you could join me for a cup of coffee this evening?"

"Well, I..."

He pulled a sad face. "Oh, no. Please don't turn me down. I've been waiting for you this past hour or more."

I must have looked skeptical, because he immediately said, "It's true. I know it's late, but what could one cup of coffee hurt? I'll take you to the nearest Starbucks and then home. Don't worry. You'll be tucked up in bed in only one more hour, sleeping the sleep of the beautiful."

He was British, I guessed, from his accent, and older than me by at least a decade. Not tall, but well made, and he matched my height in heels. He was not actually handsome, but he was distinguished looking. His clothes were immaculate and very expensive.

"Should I recognize your name?" I asked, because it was unfamiliar to me.

"Only if you read the American edition of the British newspaper, *Financial News*. I'm one of their least important reporters, and Wall Street is my beat. Come on. My driver is waiting." He indicated a limousine parked illegally in front of the hotel.

"Okay." To this day, I will never know what possessed me to accept his offer. I should have known better.

We drank our coffee. We had a pleasant time, and then he delivered me to my door. He behaved like a gentleman. He shook my hand, and said he hoped to see me again very soon.

I went upstairs, got ready for bed, and thought nothing more about him.

☾

Early the next morning, several huge bouquets of red roses were delivered to my apartment. When I arrived, late, at the office, I discovered my little cubicle also was filled with roses, pink ones this time. There was hardly room to turn around in either place.

"Looks like you have an admirer," my boss's secretary whispered. "Who are they from?"

"I don't know. There was no card in the flowers that came to my apartment this morning. Maybe there's one here?" I began to examine each bouquet.

"You mean… flowers were delivered to your apartment this morning, too?"

I nodded.

"You must have made quite a conquest. Let me know when you find out who sent them. Everyone in the whole office, and I do mean everyone, including all the bosses, is dying to know.

That was just the beginning. The next day, more flowers arrived, along with a box of expensive Belgian chocolates. There were so many flowers in my small condo, it was hard to get around them to get dressed. The additional bouquets in my tiny office cubicle made it almost impossible to reach my desk, let alone do my work. I gave away as many as I could, both to other condo owners in my building and to my co-workers.

Who were they from? I was mystified, and more than a bit creeped out. The last thing I wanted was to accept gifts from some anonymous man. I assumed the gift-giver was a man.

The next morning, I was again running late. In my hurry to get to the subway, I passed a limousine parked in front of my building without noticing it. Jay suddenly appeared at my side, and grasped my arm. I was startled and gasped, "Let me go! What are you doing here?"

"Waiting for you."

"What on earth are you talking about?" I looked around for a police officer.

"Let's have dinner tonight. I'll pick you up at seven and we'll go wherever you'd like."

"I'm working late tonight."

"That's all right. I'll be waiting in my limo outside your office building. See you later."

He popped back into his car and off they roared. I stood rooted to the sidewalk, staring after them.

To my surprise, he *was* waiting for me in the limo that evening, and every other evening over the next three weeks. That first night, I told him I only wanted a fast food hamburger. Gamely, he took me to a neighborhood burger joint.

After that, *he* chose the restaurants. They were varied, both upscale and plain, specializing in succulent Italian, Greek, Asian, Indian, and American cuisines. He was partial to steak; I preferred seafood. He managed to find both of those items on the menu of each restaurant he chose.

Over the same three weeks, more gifts arrived. I knew, now, they were from Jay. He sent more roses, perfume, designer scarves, and other expensive name-brand goodies. They were becoming a nuisance, an embarrassment of riches, so to speak.

Finally, a bracelet set with what looked like diamonds arrived, tucked into yet another bouquet of roses. I was astonished. Could the "diamonds" possibly be real? I was no expert. They could have been glass for all I knew.

&

On Monday morning, at the beginning of the fourth week of our acquaintance, he showed up in his limo outside my condo building. When I emerged, ready to catch my train to work, he got out of the car.

"Come with me, Suzi. I'm taking you on a little trip."

"What? No, you are not! I'm not going anywhere today except to work!"

"Oh, come on. Don't you have at least a week of vacation coming to you? I have a house and staff on St. Lucia in the Caribbean. They're waiting for us."

"Just like that? You didn't think to ask me first, or even get to know me a little more? I've only known you three weeks." I was shocked at his audacity and starting to become angry.

"Don't be angry. Think about it, and then come with me."

"Wait. Did you just send me a diamond bracelet? It is real?"

"Yes, guilty as charged."

"What? I can't accept that! And, you've got to stop sending me all those other gifts. What do you take me for?"

"I take you for the beautiful young woman who has stolen my heart. Come with me. Please."

I am still unable to explain why I suddenly stopped protesting and agreed to think about going with him. "Okay. I guess I'll think about it. Ask me again in two weeks." Obviously, I had lost my mind completely.

"All right, if you insist. The house will still be there in two weeks. I'll see you tonight."

Over the next two weeks, Jay behaved like a model citizen, and a very entertaining escort. He told me about his family, his work as a journalist, his interests, his likes and dislikes, and even asked me about mine. He also slowed down the gift-giving, only presenting me with gifts two or three more times. Despite my misgivings, and I still had some, he was beginning to charm me.

There was another thing. So far, he had only kissed me, very chastely, good night. He kept his hands to himself, and always behaved like a gentleman. I was beginning to feel safe with him.

At the end of the second week, he asked me again to go with him to visit his house in St. Lucia. Since the first time he had asked me, I had spent most of my free time trying to decide what to do. I wanted to go, but I was hesitant. It was not Jay, himself, who made me hesitate. Now, it was a financial concern. I knew I would need to bring tropical clothing, and resort wear was beyond the limits of my tiny budget. When I mentioned my concern, he laughed.

"You'll only need traveling clothes. Something light. Tell me your size, and I'll have my housekeeper find a swimsuit for you. You won't need anything else."

I looked at him. "Just traveling clothes?"

"Yes. We'll be flying in my private jet. Only the pilot, and I, will see you. And, on the island, it's very casual. A swimsuit or two will be all you'll need."

It seemed so simple. "Okay, I'll go. And you don't have to buy me any swimsuits. I have my own."

"Can you get away from your office soon?"

"I'll talk to my boss. I do have some time accrued, and I should be able to go in a week or two. Is that okay?"

He shrugged. "I'd like to spirit you away today, but I'll wait."

When he picked me up at the end of the day, I had good news. "I was able to get a week off starting next Monday. That means we could leave on Saturday morning, if that's okay with you."

He took my hand and brought it to his lips. "Perfect. St. Lucia is gorgeous and I can hardly wait to show you the house. It's been in my family for three generations. The ocean views are amazing."

The next four days passed in a blur. I packed both of my swimsuits, and agonized over what to wear on the plane. When Saturday morning dawned, I was ready.

Promptly at eight o'clock, Jay's limo drew up in front of my building. I was waiting in the lobby, and when I came outside, he stepped out of the car. Grasping my hand, he pulled me into an embrace. "You look wonderful. Are you ready?"

I nodded, smiling broadly. He helped me into the car and we were immediately on our way to an airport in Teterboro, New Jersey, where he kept his private plane. A few hours later, we arrived in St. Lucia. The driver of a very clean and well-kept open Jeep met us at the airport and drove us through a tropical paradise.

Jay's family's property, a "plantation," he called it, covered more than three hundred rugged acres, mostly planted in bananas and avocados. Dozens of native servants lived and worked on the property. Jay claimed it was the largest private plantation on the island.

The "house" turned out to be a mansion so huge it was like Tara on steroids. Swaying palm trees and lush flowering plants were laid out in manicured beds surrounding the house. I guessed it must take around the clock supervision to keep them all in check. I soon found out I was right. Twelve gardeners worked in shifts to keep the plants from swallowing the house.

Taking my hand, Jay escorted me up the broad front steps and across an enormous portico whose roof was held aloft by massive white columns. Then, he led me through an intricately carved double door twice my height, and into the foyer.

I looked around in awe. The inside of the house was magnificent. In the foyer, and in each surrounding room except the dining room, there were bamboo couches and chairs upholstered in tropical print fabrics. Beautiful Oriental carpets and exotic fur rugs softened the white marble floors throughout the main living areas. There were also bamboo chests, side tables, and buffets, each holding exquisite gold, ebony, and ivory accessories.

The dining room contained a vast ebony table surrounded by at least two dozen ebony Hepplewhite-style chairs whose seats were upholstered in a shimmering golden fabric. The room was lit by gold and crystal wall sconces and an enormous antique crystal chandelier hung over the table.

One whole wall in the gigantic library was lined with floor-to-ceiling Chinese lacquer bookcases whose hermetically sealed glass doors protected valuable books and other precious objects from dust and humidity.

I had only a few moments to take it all in before a butler entered and bowed, and a housekeeper bustled in and curtsied. I had never seen that before in real life, only on TV and in the movies. The housekeeper, whose name, she said, was Matilda, escorted me upstairs to an exquisite bedroom suite, decorated in shades of blue and aqua.

The windows were open, as was a door leading to a wide balcony, and I could hear the crashing of waves. Irresistibly drawn to that open door, I stepped through it and drew in my breath in awe. The balcony overlooked a spectacular view of the ocean, a white-sand beach, and a rock and concrete jetty. Just down the beach, probably less than half a mile away, there was a colorful village and a marina full of yachts and smaller boats of all kinds.

Matilda showed me the contents of the suite: the sitting room, bedroom, and the adjacent bath, where plush towels that matched the décor, a white robe of the same toweling material, and exclusive toiletries were waiting for me. In the bedroom, three different bathing suits with matching cover-ups were laid out on the wide bed.

"Miss," said Matilda, indicating a button on the wall near the door of the sitting room, "ring for me if you need anything. Lunch will be at one o'clock on the verandah. Mr. Jay suggests you wear one of the bathing suits, its matching cover-up, and a hat. The sun is quite strong here. You will find sunscreen in the bathroom."

"Did Jay tell you my size?"

"Yes, he did. Please let me know if they do not fit. I will exchange them for the correct size."

"That won't be necessary. I'm sure they'll be fine. Thank you."

She curtsied again and backed away toward the door. "I will leave you now to freshen up and get ready for lunch."

I had been speechless while she showed me the contents of the suite. In the sitting room, there was fruit in a cobalt blue glass bowl on a glass-topped cocktail table in front of a bamboo sofa. A side table held a small dish of assorted wrapped chocolates. Bottled water rested in a huge ice-filled bucket along with champagne and other wines, waiting to be poured. I felt as if I had been dropped into a fairy tale. This could not be real!

I went back into the bedroom and stood

contemplating my swimsuit choices. These were much nicer than the ones I had packed.

Suddenly, a door, set so cleverly into the wall that it was almost hidden, opened, and Jay came through. "Aren't you going to change into a swimsuit? The water in the pool is kept refreshingly cool. Or we could go down to the beach. There's a cabana stocked with towels and sunscreen."

"This house, this suite, they're amazing. How come you invited *me* here? It must be obvious that I'm not of your economic class!"

"I thought I made it clear. I'm in love with you. I want to spend uninterrupted time with you and this is the best way to achieve that. Away from Manhattan, your job, and all your other obligations, you can relax and just be. I want to be with you."

"But… You don't know me yet!"

"Maybe not yet, not completely, but I will. I'm going to start getting to know you right now."

He came closer until he was standing directly in front of me. He took my hand and pulled me against his chest. I opened my mouth to protest, and he covered it with his own and pulled me closer. His kiss was sensual, his tongue playful. I tried to turn my face, but he was too strong. Then, without conscious thought, and completely against my better judgment, I relaxed into him and began to kiss him back. Dizzily, I swayed in his arms. It had been a long time since I had allowed a man to kiss me like this, and I knew we were not going to stop with one lustful kiss.

He was going to seduce me, and I was going

to let him. I have no defense for my idiocy. I knew I had no business letting him seduce me. But, I guess, that is why it is called seduction. I turned off my protesting mind and gave myself completely to him.

Soon, we were on the bed. The suits and cover-ups fell unnoticed to the floor. We missed lunch. Or, rather, we had lunch later. Much later.

The week flew by. We spent most of it either in bed, in the pool, or walking on the beach. But mostly, we were in bed.

All too soon, Sunday morning came. I needed to be back at work on Monday, and Jay and I made the most of our last morning together on the island. After lunch, the Jeep's driver took us back to the airport and we landed in New Jersey just as the sun sank into the western sky. The limousine was waiting. Our romantic tropical idyll was over.

During the next few weeks, Jay continued to take me out to dinner in a different restaurant each evening, and then to his luxurious apartment on the Upper East Side of Manhattan. He insisted on having the limousine drive me to work each day and pick me up each evening when I was finished for the day. He was always in the car in the evening, waiting to give me a new trinket: diamond earrings to match my bracelet, more flowers, a delicate dessert from an exclusive patisserie, a designer scarf, or bag, or shoes. He said he loved me. Locked in an unquestioning daze, I accepted it all, no longer protesting the gifts.

❦

At the end of the third month, he proposed, giving me a huge and dazzling emerald and diamond ring he claimed had belonged to his grandmother. I was dazzled enough by now to agree. And so, we were engaged.

Did I love him? I thought so, at the time.

We set a date, invited friends and relatives, and I went shopping for a wedding gown. Ellen, of course, went with me. She was concerned about the swiftness of my decision to marry Jay, but I finally convinced her that I knew what I was doing.

My grandmother was undergoing treatment at Sloane-Kettering Cancer Hospital in Manhattan, fighting gallantly against her colon cancer. She promised to come to the ceremony if she was up to it physically, but she was not able to shop for wedding finery.

Jay's family was spread over five continents. His older brother in France might come, his father was based in Bangkok, his other brother ran a company in Johannesburg, one sister lived in Buenos Aires, and another was in Toronto. His mother was dead.

He booked St. Patrick's Cathedral despite our tiny guest list. Few people would be able to attend, though my entire office was coming. They were ecstatic to be invited. Two or three people from the *Financial News* also were planning to come. Ellen agreed to be my Maid of Honor. She and her boyfriend, Jon, were coming, as was my brother, Ron. Jay's brother, Peter, finally consented to fly in from Paris for the day. He was to be Jay's Best Man.

By the time the great day arrived, I was having serious misgivings. Jay brushed them all aside and took me to bed.

He was, as usual, persuasive. I gave in and agreed to go through with the marriage. I even smiled as I walked down the aisle on my brother's arm. Had I known what would happen only eight weeks later, I would have flown away as swiftly as a bird heading south for the winter.

The ceremony was a blur. I am sure it was lovely, but I was too stupidly blind to remember much. I do remember the limousine driving us to the wedding breakfast, in a small, exclusive hotel. We honeymooned in Venice. It is a romantic city, and we toured the magnificent museums and galleries, rode gondolas in the moonlight, and feasted on delicious Italian cooking. And we made passionate love.

After two weeks, we flew home. I had moved into his apartment soon after we returned from St. Lucia. Instead of dropping my lease, I had decided to try to sublet my apartment, wisely keeping the lease in my name. It was the only smart thing I did during those whirlwind months of insanity. Luckily, no prospective tenant had met my requirements.

We both went back to work. Five more weeks passed while I was busy with the usual work-related parties, and occasional overtime. The limousine was at my disposal. Jay traveled to his office by taxi, but was always in the limousine when it picked me up after I finished work.

The eighth week of our marriage began as usual. It ended very differently.

On Friday evening, there was to be a party in the *Financial News* offices to celebrate their acquisition of a small, but well-respected, German financial newspaper. I never learned the name of the paper.

After a tiring day that seemed to go on forever, the limousine was waiting outside my office building as usual when I finally was free to leave. To my surprise, Jay was not inside.

The *Financial News* party had been underway for several hours by the time I arrived. I took a glass of champagne from a passing waiter and looked around for Jay. He was nowhere in sight, so I asked his boss where he was. The man had turned red when I approached him, tried to cover it with a fake coughing fit, and finally said, "Oh. He's around somewhere. Probably in the loo."

I decided to look for him in his office since there was no way I was going to search the men's room. His office door was closed, but I could hear muffled laughter.

I tapped on the door and there was silence for a moment, followed by shushing noises and more muffled laughter. I opened the door, and there they were, caught in the act. My husband's hand was up his executive assistant's skirt. If his hand had been the only part of his anatomy up her skirt, I might eventually have forgiven him. To his credit, Jay looked startled and slightly ashamed. His assistant, however, grinned triumphantly, and stayed astride his lap.

I left.

I spent that night in my own condo and next morning I called Ellen with my news, and asked if her corporate attorneys could recommend a good divorce lawyer.

Jay tried to explain. He was drunk, she seduced him, it meant nothing, it was not his finest hour, could I not forgive him, etc., etc. I was having none of it, or him.

Six weeks later, I was a free woman. I gave him back everything he had given me, except the flowers. They were all dead anyway. He told me to keep the diamonds and the emerald ring, since it was not really his grandmother's after all.

When I had them appraised, the ring turned out to be a fake, along with the "diamond" bracelet and earrings, just like the romantic love I thought we had shared.

So, that was the end of my brief foray into marriage. About a year later, a small article appeared in *The Wall Street Times*. The piece stated that Jeremy Davidson Porter IV, until yesterday employed by the American edition of the British newspaper, *Financial News,* had been summarily dismissed. He was accused of plagiarism and of submitting false personal information to the paper. He was reported to have gone back to England, bankrupt, and in disgrace. His share of his family's money was gone. He had frittered it away.

Frittered is not the word the venerable *WST* used in their article, but that was what they meant.

I could find no sympathy in my heart for Jay. But worse, I wondered if I would ever again be able to trust a man with my heart.

❦

That was eight years ago. Even after all this

time, thinking about Jay, and my ridiculously naïve behavior, always made my head hurt.

I took two aspirin and tried to banish any thought of the deceitful Jay from my mind. It was time to sleep, if I could. I had to drive back to Atlanta in the morning to catch my flight.

# CHAPTER 7

*C*

THANKFULLY, MY HEADACHE WAS GONE by the time I drove away from Blue Ridge, early on Friday morning. I left my rental car at the Atlanta airport, and, much later that day, returned to my condo in Manhattan.

I loved New York City. And, I liked my job. But, by Monday morning, riding the subway to work, I knew I was going to find it hard to settle back into my usual routine. I was feeling restless. And lonely.

I dated occasionally, but for a fun social life I depended on a small circle of friends and co-workers who hung out together after work and on weekends. Some, or all of us, often went together to concerts, Broadway shows, movies, and our favorite restaurants, or to try new ones. I took classes in various subjects, from cooking to Tai Chi, at a branch of the public library near my condo, but I enjoyed solitary pursuits too: reading, needlework, and taking long walks in the city to window shop.

For a short while, I had entertained romantic thoughts for my boss, Alexander Whiteside. He was a handsome, youngish man who treated me fairly and never led me to believe that he found me the least bit attractive. I was pretty sure Alex was straight, not gay, but he wore no wedding ring, making me think he might be free. With absolutely no encouragement, I soon came to my senses and began to see him as he really was: my boss.

I was happy, more or less, with my life as it was, but I wished people would stop trying to set me up with single men. That had happened quite often since my divorce, but none of the men I had dated so far had fulfilled my notions of a suitable lover, let alone of husband material. Was I expecting too much? I thought not. Besides the trust factor, I simply wanted my dates to be my equal in intelligence and earning power, and be honest, reliable, charming, and cheerful. A shared sense of humor would be good and, oh yes: he should also be a thoughtful and exciting lover. Most of the men I had dated were nice enough, but the spark I was looking for was missing.

Now, I was feeling that spark from a totally unsuitable man. Snapshots of him kept popping up in my memory: Tom showing me condos and cabins, both of us enjoying the gluttonous barbeque dinner at Billy's, Tom building a fire in his fireplace while dazzling me with his gorgeous body, serving that delicious lunch after I had signed the papers to "rent" Margaret's cabin rent-free, and then driving me to Dial.

Most dangerous of all was Tom pulling me into his arms and our passionate kiss. We had both been swept away, until we came to our senses and reared back in horror. He was, obviously, not auditioning me for the role of his next bedmate. So, what was the meaning of that kiss?

Sparring with him had been both infuriating and stimulating, in more ways than one. But, he was all wrong for me. There was no way he would move to New York. And I was not about to leave my job—my career—to move to Georgia. What would I do there?

⁕

I had been sunk in contemplation of my life, career goals, and my non-existent love life ever since I left Blue Ridge. Now, the subway train screeched to a halt at my stop. It was time to focus on my job.

I pushed through the crowds exiting the station and discovered that it was raining. Except for that, it was a typical Monday morning in Manhattan. I dashed the three blocks to my office building and, damp and breathless, I took the elevator to the eleventh floor. When I walked into the reception area, Judy, my assistant, was chatting with our receptionist.

Practically in unison, they said "Hi, Suzi, how was your vacation?"

"Great," I answered with a smile, and motioned to Judy to follow me to my office. On the way, we grabbed coffee in the lunch/break room, and she started to fill me in on the latest news and gossip. Her behavior was odd, though. I could tell she was holding something back.

I soon found out what it was. Alex, my boss,

called me into his office, closed his door, made sure I was sitting down, and gave me the news.

Our firm was merging with its closest rival. There were going to be redundancies, and my job was being given to a woman from the other company. Apparently, she had years more experience than I had. Alex was apologetic, but he could offer me only a lesser job and a drastic pay cut. His hands were tied. He had tried to convince upper management that I was a valuable asset to our company, but they wanted the more experienced candidate.

I was shocked. This happened to other people. Not me. There had been no indication before I left, only a week ago, that I was a candidate for my own job.

To his credit, Alex behaved in a completely matter of fact manner. He explained that I would have to clear out my desk and leave that very day. There were papers to be signed in the Human Resources office and I should go there now. Packing boxes would be delivered to my former office by the time I finished. The company was "generously" providing transportation to see me home with my belongings.

He left me then, closing the door behind him, to give me time to compose myself.

I was finding composure difficult to achieve, however. Alone now, my body began to shake. The fact that this had happened to millions of people before me, especially since the recession that began in December of 2007, was no consolation.

What would happen now? I was committed to staying in Margaret's cabin this summer. I had to find a job, but a new employer would never agree to the ten-week leave of absence I had just lost. Even if I thought I could afford a summer in Georgia using my meager savings, how could I pay my New York condo fees, mortgage, taxes, and all the rest? My mind played out one chaotically fantastic scenario after another.

Finally, I wiped the tears of anger and grief from my face, reapplied my lipstick, and tried to appear calm as I exited Alex's office. The Human Resources department was located on another floor, and hoping to avoid being seen, I took the stairs.

Luckily, I met only a few of my colleagues on the way. Most of them gave me a sympathetic smile or an encouraging pat as they passed. Only one averted her eyes, but we had never been friendly.

I paused in the HR department's doorway, and caught the receptionist's eye. She beckoned to me and told me to go right in to see Karen Rogers, the Vice President of HR. I squared my shoulders and did so.

I had worked with Karen numerous times and we had a cordial, respectful relationship. She was nothing but professional as she took me step by step through the details of my departure. I was amazed to learn that my severance package included full salary for six months, medical and dental coverage for one year, and both personal counseling and relocation help if I needed either service. I shook her hand after I signed the last document, and she came around her big desk to give me a good-bye hug, and to wish me well.

Still in semi-shock, I found my way back to the

office I had thought of as *mine* for three of the last five years. When I was promoted, after two years in a lower position, I had decided to decorate my new, larger domain to suit my taste. On the walls, I hung a portrait in oils of my grandmother and family photos of my grandparents, my parents, and my brother and me as kids. I bought blue and creamy white striped cushions to dress up the utilitarian beige sofa, placed a few treasured books, held up by bookends made of two slices of a sapphire-colored geode, on the credenza behind my desk, and decorated both with a few of the fossils I had collected. While in college, I had dated a Paleontology major for several months. I fell in love, not with him, but with the intricate designs of tiny ancient plants and animals. They had given me much pleasure over the years since then.

As Alex had promised, there were two large cartons sitting on the floor inside my office door along with packing materials. There was also a security guard. He stood impassively while I took down the portrait and the photos, and tearfully shielded them in bubble wrap. The books, geode bookends, and fossils went into the other carton, along with the box of tissues I kept in a desk drawer, and several other personal items. I decided to leave the pillows. In a matter of minutes, my history in that room was deleted.

I closed the cartons with sealing tape and watched the guard place them on a dolly. He waited as I grabbed my pocketbook and looked around one last time. Then he walked me down to the lobby.

About fifteen of my former colleagues were waiting there. They hugged and kissed me, and wished me good luck, but I could scarcely take it all in. I managed a brief thank you to everyone, and a promise to keep in touch, but I was unsuccessfully trying to keep my tears in check.

My transportation, a prepaid yellow cab, was waiting at the curb. After the cartons were loaded, there was nothing more to do or say. I got into the cab and the driver pulled away from the curb into traffic.

# Chapter 8

W HEN WE ARRIVED AT MY condo, the driver lifted my cartons out of the taxi and left them on the wet sidewalk. The rain had slackened off a bit, but it was now coming down in big spring drops.

I was able to pull the cartons close to the entrance before the building manager's 18-year-old son, Stewie, saw me and came out to help. He knew he would get a nice tip from me. Otherwise, I would have to drag these cartons in and out the elevator and into my condo myself, hoping all the while that no one would steal the carton I was not currently dragging.

Between us, we accomplished the task in only two trips, with me standing guard over the second box, while he rode up in the elevator with the first. I thanked him, and got a lascivious grin in return for my generous tip. He fancied himself quite the ladies' man with the high school girls in the building.

Once inside, I threw down my pocketbook and collapsed on the sofa. I looked at the cartons and howled in pure anguish. I had tried so hard to keep my grief bottled up inside after I left Alex's office. Now, I wept until I could weep no more. Only then did I get up, wash my face, and change into dry clothes. I was still so angry I could spit, but there were no more tears, at least for now.

I glanced at the clock hanging in the kitchen, I could see it from almost anywhere in my tiny condo, and was shocked to see it was only ten-thirty. It was not even lunchtime yet. It seemed impossible. I felt as if I had aged ten years since I left for work this morning. My whole world was upside down.

How I missed my Grandma Rose. Always, memories of her were in the back of my mind, and it seemed especially cruel not to be able to pour all my current woes into her sympathetic ears. She would have listened to me, given me a hug, and then told me to stop feeling sorry for myself and start looking for a job.

So, I got up off the couch and washed my face again. Contemplating my red and swollen eyes, and my sullen expression in the bathroom mirror, I knew I had better listen to Grandma.

It seemed that I had two choices. I could cancel my summer "rental" in Margaret's cabin and start looking for a new job at once, or I could go to Georgia as planned. Thanks to my former company's generous severance package, I was no worse off financially now than if I had been able to take their promised leave of absence, except, of course, I had no job to come back to when my "rental" period was over.

My confidence had been severely shaken. I was probably not in the best frame of mind to go job hunting just yet. I needed time to recover, to examine my goals, and try to map out a new future.

Where better to do that than in Margaret's inviting cabin? I wondered whether I could come a week or two before the date Tom and I had agreed on.

At least for now, my financial picture was less bleak than it might have been. I had some savings, not much, but unlike many of my peers, I had been putting a small amount from each paycheck into a savings account. I also had inherited some money from my grandmother's estate, which I had invested.

But now, it was becoming much more urgent to find someone to sublet my condo. I had already advertised in the neighborhood weeklies, but with no success. I would have to try again.

I spent the next few days placing more newspaper ads and putting notices on the community bulletin boards in my bank, the food market I patronized, and the laundromat I visited each week. I received several responses, but again, no one was suitable.

By the end of the week, when I was calmer, I called Ellen. She still had not left for Africa, and though she and I had texted or spoken every day as usual, I had not told her my sad news. When she called me back later that evening, we made a lunch date in Manhattan for the following Friday.

❧

We embraced and the hostess seated us. The restaurant was crowded, but the noise level was not as loud as I had feared. When I told her my tale of woe, she responded just as I had imagined.

"Oh, no! What were your supervisors thinking to let you go? I know how hard you work, and your work is good. Very good! I hope they gave you a good severance package at least!"

"Well, I was surprised. They were very generous, in fact. There might have been some guilty feelings there, though when my boss broke the news to me, I was pretty sure they had no feelings at all! There have been several other layoffs while I was in Georgia, but I was the first person in my division to be fired."

"Uh, oh. What about that group you meet all the time to play with? Have you seen any of them since you were forced to leave?"

"Well, no. But it's only been a couple of weeks. I did get some calls. They were very supportive over the phone. But, I don't know. It'll be awkward, I guess. We'll see."

We gave our orders to the waiter, and while we talked, a colleague of Ellen's came over to our table to greet her and ask a few questions. That almost always happened when we were out together in Manhattan. When she finished her architecture degree in the prestigious Cornell University Master's program with an even higher average than her father's, she became an instant celebrity within the architectural community. Now, she was becoming better known among the rest of the world.

She had been featured in newspaper and magazine articles ever since she took over her father's firm. While her looks probably helped, it was her architectural talent, business acumen, and appealing character, that gained her the respect of her clients and other architects.

The man shook hands with Ellen and returned to his table. She looked at me, shrugged, and said, "Now, where were we? Oh, yes. I was about to ask you about your mysterious Tom."

I could feel my cheeks warming. "He's not my Tom!"

"Oh, boy. She's protesting a bit too much, methinks! Sorry, Shakespeare." Laughing, she shook her finger at me. "Go on, girl. Spill it!"

The food came, and we spent the rest of our lunch talking about Georgia, the town of Blue Ridge, the mountains, the cabin I would be staying in this summer, and finally, my impressions of Tom.

"He's much too gorgeous and charming, and he's not above flirting with every woman in sight. But, he's obviously been well trained in etiquette and the culinary arts by the multi-talented Margaret, his teacher, friend, and substitute mother. He's also doing very well financially, thanks in part, he says, to a college friend who has become a Wall Street tycoon and sends him pointers now and then. He's used some of his money to help friends who were down on their luck. I saw a couple of examples of that while I was there."

"Okay, but how does he make you feel?"

"Oh, wow! He makes me feel all shivery and ready to melt at his feet one minute, then a few seconds later, he ruins it by saying something so patronizing that I want to slap his conceited face. And, who is Sheila? And who, surely not Margaret, decorated his house? It's a showpiece of backcountry chic! You should see it! It's all Tiffany-style lamps and red wool upholstery. His kitchen has commercial quality appliances and is about as big as my whole condo. He drives a convertible sports car so expensive that I've only seen photos of them in upscale magazine ads. It's hard to believe he's for real!"

"Oh, my. You've got it bad. He's certainly a fast worker. I haven't seen you this interested in a man since you divorced the faithless Jay. That was how many years ago?"

"Please don't bring *his* name up again! Last time I thought of him, I couldn't get him out of my head for hours. I kept replaying our so-called courtship, engagement, and marriage over and over 'til I wanted to scream!"

Ellen reached over and grasped my hands. "Oh, Suzi... I'm sorry. I won't mention him ever again. He's a bad memory for everyone who loves you."

I knew she meant what she said. Busy as she was, Ellen had given me as much of her time and attention as I needed during my divorce ordeal. She listened to my tearful complaints and sometimes wild accusations without once telling me to grow up and be a woman. Instead, she gave me good advice, and kept repeating it, until I was ready to listen.

I steered the conversation to Ellen and her latest project in Africa. She was excited about it, though she was unsure when it could be completed. She had designed a hospital in Nairobi, Kenya, a much-needed state of the art facility funded by charitable donations from all over the world. It was to be built in three stages, and Stage I was already underway.

Like many countries in Africa and the Middle East, Kenya often had to deal with multiple challenges, including high unemployment, poverty, crime, corruption, violence, ethnic diversity, devastating droughts and flooding, and the threat of militant uprisings and invasions. When problems escalate to dangerous levels, the U.S. State Department temporarily banns travel to the affected areas. Ellen had been in tight spots before, however, and she was determined to go back as soon as the current travel ban was lifted.

At last, she glanced at her phone and saw the time. "Suzi, I love you, but I've got to go. Let's get together again next weekend. I'll text you, okay?"

I nodded, we embraced, and she was gone. I discovered that she had grabbed the check, and paid it on her way out. She was generous like that, and I appreciated it. Especially now.

☾

I walked back to my apartment and, just as I put my key into the lock, I could hear my house phone ringing. Maybe it was my former boss. Had they realized their mistake? Was I going to be given my job back? I managed to answer the phone before it stopped ringing.

No, I was not going to be given my job back. But, if I could believe my ears, the woman who was replacing me needed a temporary place to live until she found the right apartment. My former boss remembered that I was planning to sublet

mine while I was on leave. Could she come and
see it today?

"What?" I thundered. "Of all the nerve! Did
you really think I would be willing to sublet my
apartment to the woman who is replacing me?
Well, you are wrong!"

I slammed the receiver down and barely
restrained myself from throwing the phone across
the room. So much for not burning my bridges.
Even if they finally did realize they had made a
mistake in hiring her, they would never ask me to
come back now.

When I calmed down a little, I texted Ellen this
bit of news. She called me back immediately with
a satisfyingly succinct "F... them!"

"Oh yeah!" I yelled into the phone. But, I had
already realized, too late, of course, how badly I
had behaved.

"But Ellen, I won't be getting a decent reference
now. What will I do next fall when I need a new
job? Who will hire me?"

"Look, I get your concern, but I'll bet your boss
knew he was asking something totally outrageous
of you. You may be worrying unnecessarily. Take
my advice, and just forget all this for now.

"By the way, I may have found a suitable
candidate to sublet your condo. Give me a couple
of days and I'll get back to you. Meanwhile, try
to focus on other things, like packing for ten
weeks in the mountains. Wow, you may need to
get some new things. If we can arrange it, I'll go
shopping with you!"

After we hung up, I walked into the bedroom
I described to people as "cozy" and opened my

tiny closet. She was right. Dwelling on what I had done to ensure my future unemployment would be counterproductive. And what a nice segue from my almost tears to a shopping excursion. Of course, it was doubtful she would be able to go with me. Her schedule was tight and it would take a miracle to free up an entire morning or afternoon. I could hope, though.

※

There was a room set aside in the basement of my building for tenants to store their excess belongings. Each condo owner had a locked, open-wire cage about six feet square. I kept the suitcases my grandmother had given me when I graduated from high school in mine, but that was all. My plan was to pack my business and dressy clothes and shoes in boxes and store them in my cage. There would be plenty of room for them.

I grabbed my pocketbook and visited my local liquor store to ask about getting cardboard boxes. The clerk told me to come back at seven o'clock Monday morning, when they restocked the shelves. I could pick out the boxes I needed before they crushed them for recycling.

Back in my condo, I was at loose ends. I could call some of my colleagues and meet them for Sunday brunch, but I wondered whether that was a good idea. Would they treat me as usual, or would there be awkwardness? I decided to wait until I had firm plans to go to Georgia. A good-bye luncheon would give us all something positive to talk about.

❧

It rained again on Saturday, but Sunday was a rare perfect spring day in New York. The month of May in Manhattan was sometimes cold, sometimes windy and rainy, sometimes sunny and hot, and occasionally all these weather conditions were featured in the same week. For today, at least, the sun was shining, and the temperature was a lovely 72 degrees. I decided to make the most of it.

I walked the southern-most part of the High Line, the amazing walkway-public park above lower and mid-town Manhattan that had recently been converted from an abandoned elevated railway. After that, I visited my favorite art gallery in Soho (south of Houston Street), and window shopped along Broadway in Noho (north of Houston).

When I was hungry, I bought street food: a delicious chicken pita, with onions, shredded lettuce, and tomato slices, all smothered in savory yogurt sauce, and finally, I arrived in Washington Square Park. The trees were in glorious bloom, and the square was thronged with musicians, rowdy children and their harassed nannies, older men playing chess, homeless people, teenagers with eyes glued to their smartphone screens, policemen and women on patrol, and people of all ages expressing their artistic personalities with extreme outfits, hairdos, tattoos, and body piercing. I loved to people-watch. I sat on the rim of the huge central fountain and enjoyed the parade of humanity. I was going to miss my city.

Eventually, the sun sank lower in the sky and it was time to go. I stopped in a café near the Square and ordered take-out sushi and a large salad. Carrying my dinner, I headed for home.

A short subway ride and a quick walk brought me to my door. Again, I could hear my house phone ringing. That was one expense I could do away with now that I was unemployed. I no longer needed a land line for my boss to call. I had never divulged my cell number. Twenty-four-seven connectivity was for those with an actual career. Besides, it was probably a salesman. I opened the door, went inside, and let it ring until it stopped.

A few moments later, the answer machine beeped, a relic of the previous owner who had lived here for more than twenty years. I took off my jacket and pushed the replay button.

Tom's sexy voice filled my condo.

"Hi, Suzanna. It's Tom Wolf. Just callin' to let you know that Margaret is leavin' soon for California, and I'll be drivin' her to the Atlanta airport a week from next Friday. Her flight leaves at eleven a.m. I wondered if you'd be able to fly south the same day. I know it's a little earlier than you'd planned, but if you could come then, I could pick you up while I'm in Atlanta and bring you back to Blue Ridge. Let me know. You have my email, or call me at the number on my business card. Hope to hear from you soon."

Well, that was food for thought. If I could just find a good person to sublet my condo, I could be on my way to Georgia the Friday after next. This was Sunday. That gave me almost two weeks to get ready.

I unpacked my dinner and searched the internet for a suitable flight while I ate. I finally found one from LaGuardia airport that would get me into Atlanta by two-thirty in the afternoon. I would have a very early start and a two-hour layover in Baltimore, but if Tom was willing to wait for me, it could work. If, I could get a tenant to sublease my condo in time.

I decided to wait to hear from Ellen before calling Tom back, or booking my flight. The airfare was already outrageously expensive. Waiting a few more days would only make it pricier, but I had little choice.

# CHAPTER 9

NEXT DAY, ELLEN CALLED ME back. She was not going to be able to go shopping with me on Saturday after all, because she finally had State Department permission to fly to Nairobi this Thursday. She was excited.

"At last, Suzi!" I could hear the grin in her voice.

"Are you sure it's safe? There's still stuff in the news."

"I'll be fine. The American Embassy is not far from the building site, and I've made friends there as well. Don't waste any time worrying about me, okay? You've got enough to think about."

"Will you promise to check in with me every day, as usual?"

"Of course, I will. I want to hear all about the progress of your almost love affair."

"There is NO love affair!"

"So you keep saying. But that's not what I'm hearing… But before I forget, I've got a prospective tenant for you to interview. He was an intern in our office last year and he finished Cornell's Master's Degree program in architecture this spring. He'll be starting his first real architectural job next week, working for my old company. He's been looking for a place to live, but hasn't found anything yet. I told him about your condo, and he'd like to see it. Subletting for a few months will mean he'll have more time to find something permanent.

"I think you'll like him. He's nice, clean-cut, and serious about his work, but he also has a great sense of humor. In fact, he's almost perfect. Too bad he's so young!"

"What...?" I knew Ellen was kidding. As far as I knew, her marriage to Jon was solid. "Okay, then. Have him call me. And thanks, Ellen. If this works out, I'll owe you!"

Twenty minutes later, my potential tenant, Bill Morrison, called. If it was convenient, he could come by to see the condo now. He was only a few minutes away.

I agreed, and when he arrived, I liked him right away. We talked for a while after I gave him the fifty-cent tour. Though the condo was small, he said it was perfect for now as it was only two subway stops from his new job. He agreed to three months deposit, and to send each month's rental check directly to me, so I could pay the condo charges, utilities, etc., as usual. I gave him a copy of both the condo association's rules and my own, and urged him to read them now before agreeing to abide by them. He looked them over, signed both copies and gave me his references. I promised to check them and let him know my decision as soon as possible.

He seemed a nice young man, and it was a bonus that he came recommended by Ellen, but I was going to take no chances. I knew the trouble a bad tenant could make for a condo owner. There were tales of woe all over social media and, probably, at least some of them were true.

To my relief, he checked out positively. He came by with his deposit check two days later. I agreed to leave my extra key with the doorman on the day of my flight to Georgia, so he could move in later that same day.

As soon as Bill left, I called Tom back. He picked up on the first ring.

"Suzanna!"

"Hi, Tom. I got your message, and I apologize for not calling back immediately. I was still looking for someone to sublet my condo, and I've finally found the right person."

"That's great. What about next Friday? Are you goin' to be able to fly in then? I know it's a bit earlier than you'd planned."

"Yes. I found a flight that's supposed to land at two-thirty. Is that too late? It means you'd have to wait around the airport for a few hours."

"It's no problem. I'll bring a book. By the way, I'll be drivin' Margaret's Jeep. She's takin' quite a bit of luggage for her six months' stay in California. And, I guess you'll have several bags too."

"I'm trying not to bring too much. I'm sure I can buy whatever I need on line if it's not available in town."

"Sure. Well, I'll see you next week. Have a good flight."

"Thanks. Bye for now."

I hung up and immediately booked my flight to Atlanta. Luckily, a seat was still available.

I tried not to feel let down by my brief and business-like conversation with Tom. Since there was no reason to have expected anything else, especially after the way we parted, I had no reason to feel sad. Nevertheless, I had hoped for more warmth. I remembered all too well my physical response to his mere presence. The electricity between us had felt like magic. I refused to dwell too much or too often on his kiss, but the memory kept intruding into whatever I was doing. I knew I would be devastated if, when we were together again, the magic was gone.

☾

I picked up the boxes I needed, and spent the next few days packing away my business and evening clothes, personal items, and some breakable decorative pieces Grandma Rose had given me when Ron and I helped her sell her Long Island house.

In my spare time, I scoured the internet, studying north Georgia's summer weather patterns. I was worried about weather extremes in the mountains. I knew I would need raingear, new hiking boots to replace my old ones, summer clothing, and some warmer things too.

The time flew by as I made and remade lists of the clothing and other items I would need in Georgia. I shopped, returned bad decisions, shopped again, and packed and repacked everything to make it all fit into the smallest number of bags. I debated whether to bring something pretty and sexy for evening wear, and finally decided to do so. Maybe

I would get lucky.

I worried about the implications of that. Did I want to get lucky? It seemed like a better idea to lay low and not go out of my way to meet eligible men at this point in my life. I had a purpose, a good reason to be in Fannin County this summer. I was not on vacation, not exactly. I was going to be quite busy with my research and writing my family's history. And, I told myself sternly, I was not going to expect anything but business from Tom. So there!

Really? Huh, I had to laugh at myself. Of course, I wanted to get lucky. Especially with Tom!

I carefully planned the outfit I would wear on the plane to show off my best assets without showing them too blatantly. My sleeveless blouse was form-fitting, with a low-cut neckline, in my favorite cinnamon brown. My jeans fit snugly, and I had new tan leather sandals with a three-inch wedge heel. In case the plane was chilly, I planned to bring a light sweater patterned with blue hydrangeas, and a blue and beige striped silk scarf. My laptop, wallet, and other personal items, including a romance novel by my favorite author, went into my leather briefcase, the same one Tom had called a "suitcase."

I finished packing last minute items just before it was time to leave for the airport. I lugged my bags down to the lobby, left my extra condo key with the doorman, and hailed a taxi. It took some ingenuity to fit all my gear into the trunk, but the driver was an expert luggage fitter. Then we were off.

# CHAPTER 10

❦

THE FIRST LEG OF MY journey was uneventful and, thankfully, on time. The two-hour layover in Baltimore was tedious, but eventually we boarded the new plane. I was, of course, nervous about seeing Tom again, and with every mile I became more apprehensive.

I had no idea what to expect. Would he be cold and distant? Too jolly? Flirty? My stomach was doing flip-flops. I jumped when the Captain announced over the PA system that we were on our final approach to Atlanta's airport and about to land.

We touched down, taxied to the gate, and slowly deplaned. I had expected to find Tom at the baggage carousel, but he was waiting for me at the gate.

"Welcome back to Georgia," Tom murmured as he pulled me into a hug. I was too surprised to react, and he quickly let me go and stepped back. He looked gorgeous, his long hair tucked behind his ears, and a big smile crinkling the skin by his dark eyes.

"Baggage Claim's this way," he said, pointing.

Taking my elbow, as usual, he set off at a brisk pace, towing me along.

Breathlessly, my arm tingling, I began to thank him for waiting for me.

"No thanks necessary. I was here anyway, and Margaret's plane was delayed. It finally took off about an hour ago."

"I hope she'll have a good flight."

"Well, she's got snacks, magazines, and her headphones. But if I know Margaret, she'll make friends with her seatmates and ever'body else within earshot of her. She'll hand out the snacks and the magazines, and never get around to listenin' to her music. That's just the way she is."

I glanced up at him and found him gazing down at me. My stomach did a somersault. He pulled me carefully onto the down escalator and soon we arrived at the baggage claim area. The carousel was already moving luggage in lazy rounds. I pointed out my first suitcase, the largest one I had, and he lifted if off.

"How many bags did you bring?"

"Just four. That one, a smaller suitcase and two gym-bag-sized duffels."

"That's it? You didn't bring the contents of four department stores with you? I know how you girls travel."

I immediately began to think of something to retort to put him in his place, but stopped myself. Did I really want to fight with him? Our verbal sparring was fun, but I wanted more from him than that. Of course, I had no guarantee that we would ever see each other socially after he dropped me off at Margaret's cabin.

That idea panicked me, and I tried to calm myself. There really was only business between us. He would contact me when he had something to report about his research into my family history, and not before.

At my direction, Tom removed my other bags from the carousel and loaded them onto a dolly. Soon we were outside in the warm Georgia air. I removed my cardigan and used my scarf to tie my long hair into a low ponytail.

Tom looked me over approvingly before loading my bags into the back of a shiny white Jeep Cherokee.

"This is Margaret's Jeep. She wants you to have the use of it as long as you're here. There's a second set of keys in the cabin, and I'll give you these," he waved a keychain in my direction, "when we get there." He opened the passenger door, and waited for me to buckle my seatbelt before getting into the driver's seat.

"Are you ready?"

I nodded eagerly. I was excited, and not only because I was sitting next to Tom. I could hardly wait to see Margaret's cabin again, and make it my temporary home. Whatever might happen, or not, with the man beside me, I relished the idea of living in that cozy and tranquil space all summer. I could gaze at the stunning mountain view as often as I liked.

With Tom at the wheel, I could compare the scenery I was seeing today with my earlier impressions. As I looked eagerly around, I noticed how the forest now seemed incredibly full and lush. Spring flowers had given way to summer blooms in gardens and meadows. When we passed the 'Welcome to Fannin County' sign, I sighed. No tears today. I was too happy to be back to shed tears.

Tom, seeming to sense my elation, kept up a monologue about the history of various towns we passed through on our route, and about some of the more colorful characters from the past as well as the present.

Gratefully, I realized he was talking to calm my nerves, and had no expectation that I would engage him in dialogue. I nodded at intervals, relaxing a little as I listened to his sensual voice. It was making me think sexy thoughts, and I wondered if, and when, I would get to hear it again.

Before I knew it, we drove through the outskirts of Blue Ridge and up onto "my" mountain. As we approached Margaret's cabin, my heart beat faster. Would I be disappointed when I saw it now? Had I built it up in my mind to an impossible degree of perfection?

Tom pulled the Jeep into the driveway next to his sports car, and my fears dropped away. The cabin *was* perfect. I felt as though it were reaching out to welcome me.

I was out of the Jeep before the engine stopped. I stood on the path and tried to take it all in. The lawn was freshly mown, the porch still held the blue painted rockers and swing, and the blue door, though closed now, would open on my new life. That this new life would end in a few months' time was only a minor blip in my excitement.

By the time I turned around to help Tom bring

my bags to the porch, he had lifted them out and was waiting by the car. It was as if he knew I needed these few minutes to myself to breathe in the scents of the pine forest and the mown grass and let the peace of the place settle my nerves. Why had I not noticed before how perceptive he was?

"Ready to go in?"

"Yes. I'm ready. Thanks for not rushing me... Thanks for everything..." My eyes filled with tears, and I blinked hard.

He touched my shoulder lightly, his eyes crinkling. "It was nuthin'. Really. There's no need to thank me."

I shook my head. "You're wrong, but if you'll give me the key, I'll unlock the door."

"Actually, it's already open. Margaret wanted me to leave it unlocked for you."

"What? I hope you don't expect *me* to leave her door unlocked. I couldn't live with myself if anything happened while I was out."

"Suit yourself, though I'm pretty sure nuthin' bad would happen."

I shrugged my shoulders and bent to pick up one of my duffels.

"Leave that. I'll bring everything in. You just go on inside."

☾

The cabin was almost exactly as I remembered it, except now there were vases of fresh flowers on the cocktail table in the great room and on the dresser in the bedroom. Next to her herb log on the kitchen table, I found a note from Margaret welcoming me. On top of the journal, she had left driving directions to her favorite supermarket, the farmers market, and the laundromat. Again, I wished we had been able to meet. Though I was more than a bit intimidated by her many skills, she had done everything possible to make sure I felt at home in her cabin. She and Tom made quite a team.

While I was looking around, Tom had brought all my belongings onto the porch.

"I guess you'll want the suitcases in the bedroom, right? What about the duffels?"

"Oh, put them in there, too, please. They're mostly clothes. I decided to buy everything else here, shampoo, lotions, you know. And, I've got to stock the fridge and cabinets. I see Margaret left me directions to the supermarket. That was kind of her... and the flowers. They're beautiful."

"They're flowers from her garden. The roses are coming into bud right now, as you'll see when you go out the back door. She'd love to plant some in the front, but there's too much shade."

He began setting my bags into the bedroom and then came back into the great room. Suddenly, the room seemed much smaller. He was taking up almost all its space and air.

"Well, I must be going. I'll call you after you've had time to get settled and I'll hope to see you soon." He stepped closer, put his hands on my shoulders and brushed his lips over mine. "Bye!" And he was gone, leaving me shivering in his wake.

I came to after a moment of utter confusion, and

mentally cursed him for doing that to me again. I gave myself a shake.

I could have sat dreaming about him all afternoon, but I had things to do. I needed to drive into Blue Ridge and find the supermarket. I checked the kitchen and bathroom cabinets and began to make a list. I needed to get going soon. I had no intention of driving anywhere around here after dark.

I opened the fridge and discovered Margaret had left me a casserole dish, a salad, and rolls for my dinner tonight. Was there any end to her kindness? I added milk and orange juice to my list.

To my relief, the Jeep handled well on the mountain road. Surprisingly, the fuel gauge showed that the gas tank was almost full. Tom must have filled it after dropping Margaret off at the airport and then returned to wait with her until her flight was called. I had a lot to thank them for.

**❦**

The supermarket was clean, bright, and well stocked. I loaded my groceries into the back of the Jeep and climbed into the driver's seat. Just as I started the engine, an attractive woman ran toward the car waving her arms. I lowered the window slightly.

"Hi, you must be Suzanna. I'm Sheila Wolf, Tom's sister-in-law. He's told me a good deal about you and I'm hopin' we can have coffee one day next week. I'd like to get to know you. And, there are some other women you might like. How about it?"

I lowered the window all the way. So, this was the mysterious Sheila. She was beautiful in a matronly sort of way. She was short and curvy, with long dark hair drawn back into a knot at the back of her head, expressive long-lashed dark eyes, and full lips. She seemed not to be wearing any makeup and her dusky skin was youthful, though I guessed she probably was in her late thirties.

I smiled. "Yes, that would be great. How about this coming Monday?"

"That's fine. If we meet around three o'clock, I can spend some time with you and still get to work on time. I'm an ER nurse at the hospital and this month I'm on night duty. I'll get your number from Tom and give you a call on Sunday, and then we can decide where to meet."

"Thanks. I'll look forward to hearing from you."

She backed away from the Jeep, waved, and headed toward her own vehicle, an older model black pickup truck.

I pulled out into traffic and smiled to myself. The mystery was solved. She seemed nice. I hoped we would like each other. It would be fun to have some girlfriends to hang out with while I was here.

☾

It was five o'clock by the time I pulled into the driveway and unloaded my packages. Margaret had specific places for certain types of foods, kitchen gadgets, utensils, plates and glassware. I carefully put away my purchases. There was no way I was going to mess up her orderly arrangements. Soon, however, I realized I would have organized the kitchen in almost the same way. It was no wonder I felt so much at home here.

Next, I began to unpack my bags. Margaret had emptied all the drawers in the dresser and night table, and the closet contained only an extra pillow and blanket. I unpacked in record time, stuffing the empty duffels inside the suitcases and stowing both under the bed.

It was time to eat. My lunch had long since worn off. I took the casserole dish out of the refrigerator and peeked inside. With anticipation, I saw it was a chicken and vegetable stew. If this was the same recipe as the one she had taught Tom to make, I would be very happy. I had fond memories of the delicious lunch he served after I signed the lease papers. A note was attached to the dish's cover, telling me to preheat the oven to 350 degrees and heat the stew for thirty minutes. I was to put the rolls in to warm during the last five minutes.

There was too much food for one meal. I put two of the four rolls back in the fridge for tomorrow morning. I was sure there would be leftover chicken stew too, giving me another delicious meal to look forward to.

When the oven chimed to tell me the pre-heat function was finished, I popped the dish into the oven, set the timer, and stepped out the back door onto the deck. Tom had neglected to tell me about the sunsets. There was a spectacular one going on just then. I ran inside to grab a sweater and went back out.

I sat down on the deck's steps, sipped a beer, and looked around. There was a hedge of rose bushes on either side of the backyard, perfectly framing the view down the mountain. According to Tom, and depending on the weather, they would begin to bloom soon in shades of deep red, pink, yellow, and white. The herb garden was just to my left, with the almost empty vegetable garden beside it. On my right was the big apple tree Tom had told me about. I had a hard time picturing Tom as a seven-year-old boy. I wondered if Margaret had any photos of him at that age.

The sun slowly sank in the orange, pink, and purple sky until it finally dropped out of sight. The evening chill was coming on, light was fading, and it was time to go back inside. Five minutes later, the oven timer beeped to let me know supper was ready. I put the rolls in belatedly, but by the time I washed up, set the table, and served a helping of stew onto my plate, the rolls were warm.

My supper was delicious. Not surprisingly, the stew was very much like Tom's. The rolls were slightly different, and I remembered Tom saying he used more garlic than she did. I was unsure which version I preferred. Both were outstanding.

I cleared away the leftovers, washed and dried my dishes and utensils, and settled in the great room with my book. Tomorrow was Saturday. I decided to see if I could get a temporary card at the library, if it was open on Saturdays. I was going to need more reading material.

At ten o'clock, I turned on the TV to get the local news, but I was yawning by then. My long day was almost over.

As I prepared for bed, I wondered where Tom was tonight. Was he thinking of me? I chuckled ruefully at my nerve. Why would he be thinking of me?

I sent Ellen a text, telling her that I had arrived safely in Blue Ridge and that I had met the mysterious Sheila. Ellen was due back from Africa next week. I could hardly wait to fill her in on the details of my arrival.

Next, I called Ron. One of my nephews bragged that he had been chosen to pitch in his Little League team's final game of their season. The other chimed in with the results of his latest spelling test: 98%. I congratulated them both, trying not to yawn audibly. I loved my nephews and missed their cheerful squabbling, each trying to outdo the other. Ron finally grabbed the phone back from them, and bid me goodnight. They had to be up early tomorrow for a charity 5K run.

Finally, I slipped into Margaret's bed and fell dreamlessly asleep.

# CHAPTER 11

By EIGHT O'CLOCK NEXT MORNING, I was showered, dressed, and on the road to Blue Ridge. It was still cool, but the sun was shining and I felt energized. According to the radio weatherman, we were in a stretch of good weather that could last at least until the middle of the coming week. I found an upbeat country station, and hummed along all the way to Blue Ridge.

I was back in Fannin County and life was good!

I had three priorities today. First, I needed to get a library card and download an app that would allow me to access library books on my tablet. Not every book was available to download, so I would be checking out print books too.

Next, I wanted to walk around the business district to discover what kinds of shops were available. I also wanted to get an idea of which restaurants I might be interested in trying, and to find a sporting goods store where I could get information about fly fishing lessons.

Finally, I wanted to hurry home to Margaret's cabin and spend time just being there. I would never be able to think of it as mine, even for the few months I would be staying in it, but I wanted to become acquainted with all its comforts and quirks, both inside and out.

The library, I discovered, opened at ten o'clock on Saturdays. Since I had more than an hour to kill, I parked the Jeep and walked up and down the business district window shopping and reading the menus posted in the restaurants' windows. There was an interesting mix of shops, from the usual pet supply and hardware stores to pricey boutiques and upscale giftware and antique stores. The restaurants varied from no-frills burgers and beer to French, Japanese, "authentic" Southern, and New American cuisines. I looked forward to visiting several of them.

At ten o'clock, I returned to the library, registered for a card, and checked out several books. When I asked about the genealogy section Tom had mentioned, the young librarian on duty pointed to a glass enclosed room across from the main desk. Lined up on the shelves were bound Fannin County record books of births, deaths, and marriages, as well as other reference materials. Several shelves held fat notebooks labeled with family surnames. I looked for "Smith" and there was one, but the information it contained was for a different Smith family. I shrugged philosophically and left the room.

Back outside, I put my library books in the Jeep, and walked back uptown to visit two of the boutiques I had admired earlier. They opened for business at ten also. There was plenty of time for a little shopping before lunch.

The boutiques were fun. Along with several

cute tops and skirts in my size, I found a gorgeous pair of high heeled sandals in pale blue leather that went perfectly with the outfit I liked best. Each item was completely out of my price range.

Reluctantly, I left them behind, and walked back to the Jeep. As I drove out of town, I congratulated myself for being so adult. I had not blown my budget on clothes I might never get to wear, either here or in Manhattan. Then came the reality check and I laughed. I was *not* too grown up to hope they would still be available later in the season, when they might go on sale.

Inside Margaret's cabin again, I dropped my books on the cocktail table in the great room and made a sandwich for lunch. I took it, a fresh peach, and Margaret's herb log outside to the back deck. From my seat at the redwood table, I had a good view of the herb garden. I paged through the log as I ate. Beside the entry for each herb, she had attached at least one photo. Using them, I found I could identify all the herbs in her garden. I was relieved. I began to think being responsible for them might not be as daunting as I had feared, though I still had no intention of planting any of the vegetable seeds Margaret had left for me.

When I finished eating, I inspected the tool shed. Hanging on a peg board over a sturdy workbench were all sorts of gardening tools. A plastic watering can and hoses hung from larger hooks, and in one corner I saw the push mower Tom, or someone, maybe Margaret, must have used to mow the grass just before I came back to Fannin County.

I took down the watering can and filled it at the

kitchen sink. Though I had to make several trips, I made sure each herb plant got a good drink. A pen was attached by string to the log, and I made my first entries: the date and time I had watered each herb.

Margaret's log was much more interesting than I had assumed it would be. She had made careful notations about the care of each herb, but she also had included recipes and tips for using them in various dishes. Some of the recipes sounded wonderful. I especially wanted to try my hand at her herb rolls. Who knew? Maybe I could come up with my own variation.

The vegetable garden looked a bit forlorn. According to the log, the early peas were finished, and the lettuce plants had begun to "bolt." I had no idea what that meant, so I looked it up using a search engine on my smart phone. I discovered that when lettuce plants bolt, they stop producing leaves for salads, etc., and put their energy into making flowers. When that happened, it was time to remove the lettuce plants and grow something else.

This was all new to me, having never planted vegetables of any kind. I looked with more attention at the seed packets Margaret had left. Radishes sounded easy enough, but carrots required loose soil, free of rocks. I could see plenty of rocks in the garden's red soil. Carrots were out, I decided, too much work. Margaret could deal with them next year.

It was too gorgeous a day to go back indoors. I strolled around the front and backyards, stopping occasionally to inspect emerging rose buds and guess what color the flowers would be when they opened.

It was so peaceful here. There was little traffic on the road and the only other sound I could hear was the whispering of the wind through the trees. On the front porch, I sat in each rocker to try them out, and then the swing. I decided to go on online to buy cushions for both the swing and the rockers. If I was lucky, maybe I could find some with blue and white stripes. With nostalgia, I remembered the blue and white striped pillows I had left in my old office. Huh. That was an unproductive line of thought.

I went inside to get one of my library books from the great room and settled down to read on the back deck. In the combined shade of the overhanging eaves and the umbrella over the picnic table, there was a padded redwood chaise lounge that looked inviting. The book was enjoyable, but after a while I began to drowse.

*C₆*

I woke up in time to see the beginning of another amazing sunset. I ran inside to get a sweater and came back out to watch the show. I stayed until the sun disappeared entirely and dusk was deepening into darkness.

As I gathered my book and Margaret's log to bring them back inside, I wondered where Tom was tonight. Not that it was any of my business, of course.

I warmed the leftover chicken stew in the microwave and sat down at the kitchen table with my book and a bottle of water. If anything, the stew was even better the second time around. I had always associated that phenomenon with Italian food, but Margaret's stew was beyond delicious. I began trying to come up with a word or phrase that topped "beyond delicious," but my brain was not up to the task.

After I finished eating, washing my dishes, and straightening up the kitchen, I decided to look for something to watch on TV. I found a favorite old movie, and by the time it ended I was feeling sleepy again. I was ready for another early night. If I kept up this clean country living, I was going to be very healthy when I returned to New York.

Tom's possible whereabouts still nagged me. It was Saturday, a traditional "date" night. Who was the lucky lady in his arms this evening?

# CHAPTER 12

IT RAINED ALL DAY ON Sunday. I stayed inside, puttering in the kitchen, reading, and watching the news on TV. Late in the afternoon, my cellphone rang. The number was unfamiliar, but I answered it anyway.

"Hi, Suzanna, it's Sheila Wolf. Remember, I said I'd call you today to set up a place to meet tomorrow?"

"Hi, Sheila. I do remember. Thanks for calling."

"There's a little café on East Main Street called The Elms. It has good lunches, and it's not expensive. It's about two blocks from the library."

"Oh, yes. I passed it yesterday when I was exploring Blue Ridge's shopping and restaurant scene. It looked nice."

"Good. Why don't you meet me there tomorrow at two-thirty? I've invited a couple of other girls to join us, but they won't come until around three o'clock. I thought you and I could use the first half hour or so to start gettin' to know each other. How does that sound?"

"It sounds perfect. I'm looking forward to spending some time with you, and it will be great to meet some other nice women from here. I'll only be in Blue Ridge for about ten weeks, but I won't be so lonely if I have people to gossip with. Not that I'm much of a gossip."

"That's okay. We'll keep the gossip on the back burner until you can appreciate it. Gossip only works if you know the parties involved." She chuckled.

I laughed too. "You're right!"

"I think I'm goin' to like you, Suzanna. Well, I'm off to work now. See you tomorrow."

"Okay. Thanks again for calling."

❧

I hung up, and almost immediately, my phone rang again. This time I recognized the number!

"Hi, Tom."

"Hi yourself. I'm callin' for two reasons. First, I made a great big salad. I kind of got carried away. There's no way I can eat all of it before it spoils. If I grill some chicken to put on top and bring it over to your cabin, do you think you could help me eat it?"

"You're still trying to feed me?" I thought the way to a *man's* heart was through his stomach, not the other way around. Or, was he just being friendly?

"You don't want me to come?" He sounded disappointed.

"I didn't say that. I'll be happy for the company, and salad with grilled chicken on top sounds great. But how will you grill the chicken? It's still raining."

"There's a grill built into my stove, so it's easy. Of course, it'd taste even better on a charcoal grill, but we can't have ever'thin'. I'll bring the salad dressin' you liked, some herb rolls, and some of Margaret's cookies. She left me with a huge tin of 'em."

"Isn't there anything I can do? You're bringing everything!"

"Sure. You can set the table, and I'll even let you clean up. But I may try to help."

"Oh, okay. I might even let you. But what's the second reason?"

"I have some information for you. Not much yet, but I've made a start. I think you'll find it interestin'."

"Really? That's great! So, what time do you want to come over?"

"Is an hour from now too soon?"

"No. I was just thinking about what to make for my supper. Now I don't have to."

"Great! See you soon."

☾

I did a slow pirouette in the middle of the great room. I remembered how immaculate Tom's house had looked, and I wanted nothing here to seem out of place. I straightened my books on the coffee table and looked around the rest of the room. Everything looked tidy.

In the bedroom, I made sure the quilt was perfectly centered on the bed, and hung my robe in the closet. In the bathroom, I refolded the towels I had used since I arrived and put the cap back on my shampoo bottle.

After examining my pale reflection in the bathroom mirror, I applied a dab of rouge, some mascara, and lip gloss, and decided to change my everyday top for something a little more attractive. I wanted to avoid looking as if I had dressed up for him, but there was no reason not to look my best. I decided my sleeveless, leaf-green, scoop-necked T-shirt would do nicely with the jeans I was already wearing. It closely matched the color of my eyes.

I set two places at the kitchen table, nervously checking the time. The doorbell rang just as I put two wine glasses into the freezer to chill. I had bought a bottle of white wine and one of rosé on Saturday, and both were in the refrigerator.

I wiped my palms on my jeans and opened the door. Tom stood there, damp and grinning, his arms full of baskets containing various covered dishes and a large tin of Margaret's cookies. There was no umbrella in sight.

"Come in. Let me help you with those baskets."

"Thanks. Mmmm, you look good." He bent awkwardly and brushed his lips near my ear. "Uh oh, be careful with that one. It's full of grilled chicken."

Surprised by his kiss, I had juggled the basket containing the chicken before pulling myself together and grasping it more firmly. I had reacted as usual: my face felt hot. I was blushing. Again. I sincerely hoped my color would subside before he noticed.

Giggling in embarrassment, I led him into the kitchen. I longed for him to sweep me into his arms and kiss me thoroughly but, of course, his casual kiss meant nothing at all.

He took off his damp jacket and baseball cap and hung them next to mine on a peg near the back door. His long, thick hair was tucked behind his ears, the ends glistening with moisture. Tonight, he was wearing a deep blue button-down oxford shirt with tan khaki trousers and brown cowboy-type boots. He folded back his sleeves and washed his hands at the sink.

His presence seemed to fill the cabin. I was having trouble catching my breath.

He dried his hands on a dishtowel and, together, we opened the baskets and put everything on the table. He chose the white wine over the rosé, expertly opened the bottle to let it breathe, and set it into the bucket of ice I had prepared.

When everything was ready, he gallantly pulled out my chair and we sat down at the table. He poured some of the chilled wine into our glasses and raised his in a toast. "To happy days in Blue Ridge, and in this cabin."

"To happy days," I answered, bemused. We clinked glasses and sipped in silence. His dark eyes were focused intently on mine, and for a long moment, neither of us looked away. Finally, I dragged my gaze from his and began to serve the food.

The salad, the chicken, the dressing, the herb rolls… everything was delicious. Maybe he really was a celebrity chef. But, though I was thankful he was willing to cook for me, I was no closer to understanding his motives.

He puzzled me. I was making no money for him

at all on my "rental" cabin. It was a gift. Why? In addition, I had not yet paid him anything for genealogical research. Maybe after his initial report tonight he would give me an invoice, but I had neglected to pin him down on his fee schedule.

I had been too dazzled by his sexy voice and magnificent body when we met in April to think clearly. I might be surprised by the amount of his hourly charges.

"You're very quiet. What are you thinkin' about?"

I looked up sharply, caught dreaming. "Um, nothing really. I'm just enjoying the food. Everything you make is delicious, and it all looks so beautiful, like a photo on a foodie website. Did Margaret teach you to do that too?"

He laughed. "Yes, well. I guess Margaret's responsible for a lot about me, my public face anyway, and some cookin' and gardenin' skills. But, I warn you, she was never able to tame me completely." He was grinning that wolfish grin again. And he was eyeing me in the way I always imagined the Big Bad Wolf had eyed Little Red Riding Hood.

I was unsure whether to laugh or die of embarrassment. My cheeks were burning, so I knew I was blushing again. I took a deep, unsteady breath.

"Well, she's done a pretty good job, as far as I can see."

Mercifully, he merely laughed. Meanwhile, I contemplated all the things he could have said. But, again, why would he? We had only a professional relationship. He probably flirted with all his reasonably attractive clients. I felt sudden sympathy for laboratory mice. My mind was trapped in a maze of my own making.

While we ate, we talked quietly about nothing much, which helped calm my nerves. I wondered if he had noticed my agitation and was deliberately steering the conversation to bland topics. He had managed to surprise me before in our short acquaintance. How many men would be that perceptive? But no, I was probably giving him too much credit. Our acquaintance had been much too short for me to get to know the essential man, however good looking and charming.

At last, the meal was over. While I cleared away the dishes and made coffee, he built a fire in the great room's fireplace. I brought in our mugs and the tin of Margaret's cookies, and we settled on the couch in front of the fire.

"This is nice. Thanks for lettin' me come over. I'm excited about what I've found, so far, about your family, though I warn you, this was the easy part. It may be difficult, if not impossible, to fill in the rest of the blanks."

"I understand. I appreciate your help. I'm sure you'll be able to find much more than I could on my own."

"I'm busy with a client tomorrow afternoon, but how about if I take you to the library in the mornin'? I can introduce you to the head librarian and her assistant. Both are good friends of mine, and they can show you around. There's quite a bit of historical data in the genealogy room. If it's okay with you, we can both do some research."

"Sure, that makes sense. Teamwork."

We were quiet for a few minutes, sipping our coffee, eating Margaret's cookies, and staring into the fire. At one point, both of us reached for a cookie at the same time, and his hand brushed mine. He seemed not to notice, but my entire arm tingled at his touch and I shivered.

While I refilled our cups, he took folded papers out of his jacket pocket and returned to the couch. When I sat down again, he handed me the top sheet. On it was a sketch of an actual tree with spaces for names. Mine, my parent's, my grandparent's, and my great-grandparent's names were already filled in. Next to my great-grandfather's name there was an asterisk. Before I could look for the corresponding star, Tom told me what it said.

"Your great-grandfather was married, fathered a son, and became a widower before he married your great-grandmother. The boy's name was John, and he was your grandmother's half-brother. He was three years old when your grandmother was born."

"My great-grandfather was married before? I had no idea. Grandma Rose did mention a brother once, but I couldn't persuade her to tell me anything about him. I gathered that he died young, but that was just my impression."

"Actually, he moved west to Colorado after he grew up. He married, and had one child with his wife before becomin' ill and dyin'. I couldn't find out what disease killed him, and in those days, it could have been anythin'. There weren't any antibiotics yet, and doctors still didn't know very much."

"I always wondered why Grandma Rose never was willing to talk about him. Maybe he was mean to her, or maybe he just wasn't interested in playing with girls. I guess I'll never know."

I shook my head in frustration. Why...? Why hadn't I asked her more questions, and pressed her for answers, while she was alive?

"Here's a copy of your great-grandfather Montgomery's obituary. See," he pointed, "it lists his brothers and sisters." He handed me another piece of paper. "Here are their names, and as much information as I could find about them. It's not much, unfortunately, but one of the brother's obits mentioned his father's name. If this man is really your great-grandfather's brother, and not some other man with a similar name, his dad would be your great-great-grandfather. It's somethin' to research further. However, there doesn't seem to be an obit for your great-grandmother, or at least I haven't found one yet."

He handed me another sheet of paper. On it were photos of cemetery headstones. I was puzzled. There were several, and two of them were of my great-grandfather and great-grandmother Kelly.

"These photos were taken at Epworth Cemetery. You already knew your great-grandfather Kelly was a Methodist minister, right?"

I nodded.

"Well, there's an interestin' story about him. After I introduce you to the librarians tomorrow mornin', I'm goin' to drive you to Epworth to visit the cemetery. I'll tell you the story on the way."

"But, why don't you tell me now? Why wait until tomorrow?"

"You'll understand when we get there. No more questions now!" He grinned, teasingly. "You'll just have to wait."

"But, how far is it to Epworth? Won't you be late getting back home for your clients?"

"It's okay. Epworth's only a few miles away. And I don't have to be back until one-thirty. We can grab some lunch in Blue Ridge before I bring you back up here."

"Why don't I meet you at the library tomorrow morning and follow you to Epworth in Margaret's Jeep? That way you can go whenever you need to and I can go back to the library. Having lunch together isn't necessary."

"Yes, it is. We should strategize our research. That's better done on a full stomach. And besides, I can't tell you the story I promised to tell you on the way if you're not in my car."

There was no way to refute that logic. Reluctantly, I agreed. I wanted to spend every moment of every day with him. But, limiting our time together to "business" was my only defense against the inevitable letdown when I no longer had a reason to see him at all.

He stood. "It's gettin' late. I'll dry our dishes if you'll wash 'em. I keep suggestin' to Margaret that she should install a dishwasher, but she's stubborn."

He reached down with both hands and pulled me to my feet. He held my hands for an extra minute and then, with a soft noise in his throat, he pulled me into an embrace. My arms slid around his waist and we stood like that, locked together, for several seconds, an hour, a day. Time seemed to stop while I barely breathed. Finally, he dropped his arms and stepped away.

"Come on. Let's get the kitchen cleaned up and my baskets ready to go back home." He turned and marched into the kitchen as though nothing had happened. I stumbled along behind him, fighting my emotions.

I hope that I functioned normally while we worked together. In an instant, or so it seemed, we were finished and he was ready to go. It had stopped raining, I saw, when he opened the door.

Turning to me, he dropped another kiss near my ear. "Good night. I'll pick you up tomorrow mornin' at nine-thirty."

I watched him load the baskets into the car, and waved good-bye as he backed down the driveway. I heard the car roar away as I closed the door.

My pulse was racing but my mind was numb. I prepared for bed in a semi-trance. For once, it never occurred to me to call or text Ellen or my brother, Ron. I fell asleep finally, after tossing and turning for what seemed like hours. At one point in the middle of the night, I awoke, and realized I still had not asked Tom about his hourly research fee. I wrapped my arms around my body and, eventually, fell back asleep.

# CHAPTER 13

❦

I WAS UP EARLY NEXT MORNING, and despite the emotional turmoil of last evening and my short night, I felt amazingly rested. I made coffee and took my cup out on the deck. It was cool, but I knew the day would soon warm.

I wanted this morning to be all business. I was going to have to stop behaving as if I were a teenaged groupie. No more pink cheeks. No more shivering whenever he accidently touched me. His embraces were friendly, that was all. Same for his kisses, brushed across my lips or dropped casually near my ears.

With these brave decisions made, I hoped my body would not betray me. Let Tom try his wiles on more susceptible females.

❦

It was exactly nine-thirty when he turned into Margaret's driveway. I ran out to his car and slid into the passenger seat before he had time to get out and open the car door for me.

"Hi, Suzanna. Ready to go?"

"Ready. Tom, I want to thank you for dinner

last night. It was really delicious." I buckled my seat belt.

"It was nuthin'. Thanks again for havin' me."

He backed out of the driveway and we were off. He had the top down today, and my hair began to fly around my head. He pointed to the glove compartment. "There's a scarf in there if you want to use it."

"That's okay. I'd rather have the wind in my hair. It feels wonderful."

He glanced at me, visibly surprised. Maybe the women he usually drove were more careful about their hairdos. His own hair was tied back into a pony tail. He had pulled it through the hole in the back of his ball cap, and it still reached almost to the middle of his back.

We were silent for several minutes as he negotiated the mountain twists and turns, and drove into Blue Ridge. The stop at the library took only a few minutes. The head librarian and her assistant were both friendly and offered to do anything they could to help me. I promised to come back tomorrow afternoon so they could help me start my research.

Leaving town, we took a road I had not yet traveled, and headed north.

"Tom, are you going to tell me the story about my great-grandfather Kelly now?"

"Actually, I think I'll wait 'til we get to the cemetery. We'll soon be turnin' off this road, and we'll be in Epworth in about five minutes."

I smiled. "Okay, I guess I can wait."

"Good. By the way, this road continues north to McCaysville and Copperhill. The Tennessee border lies between the two towns."

"I've already planned to drive up there one day. And I want to take the scenic train ride, too."

"Well, if you remember, I did promise to take you on the train ride. So, pick a day, and we'll do that."

"You don't have to. I can go by myself."

"I insist. A scenic ride on an antique train can only be properly enjoyed with a friend."

"Really!"

"Yes. Really." He reached over and squeezed my hand. "Really," he repeated, softly.

I was about to snatch my hand back, but he released it to turn the car off the highway onto a narrow, one lane road. A small green sign read 'Epworth.'

&

In a matter of minutes, we arrived at the cemetery. There was an attractive, white-painted Methodist Church with a graceful spire directly across the road. Tom parked in the empty church parking lot and we walked across to the cemetery, his hand on my elbow as usual. Marking the entrance, there was a small, brick-enclosed flower garden in front of a stone monument that read "Epworth Methodist Cemetery."

It was warm and very still. I could hear only the sound of insects, busy in the grasses. Tom took my hand, and led me to two stones near the entrance. The stone on the right read "Rev. C. J. Kelly 1874-1954." On the left, there was a stone for someone named Janella Kelly.

I looked at Tom in bewilderment. "Who is that?"

"She was Reverend Kelly's second wife. He married her several years after his first wife, your great-grandmother, Mary Catherine, died of tuberculosis, or consumption, as it used to be called. Mary Catherine's stone is over here."

Still grasping my hand, he led me to a tall, stone monument with a large, beautifully carved angel over Mary Catherine's name. "You can see how much he must have loved her. That stone really says it all."

In addition to her name and dates, there was an inscription. It was a few lines of a poem that was so intimate that there was no doubt how he felt about her. My eyes filled. How amazing to be able to see this evidence of his love so many years after their deaths.

Tom stepped away to let me have a few minutes to compose myself. When I was ready, he took my hand again and led me to a low wall near Rev. Kelly's grave. We sat and he began to tell the promised story.

"You probably already know part of this. Your great-grandfather was born in eastern Georgia and when he was a teenager, he felt 'the call' to serve God. He was accepted as a Methodist preacher on a trial basis when he was nineteen, and began ridin' a circuit on horseback. Each Sunday, no matter what the weather was, he rode from one church to the next on his circuit. Usually his congregations were small, and sometimes there were only a few people, but he would lead 'em in prayer and preach a short sermon.

"He did well, married Mary Catherine when he was in his mid-twenties, and a few years later, already the parents of several children, one of whom was your grandfather Kelly, the Church hierarchy sent him to St. Louis County, Missouri. Over the next few years he led congregations in several different towns. But, while they were in Missouri, Mary Catherine became ill with tuberculosis.

"He must have been frantic, willin' to do anythin' in his power to help her heal. A doctor they consulted suggested that he take her to Colorado. There was a theory back then that cold mountain air could cure tubercular patients. In her case, the treatment didn't work, and she gradually got worse. Epworth was her hometown, and she begged your great-grandfather to take her home so that she could die among her family and friends. They returned to Epworth in 1927 and she died a few months later."

"What a sad story. I can't imagine how he must have felt, but you're right. He must have loved her very much. But what about this Janella?"

"Patience, please. I'm gettin' to her. Rev. Kelly retired from the ministry when he and Mary Catherine made the decision to move to Colorado. When they moved back to Epworth, he became the town's Postmaster, a job he held until his death. And, though he never led a congregation again, he continued to officiate at weddin's, baptisms, and funerals. Several years after Mary Catherine died, he married Janella.

"I would have thought he would be buried next to Mary Catherine, and with Janella buried on his other side. I can only guess the congregation wanted him to be buried near the entrance, as a sort of guardian angel, I guess, or somethin' like that.

"And, as you can see, Janella's not buried close beside him. In fact, there's quite a bit of space between 'em. I don't know if that means they didn't get along or not. But, she lived longer than he did, and it's possible, I guess, that her family didn't like him for some reason. I couldn't find anythin' about their relationship, good or bad."

"I hope it was a happy marriage," I said. "It's interesting that he's buried so near the entrance to the cemetery. I agree that it's almost as if he's guarding it. But what about my grandmother's parents? Aren't they buried here too?"

"Yep. Come on over here."

He took my hand again, and led me up a slight rise to a different part of the cemetery.

"Here they are." He stepped away to give me time to read the inscriptions and absorb the implications of what I was seeing.

Rather than standing monuments like the Kelly's, these were flat to the ground. To my surprise, there were five stones. Next to Mr. Ralph Montgomery, Jan. 7, 1885 to Jan. 5, 1951, was Mrs. Sarah Montgomery, wife of Mr. Ralph Montgomery, Aug. 9, 1889 to Apr. 3, 1958. The three other stones were for a son and two daughters who apparently died in infancy. There were no names on the stones. The boy's stone read Son, 1920. The two baby girls both died in 1921. Their individual stones read Dau. with the year. I stood there for several minutes, thinking about these tragedies, wondering why some babies died before they had a chance at life, and how losing three children in such a short time must have affected their parents.

"Were they stillborn, or did they live for a few hours before death overtook them, I wonder? I guess I'll never know." I must have spoken aloud because Tom took one step toward me and stopped, hesitating. I took a deep breath, my eyes swimming in unshed tears.

Grandma Rose was about four years old when her little brother died and a year older when her two little sisters passed away. She might have understood a little about her family's loss, though she had never spoken of it to me. Maybe she was told not to ask about them, or even to mention them at all. Perhaps that was how her parents were able to cope. How I wished I knew more about these people, my unknown, unknowable family. I felt Grandma Rose's love all around me today, even more strongly than before.

I finally turned to Tom, waiting patiently a few feet away.

"Thank you, Tom. I'm so glad you brought me here."

He came closer and put his arm around my shoulders. At his touch, the emotions I had been trying all morning to contain broke free, and I was sobbing in his arms. He swept me up and carried me back to the stone wall. Setting me down with his arms still around me, I struggled to compose myself again. Eyes still full of tears, I failed to notice that he had taken off his cap and untied his hair. I peered up at him just as his mouth descended on mine.

It was a sweet kiss at first, full of compassion. Our lips lingered, he hugged me closer, and with a low groan, his kiss turned passionate. Desire washed over me like a spring tide. Somewhere, deep in my mind, I remembered promising myself that I would not to fall again for his charms. With an inward laugh at that ridiculous promise, I kissed him back, meeting his need with my own. My arms circled his neck, one hand reaching up to thrust my fingers into the long, inky-black hair at the back of his head to pull him closer.

Suddenly, he broke away.

"I can't do this." He groaned again, this time in pure frustration.

"Why? What? What do you mean?" I was bewildered. What had just happened?

"There's somethin' I have to do. Come on, we need to go."

"What are you talking about? Do what?"

"Suzanna, there's no point in keepin' this a secret. You're goin' to see my sister-in-law, Sheila, this afternoon, and you'll hear all about it anyway."

I was mystified and angry. "What are you talking about?" Tears filled my eyes again, but now they were of frustrated disappointment.

"Do you remember the blonde woman behind the desk at your hotel last April? She was the receptionist on duty when I came to pick you up to take you to dinner at Billy's Barbeque, and again next mornin' when I came by to show you the rental properties you'd picked."

I nodded. I remembered her vividly. She had glared daggers at me both times Tom and I left the hotel together.

"Her name is Colleen Jenkins, and I've been datin' her off and on for almost a year. Before you arrived, we had become pretty close. She expects a ring. She's a nice girl, fun to be with, and I began to think I was in love with her. But, spendin' time with you... I saw what I was missin' in my relationship with Colleen. I knew I couldn't settle for her."

I was stunned. No wonder she looked at me with such venom. She must have sensed something, even though Tom and I had just met. There had been an immediate spark between us. I had recognized it, as had Tom, and apparently, so had Colleen.

"So, you see, I have to break it off with her. Let her down as easy as I can."

"I do see. I think it would be better if you dropped me at home today instead of taking me to a restaurant in Blue Ridge. If... If you truly mean to stop seeing her, I mean. I know how small towns work. If we have lunch together, it will get back to her before the end of the day."

"You're right. Okay. Let's go." He put on his cap, not bothering to tie back his hair. As we walked back to the car, he held my hand, our fingers entwined. Before opening the passenger door, he kissed my palm.

We were silent during the first several minutes of the drive back to Blue Ridge, but the atmosphere in the car was charged. I desperately wanted to discuss something completely unrelated either to my family's history or Tom's relationship with Colleen. I searched for a topic, and finally found a safe one, or at least I hoped so.

"I still want to learn fly fishing. Can you recommend a good teacher?"

"Other than myself, you mean?"

"Well, yes. You're busy with clients. After I take some lessons, we can fish together. Maybe."

"Not maybe! Definitely! Saunders Tackle and Bait on the road to Ellijay is probably your best bet. His place is on the left as you leave Blue Ridge and just before you hit the city limits of Ellijay. Jim is gettin' on now, but his son, Dan, is one of the better fishermen in the area and gives regular lessons, both private and in classes of three or four. Tell Jim I sent you."

"Thanks. I will."

Silence fell again, but this time it was calmer. We both had plenty to think about. I assumed he was planning how to let Colleen down. I was busy wondering whether my attraction to Tom was purely physical, or whether I was actually falling in love with him. I had several weeks to find out. But was it fair to either one of us to get involved when I was going back to Manhattan at the end of the summer?

☾

It was eleven-thirty when we arrived at Margaret's cabin. We had been together only two hours, I realized. So much sorrow, passion, regret, elation, frustration, and anger, had been exchanged during our short time together.

Before I got out of the car, he reached over for a kiss, deep, but sweet, and full of promise.

"Please tell Sheila not to divulge all my secrets, but I'm sure you'll get an earful. Tell her 'Hey' from me, okay?"

"I will. Good luck with Colleen. When will I see you again?"

"As soon as that's settled. I'll call you."

I had to be content with that. I ran into the cabin as he reversed down the driveway.

# CHAPTER 14

INSIDE, I FLOPPED ON THE couch. My head was beginning to ache, due no doubt to lack of sleep and a scanty breakfast, not to mention, anxiety over my fledgling relationship with Tom. The last thing I wanted to do at that moment was to rehash the morning's events.

Finding, to my astonishment, that I was hungry, I raided the refrigerator. I found an apple, some Swiss cheese, and a bottle of water and took them out to the deck. I ate standing at the rail, looking out at the spectacular view. Of course, it was impossible to stop thinking about what had happened this morning. Though Tom's face intruded occasionally, it was a welcome break from the churning in my head. I wanted to enjoy looking at his face for a long, long time, but I would prefer to do it in person.

When I was done eating, I went back inside. I needed to leave no later than two o'clock if I wanted to be on time to meet Sheila. It would be rude to be late, but despite the chaos going on in my head, I was having trouble keeping my eyes open. I set the alarm on my phone for one-forty and lay down on top of the bed.

When the alarm sounded, I awoke refreshed and realized my headache was gone. There really must be something special about mountain air.

As I washed my face and brushed my tangled hair into a low ponytail, I smiled ruefully into the bathroom mirror. Getting to know Sheila would be interesting, to say the least.

☾

The Elms was quiet on this post-lunch hour Monday. Sheila was already there, sitting at a table for four. She rose as I approached. She had ordered two cokes, one for her and one for me. She leaned forward and grasped my hands.

"I'm so glad you could make it. Also, I hope you like coke. If not, I'll drink it."

"No, that's fine. Thanks, Sheila."

We sat, and Sheila looked at me frankly. "I feel like I know you a little bit already. Tom's been braggin' about you at every opportunity. And I hope you don't mind, he's told me some of your background information. He likes to talk about you, a lot! You've made quite an impression on him."

"Well, he's pretty impressive himself. Thanks to Margaret, I guess, and probably you as well. I know you were married to his older brother, Mike. Tom hasn't talked about him very much, but I've gotten the idea that Tom really looked up to Mike, and that he misses him very much."

"That's true. Tom spends a lot of time with my son Matthew. He's four, and very much like his dad. I'm so grateful for Tom's presence in Matt's life. He's a great role model. Mike was quite a bit wilder."

"In what way, if you don't mind my asking?"

"Oh, I don't mind. It's not often I get to talk about him, and it helps a little to do that."

I reached over and touched her clasped hands. She looked up, gave me a tiny smile and took a deep breath.

"So, here goes. Mike ran away from home when he was 13. Has Tom told you the story?"

"Yes. Mike didn't want to be forced to go to school, right?"

"Yeah, that was part of it. He was beginnin' to rebel against *any* authority, and he and his grandpa didn't always see eye to eye."

"Where did he go after he ran away?"

"He hitchhiked west, mostly with truck drivers, and got as far as a truck stop in western Tennessee. That last driver wanted somethin' from him, and Mike was havin' none of it. So…"

"You mean, sex?"

"Yep. Mike had lied about his age, but the driver figured he was younger than he'd said, and that got him excited. Luckily, Mike was able to get away from him. He'd brought his knife from home, and he was always pretty handy with it. I don't know all the details, Mike wouldn't say much about it, but he apparently cut the driver somehow, and managed to escape. He hid until the man finally drove away."

"What did he do then?"

"It was nighttime, and he was pretty shook up. He needed food, and what little money he'd started with had run out. He walked away from the truck stop along a secondary highway and finally came to a gas station. It was very late, but he asked for a job anyway. The night manager told him to get lost. I'm sure he was lookin' pretty scruffy by then, and probably didn't smell too good either. Mike was beginnin' to realize that the world could be a harsh place for a kid like him. Then, he got lucky."

"Lucky?"

"Yep. He slept rough that night, and in a sort of funny coincidence, he got caught stealin' apples at a farm he came to next mornin'. The farmer hauled him back to the farmhouse and told his wife to feed him and let him take a bath. They burned his clothes and give him some of their sons' things to wear. Their boys were already grown up and had moved away, so he wasn't takin' anythin' they'd want."

"That was nice of them. But what happened next?"

"The farmer and his wife made a deal with him. He could sleep and eat in the house in return for helpin' with farm chores. He also had to agree to be home schooled by the farmer's wife. I don't know how they got away with just adoptin' him like that, but he told them he was an orphan, which was, of course, technically true."

"So, he agreed to that?"

"Well, he didn't have much choice. He could stay there, or he could come home. Stayin' there seemed better than comin' back to face his grandfather. He told me that he was grateful to them. He felt they had treated him fairly, though there was no real affection between them. It was more like a business deal."

"Wow! How long did he stay?"

"Almost four years. He enlisted in the Army as soon as he turned 18. He passed all his tests, and scored high enough that they offered him officer trainin'. He turned that down, but when they gave him a chance to join the Special Forces, he jumped at it. He did well, survived several tours in rough places, got his GED, and began workin' on a college degree. He was wounded twice, not too badly, and both times he went back into combat as soon as he healed. He was a Staff Sergeant when he left the service. He'd also finished his degree in Criminal Justice."

"He sounds like a hero."

"He was to me, and his men adored him, too. I think they would have done just anythin' for him. I heard from a lot of 'em after he died. They couldn't say enough about how good he was to 'em and how they loved bein' with him."

"How did you meet him?"

"I knew him from the time before he ran away. I was a couple of years younger than he was, but I knew him. I liked him, even then, though he never took any notice of me. That changed when he came back. He hadn't been a saint. There had been other women, of course. But, one Friday night I had gone to a dance at the fairgrounds in Ellijay with some of my friends, and he was there."

She paused, a dreamy smile lighting her face. "He saw me dancin' with a guy I went to high school with, and came over to cut in. I took one look at him and my heart almost stopped. He was so handsome. I didn't recognize him at first, and he didn't know me either. But we knew right from that first moment that we belonged together. When he died, I not only lost my lover, but also my best friend."

"Oh, Sheila. I'm so sorry. That sounds so trite, but I…"

"I'm sorry too. I didn't mean to get so carried away, but…"

But how could she not? It was such a sad story. She wiped tears from her cheeks and blew her nose.

"After that evenin', we spent every spare moment together. He was home for a few weeks between endin' his tour of duty with the Army and joinin' the Bureau of Alcohol, Tobacco & Firearms. When he left for his first twelve weeks of trainin', he took me with him. We got married six weeks later."

"Wow. That was pretty fast."

"Yeah, but we knew. There was no doubt that we were meant for each other. But, anyway, at the ATF trainin', he did extremely well. Of course, I knew he would. He went on to become an outstandin' agent. He was commended twice for exceptional valor. I'm sure he would have earned many more honors if he'd lived."

"What happened to him?"

"I'll never know the details, but the official Bureau notification said he was killed in the line of duty durin' a shootout with drug traffickers. You can imagine how I felt. I wanted to die too. But, there was no way I could do that. We had been married for four years by then, and I was six months pregnant with Mike's son. Matt became my whole focus. I had a responsibility to stay alive for his sake."

Now we were both fighting tears. "Sheila, I don't know what to say. You hear stories like yours, and you think, how sad, and then you change the subject. It's entirely different when you know some of the people involved. How old is Matt now?"

"He's just turned four. He reminds me of Mike so much. He'll look at me and I'll see Mike in his expression, whether we're laughin' together, or if he's mad at me, or even when he's sleepin'. It's strange, I feel Mike's presence close by me sometimes, just out of sight. And, when I dream about him, I can't see his face."

"Not so strange. I'm having similar feelings and dreams about my Grandma Rose. I can, sort of, relate."

"Well, thanks for listenin'. Like I said, it helps a little to talk about him. I couldn't do that at first, but now, it's gettin' a little easier."

We were silent for a few minutes while we mopped our eyes and finished our cokes. She glanced at her watch. "Oh, look at the time. My friends will be here soon. I hope you'll like 'em."

"If they're anything like you, I'm sure I will."

☾

Five minutes later, two women came in and approached our table. We both stood while Sheila introduced me. Janet, the older of the two, worked with Sheila at the hospital. Her uniform, sprinkled with pink and blue baby bottles, was perfect for her job as night nurse in the maternity ward. Katie, who was dressed in a pretty lavender blouse and coordinating print skirt, was manager of a boutique on West Main Street, across the train tracks from The Elms. She had only about fifteen minutes, she said, before she had to get back. They were short-handed in the shop today.

We chatted and laughed, having a good time. The three friends poked fun at each other and still managed to include me in the conversation. It was obvious they had been primed with my basic information, so there was no need to ask me many questions. They seemed down to earth, not snobbish or the least bit unfriendly. I relaxed. I felt comfortable with them.

Katie's fifteen minutes stretched to twenty, but before she left, we decided to get together twice a week, here at The Elms, for a light bite and conversation. I was looking forward to our next get-together, on Thursday afternoon. At three-thirty, Janet left to do a quick errand before her hospital shift began at four o'clock. Sheila stayed behind to talk with me for a few minutes before she had to leave for the hospital.

"So, what do you think? Want to hang out with us?"

"Yes. This was fun and I'd like to get to know all of you better. I only have until the end of the summer, but I don't want to be a hermit. It's so nice of you to include me."

"It's nuthin'. I was dyin' to get to meet you, and this seemed the best way."

"Tom told me to tell you 'Hey,' by the way."

"Ah. Well. 'Hey,' to him, too."

"I don't know when I'll see him again, but I'll pass that on!"

"Oh, I'd be very surprised if you have to wait very long to see him again."

She waved and blew me a kiss on the way out. Smiling and waving back, I gathered my pocketbook and sweater and followed her.

☾

Before I headed back up to Margaret's cabin, I found my way to Saunders Tackle & Bait. Jim, the owner, was there, but his son, Dan, was out giving a private fly casting lesson. Jim gave me a printed sheet with Dan's schedule of classes and fees. I could use Saunders' equipment for free during class sessions, and would receive a 20% discount on any equipment I bought from the store for my own use. It seemed like a good deal.

I decided to sign up for a five-day, two-hour-a-day class that started the following Monday. I paid for the lessons and Jim gave me directions to the spot on the Toccoa River where I would meet Dan and the others in the class.

When I left the store, I decided to drive by the meeting place to see where it was and, hopefully, figure out the best way to get there from Margaret's. It was a beautiful late afternoon, still warm and sunny. I knew there was going to be a lot of heat and humidity here during the summer. Right now, the late afternoons and evenings were still cool, but they would soon begin to get warmer.

Jim's directions were good. I found the place easily. There was one car and a green pick-up truck, with the Saunders name and logo on the side, parked in a small clearing next to the road. I had no intention of intruding on the lesson, but I spotted Dan immediately because he was dressed for fishing: hat with flies pinned to it, fishing vest with a multitude of pockets, and tall wading boots. He was demonstrating a cast to his student, a youngish man in regular clothes.

Satisfied, I drove away and found my way back to Margaret's cabin with no trouble. I looked forward to next Monday. We were to start at eight-thirty and finish around ten-thirty. There would be plenty of time to have lunch, do a little research in the library, and still meet Sheila and company on Monday and Thursday afternoons. At least for next week, I had a full schedule during the day. Maybe Tom would fill my evenings.

# CHAPTER 15

☾

THE DAYS BEGAN TO SLIP by, but I had no word from Tom. I met Sheila, Janet, and Katie at The Elms on Thursday as promised, but Sheila said he had not called her since he came by on Tuesday morning to spend an hour with Matt.

We had a good time, but I came home slightly deflated. How long could it take to tell a girlfriend you no longer wanted to see her?

Each day that week, as I went about my business, doing research in the library, shopping for groceries, visiting the laundromat, watering Margaret's herbs, and keeping her cabin clean, I expected to hear from him. But, each day passed without his call or presence.

I kept in contact as usual with Ellen and Ron, but I was finding it hard to be cheerful. I wanted to let Ellen know what was going on, but since I had no idea what was actually going on myself, I kept the tone of our rare conversations and my everyday texts light and on other topics. To my relief, I found it easy to deflect Ellen's curiosity about my non-relationship with Tom. She was excited about how her African project was progressing and was planning a trip to Brazil to discuss a new conference center in Sao Paulo.

Ellen called me on Sunday to tell me her trip to Brazil was finalized.

"I'll be leaving here in two weeks, and coming back home via Mexico City. I've got plans for a new concert hall to show the Mayor and his committee, but that's not all. I've got a hospital project there in the first stages of construction, and it's already been delayed by weather and labor problems. I hope both situations will be resolved and construction restarted there in a week or so, but it might extend to two weeks or more. Luckily, I really love Mexico City!"

"But, my most exciting news is that Jon and I are planning to take a romantic week's holiday in Rome to celebrate our sixth wedding anniversary. I'm hoping to reignite our marriage, and maybe even entertain the idea of starting a family. Jon's been a bit distant lately, and I've been gone a lot. It's time to get some flames going again."

"Sounds like you've got your summer mapped out, pretty much. Didn't you say something about coming to visit me here in Fannin County this summer? When will that be?"

"It's going to have to be after we get home from Italy. I'll get that all finalized and let you know exactly when I can come. I'm really looking forward to seeing you in Georgia, and in Margaret's place, since you've told me so much about it. And, to meet that hot number you keep talking about. How is Tom these days?"

"Oh, the usual. There's nothing actually going on, you know."

"Oh, sure, sure. Tell me another story."

She went on talking about her plans for several more minutes, while I listened. I had never been envious of her. She had so much talent, it would have been ridiculous to be jealous of her success.

At the same time, however, I was stuck. No job, my career stalled, and no Tom. I was immensely grateful for Margaret's generosity in letting me stay all summer in this beautiful place, not only her cabin, but this whole area of gorgeous Blue Ridge mountains, rivers and lakes. But, except for Sheila and her friends, I was without a support system. I was lonely in a way I had never experienced before.

After Ellen said good-bye, I texted Ron to see how he and his family were doing. All was well, I was happy to read, and I went to bed wondering what Tom was doing.

Apparently, wondering what Tom was doing, where he was, and with whom, was going to be taking up a major portion of my time here. I should never have let him kiss me in the first place!

Tomorrow, I would start my fishing lessons. Maybe they would give me a new focus.

☾

I was up before seven o'clock and was the first to arrive at the meeting place on the Toccoa River. I got out of the car and sat down on a log to enjoy the peaceful sight and the roaring of the water rushing by. A few minutes later, Dan parked his truck next to Margaret's Jeep and walked over to introduce himself.

"Hi, I'm Dan. I take it you're here for fishing lessons?"

"Yes, I'm Suzanna Smith. How many people are signed up for this session?"

"We've got two others. Countin' you and me, that's four."

I nodded. He could count.

"Come on over to the truck, and I'll get you set up with a rod and reel."

I followed him dutifully and watched him pull out four rods and a large tackle box. He handed me one of the rods. "Here, you can use this. We'll get you set up and..."

A car had pulled in and parked next to the truck. A middle-aged man and woman got out.

"Oh, these folks must be the other students. Excuse me a minute."

Dan put the other rods back into his truck and went over to meet them. A few minutes later he brought them over to me.

"Suzanna, this is Harold and his wife, Linda." We shook hands.

"So, okay. Today, we'll begin by goin' over basic equipment. Next, I'll introduce you to some of the flies I've found useful, and then I'll demonstrate castin' techniques. Don't worry. Fly fishin' may seem confusin' and difficult to master at first, but by the end of the week, you'll surprise yourselves with your abilities. Okay? Ever'body ready?"

We all nodded and watched as he handed rods to the newcomers and laid out mysterious bits of equipment and explained their uses.

At one point, Dan lifted his hat to wipe his brow and removed his sunglasses just long enough for me to catch a glimpse of deep blue eyes and wavy blond hair, cut short on the sides. His tanned face was lean, with a dimple in his chin and creases on either side of his smiling mouth. He looked like he was about my age, maybe a bit older. He was only slightly above medium height, but strongly built. His shoulders were broad and his arms heavily muscled. I figured him for a gym rat. He was dressed as I had seen him last week.

The lesson went just as he described, with plenty of time for questions. Harold and Linda were from nearby Morgantown. They had taken fishing lessons several years before, when Dan's father was still doing the teaching. At that time, they both worked full-time and with teenaged children still living at home, they found they had little time for fishing.

Things were different now. They had recently retired, their children lived elsewhere, and they were eager to relearn the basics.

Dan was a good teacher, patient with multiple and repetitious questions, and able to restate a point in a different way when we were confused. He also had a sense of humor, and though it was not exactly to my taste, Harold and Linda loved it.

The two hours flew by faster than I expected. I was going to enjoy fly fishing.

❧

After the Tuesday morning lesson, I drove back to Margaret's to eat a quick lunch, and was almost ready to go back to Blue Ridge to do more library research when my cell phone rang. It was Sheila.

"Hi Suzanna. I was wondering if you could come to The Elms a few minutes early this afternoon. About two-thirty? I have something to tell you."

My heart sank. Did she have a message for me from Tom?

"Hi, Sheila. Yes, I can do that. But, can't you tell me now what this is about?"

"No. Not over the phone, okay?"

"Sure, I'll see you soon, then."

To distract myself and kill time, I drove straight to the library. Naturally, I was alarmed. Maybe Tom had decided to stay with Colleen after all, and was too cowardly to face me. I hated to think that about him, but what else could it be?

My research had been unrewarding so far, but I still had several volumes of County records to go through. I was finding it difficult to pin down exactly what my great-grandfather Montgomery had done for a living. Census documents variously listed him as farmer, copper miner, and laborer, but I could find no information about where he worked or for whom. It was certainly possible that he had done all those things, trying to make a living for his large family of mostly females.

I was also curious about the farm Grandma Rose had so often described to me. I had found a copy of a deed for property her father bought from his first wife's father, but it was in another town, not Dial. I could find no other property records for him. Was he a tenant farmer when Grandma Rose was a young girl? Had there been a deed, but somehow it was lost, or never recorded?

There were so many possibilities, and though I had more questions than answers, I still hoped to fill in at least some of the blanks. Maybe Tom was having better luck with his online research. I was anxious to discuss all of this with him.

At last, it was time to go to The Elms. I walked the two blocks, and arrived before Sheila. The lunch rush was over, though there were still a few people lingering over their food. The Elms was more a local diner than a tourist's restaurant, and it was very plainly decorated, but the food was delicious. I chose a table for four and sat down to wait.

Suddenly, the door slammed open, and a blonde woman rushed in. She looked around, spotted me, and headed directly toward me, a scowl marring her pretty face. She pointed her finger at me, shook it in my face, and began shouting.

"You! You stay away from my Tom! He's mine! You, bitch! Get out of town! You're not wanted here!" She was screeching now. "Tom wants me, not you!"

I stood up, facing her. "You must be Colleen…"

The other diners stared at us, shocked expressions on their faces. Sheila arrived just in time to hear what Colleen had shouted, and to cut off my reply. "Colleen, get out of here. You can't do any good here!"

"Sheila, you're a worse bitch than she is! You get out of my way, and tell that ugly bitch there to leave my Tom alone!" She was still shouting, shaking her finger at both of us.

"Colleen, go home, or to the hospital. Now!" Sheila grabbed Colleen by the shoulders and turned her around, shoving her toward the door. "Just leave!"

Colleen started screaming obscenities and crying loudly, while Sheila kept pushing her toward the door. Finally, Colleen was outside on the sidewalk, still shouting and crying.

Shaking her head, Sheila came back to our table and sat down. Looking around at the other people, most of whom were still eyeing us, she spoke softly. "Now you know what Tom's been doin' for the last several days. He's been tryin' to calm her down enough to talk sense to her. It's not workin', unfortunately."

She looked disgusted. I took a deep breath. I was deeply shaken by Colleen's abrupt appearance, her language, and her sad dependence on the fiction of Tom's love. And, there was another thing. Granted, I had seen her only twice before, but both times she had been immaculately groomed, with perfect hair and makeup, and a put-together chic. Now, her clothes were wrinkled as though she had slept in them, her hair was disheveled, and her makeup looked as though she had applied it in the dark. Her eye liner and shadow, as well as her lipstick, were smeared.

"Suzanna, I'm so sorry this happened. Colleen's behavior is totally irrational."

I agreed. Colleen had seemed completely crazed. But, though I was stunned by what had happened, I was also feeling ashamed of myself. How could I have doubted Tom's efforts to call off his romance with her?

But then, something else occurred to me. "Sheila, how did she know I'd be here now? It's not our usual time?"

"Oh! That's a good question. Do you think she could have followed you here?"

I buried my face in my hands. "I guess it's possible, but how scary is that? Wow!"

I shuddered. Being stalked by Colleen was a possibility I would never have thought to consider. I decided to think about that later. First, I had to know why Sheila asked me to come here early.

"Sheila, what did you want to tell me?"

"Oh, honey, I'm sorry it's not better news." She paused to take a deep breath. "Tom stopped by this mornin' to spend some time with Matt. I could tell right away that somethin' was wrong. He wasn't his usual cheerful self. In fact, he was upset, disappointed, and really angry."

"Is this more about Colleen?"

"Yeah, I'm afraid so. She's makin' his life a hell! As you heard just now, she won't accept that they're through. She's behaved so badly, made so many scenes, one or two even in public besides this one, that anythin' he once felt for her is gone."

"She's making other public scenes? How does she think that will help her?"

"Your guess is as good as mine. First she told him they couldn't break up because her mother was ill."

"Is she, really?"

"Yep, at least that part is true. Mrs. Jenkins has a rare form of a deadly cancer, and the word is that she doesn't have much more time."

"That's awful. What did Tom say?"

"He was sympathetic about her mother's illness, but he didn't think that was enough to keep them together. But, with all the cryin' and carryin' on, he wavered and she took advantage."

"How?"

"She got him to agree to stay with her until Mrs. Jenkins either goes into a coma or dies."

"But, that's terrible. Is she a ghoul?"

"Well, it sounds awful, but she told him she wanted her mom to continue to think they were goin' to be married soon. That way her mom's last days would be happy."

"What? He fell for that?"

"Yep, but it gets worse. Yesterday her mom did go into a coma, and then Colleen told Tom that she's pregnant."

I covered my eyes with my hands, and sadly shook my head. Then, bending forward, I looked up at Sheila through my spread fingers. "Does he think it's possible? *Could* she be pregnant?"

"Tom says they were very careful. He doesn't see how it could have happened."

"I don't suppose she was seeing someone else at the same time as Tom?"

"It's possible, I guess, but I don't think she'd risk it. She was too intent on capturin' Tom."

"Could it be a mistake? Or, a lie?"

"Either one is definitely a possibility. I told Tom to take her to see a gynecologist, and if she is pregnant, to get a DNA test. He agreed to do that, but he's goin' to have to wait until Mrs. Jenkins dies. Colleen's spendin' most of her time now at the hospital with her mother."

"Where's Tom now? Is he with her?"

"No. This morning he met with some clients, but now he's at his grandfather's. He's tryin' to stay away from the hospital as much as he can durin' the day."

I was fighting tears, but the mention of Tom's grandfather reminded me to ask about him. "Oh. Sheila, I've been wanting to ask about his grandfather. Tom only mentioned him when he told me how he met Margaret."

"Well, he's gettin' on, but he's very much alive. Gramps thinks Tom's too modern. He says Tom's forgotten the old ways Gramps taught him as a child. Of course, Tom thinks the old ways are for the elders to follow, not necessarily for younger men like himself. Gramps argues that when Tom's an elder, he won't remember the old ways. They go around and around that same argument."

"I'd like to meet him someday."

"After all this is over, I'm sure Tom will take you there."

"Poor Tom. He has a lot to deal with."

"Gramps and he'll get their problems sorted out. It's this business with Colleen that's makin' him 'poor Tom.' I kept tellin' him that I didn't like her. She's not right for him at all. That's why I was so anxious to meet you. And now that I have, I know you're the one who's right for him." She stopped and smiled at me. "I'm hopin' you think so too."

"I don't know what I feel right now. I'm sad, angry, naturally envious of the time Tom and she have spent together, and curious about why he was willing to settle for her. That was his word, 'settle.' With his looks and personality, he could probably have just about any woman he wanted."

"That's part of the problem. He doesn't want

just any woman. He's 33 now, and he's begun to get restless. He's ready to settle down, and wants somebody to love who'll love him back with her whole heart, just like he'll love her. Also, he wants someone he can start a family with. But, Colleen wanted him, and there seemed to be nothin' actually wrong with her when they started datin', so…"

"Wait! He wants children?"

"Oh, yeah. You should see him with Matt. It's enough to bring tears to your eyes. Uh oh, look at the time. The others will be here pretty soon. Why don't you go to the Ladies' room and freshen up? No reason they need to know anythin's goin' on until they have to, right?"

I nodded, embraced her, and stood up. "Thanks, Sheila. I really appreciate your telling me all this. Not everybody in your shoes would do that."

"Maybe, but you and he… Well, you *do* belong together. Don't worry too much about Colleen. She'll have to give up eventually."

I gave her a watery smile and headed for the Ladies' Room.

❦

If I was quieter than usual, Janet and Katie seemed not to notice. When it was time to go, Sheila lingered a moment to give me another hug. "Don't you worry. This is just a temporary setback." She gave me a bright smile and left for the hospital.

I sat alone for a few minutes, finishing my coke and wondering how I would fill the next few days.

Fishing lessons, genealogy research, and meeting my new friends at The Elms left plenty of time to worry about Tom.

Finally, I got up and drove back toward Margaret's. On an impulse, I decided to take a detour past Tom's house. I would just look. I would drive by once and then go back to Margaret's.

Two minutes later, I realized how foolish that would be. What if he were home, outside, doing something with his horses, and he saw me? How could I explain why I was there?

Turning the Jeep around, I drove home to Margaret's.

# CHAPTER 16

❦

I WAS ALREADY UP AND DRESSED when Friday dawned, ready for my last fishing lesson. It had been a welcome distraction this week. I had only worried about Tom and our "relationship" during the other twenty-two hours of each day.

As usual, I arrived before the others. Staring into the water today, however, was not as soothing as it had been at the beginning of the week. I kept replaying my talk with Sheila in an endless loop in my head.

Dan arrived next and Harold and Linda followed five minutes later. Dan had promised that today he would observe our casting form, review basic equipment, and give us his "25 Best Fly Fishing Tips," a double-sided printout to take home. As he kept reminding us each day, Saunders was prepared to give us a generous discount on fly fishing equipment when we bought new gear at the store. There was a discount coupon on the printout.

We demonstrated our casts for him, and he gave us pointers to work on. Mine went well, and he gave me a big smile, a wink, and a pat on my back.

Harold did well too, but Linda was struggling. Dan suggested she sign up for more lessons. Harold disagreed, but apparently decided not to make an issue of it with Dan. Instead, he argued heatedly with Linda while Dan and I pretended not to notice.

After a few moments, Dan raised his voice and began his promised review of equipment. Well before our two hours were up, he handed out his 25 Tips list. He told me I could leave if I wanted to, as he was going to spend the remaining time helping Linda with her casting.

I was relieved to go. Harold was still angry, and I wondered whether he was more upset with Dan or with Linda. I felt sorry for her if his ill temper was something she often had to put up with.

I drove to Saunders and asked Jim to help me choose the right gear for a beginner. When we were finished, I left with a new rod and reel, waders, fishing line, an assortment of flies, and other necessary tackle. To my relief, the discount helped me stay within the budget I had set for this purpose. I could have rented what I needed, since I was going to be leaving Blue Ridge, probably forever, in a few months. However, I had decided they would be a good investment. There were several fly-fishing attractions in the Catskill and Adirondack Mountains in upstate New York. I would have to try some of them next spring and summer.

Back at Margaret's, I stowed my new gear and made a light lunch. After I finished eating, I watered and weeded the herb garden and, flinging caution to the four winds, I planted two baby tomato plants in the vegetable garden. I had seen them for sale at the grocery store, and decided to try my luck. One label showed big, red, luscious-looking beefsteak tomatoes, and the other featured a profusion of tiny, red, grape-like tomatoes.

I was sure I would manage to kill them before they produced a single tomato, but I decided to put my pessimism on hold. I surfed the internet for information and advice and discovered that I needed tomato cages. There was a gardening department at the only big box home improvement store in Fannin County. I could go there after I finished at the library today. Hopefully, they would have tomato cages in stock and someone who could show me how to use them.

My library research was finally beginning to bear fruit, so to speak. Thanks to Tom for finding the obituary that listed my great-grandfather's four brothers, I was fairly sure I had found their father, my great-great-grandfather, Ben Montgomery. I was hunting for his wife's name, when I came across mention of my great-grandmother Sarah's parents' names. Today, I would be tracing them, too, if possible.

I had already exhausted the resources readily available in the Genealogy Room, so yesterday I had asked the head librarian, Cynthia Browne, what to do next. She immediately called the library's technology geek, Jackson Stevens, to come in this afternoon to set me up with an online research account, and be there to guide my first forays into genealogical cyberspace.

Jackson was a college student at Georgia Tech in

Atlanta, but was home this summer working on his senior project. He was on-call for tech help at the library until September when he went back to school to finish his degree.

He was already there when I arrived. Clad in shorts, tank top, and flip-flops, and sporting a black goatee and a tattoo on his wrist, he looked like a typical college student. He greeted me cheerfully, and went back to work setting up my account. He ran through basic instructions, and turned me loose to work on my own. I found the first program he recommended to be user-friendly, though it yielded no new information. He was lounging in the magazine section while I worked, but came over to help when I was ready to try another program. He gave me a list of other possibilities, and told me to call him if I needed more help.

I thanked him and Cynthia, and worked until it was time to go back to Margaret's. My phone had been quiet all day. There had been no calls from Sheila or Tom. I hated the prospect of another evening alone, but I had plenty to do. I could cook supper, read, watch television, and call Ellen and Ron. There, my evening was planned.

❧

I pulled into the driveway and just as I got out of the Jeep, my cell phone rang. To my surprise, it was Dan.

"Hi Dan. What's up?"

"Hey, Suzanna. There's goin' to be a square dance at the Veteran's Hall Saturday evenin', um, that's tomorrow night. Would you like to go?"

"Oh! I don't know how to square dance."

"Well, don't worry about that. It's easy to learn and a lot of fun. Maybe we could go for coffee afterward?"

"I don't know. What time does the dance start?"

"Seven o'clock. I'll pick you up at a quarter to. Okay?"

"Are you sure I won't embarrass you? What if I step all over your toes?"

"No way. You'll be fine."

"If I say yes, what should I wear?"

"Well, some folks come in Western type clothes, and some of the women wear skirts. You don't have to though. You can just wear jeans. But, be sure to wear shoes you can dance in. No sneakers. Okay?"

I was surprised. I had not expected this. He had been completely professional during the fishing lessons. There was that wink this morning, though. On impulse, I decided to go.

"Okay. I'll see you tomorrow evening at six-forty-five."

After we hung up, I began to have second thoughts. Why had I said I would go? I felt no real attraction to Dan. There was no shivering of frustrated desire like there was between Tom and me. On the other hand, he said it would be fun. Maybe it would be. I could use some fun.

Tom certainly had no claim on my time. Not to mention, I had no idea when I would see him again, if ever. Maybe Colleen would win after all.

It was hard to be left in the dark about what was going on. I had no idea whether Colleen's mother was still expected to die any day. Maybe her treatments had recently been more successful. But Mrs. Jenkins' health was far from my most important worry. What if Colleen were really pregnant? Tom might decide he had to marry her. And, with a baby involved, maybe he would want to.

☙

My evening progressed as planned. There were no updates from either Tom or Sheila.

Before I got into bed, I called Ron. He always had family news and tales of what of my nephews were up to. I even managed to laugh with him.

Next, I texted Ellen. There was no immediate answering text, but I knew she would respond when she could. I was used to that.

To my surprise, she called me ten minutes later.

"Hey Suzi. What's up? Everything still status quo in Fannin-land?"

"Hey, Ell. Yes and no. I met Sheila early on Tuesday, before her friends came. She had some news for me…" I repeated my conversation with Sheila.

"Look Suzi, you have two choices. Number one: Forget about him."

"Ell…!"

"I know, I know. He's not really forgettable, is he? So, number two: wait for him. Sheila's right, this can't go on forever. But, the real number one is you. Do you love him? Do you want to spend the rest of your life in Fannin County with Tom?"

"Ah, that's what I don't know. It's like a

nightmare. I wish I could wake up and everything would be the way it's supposed to be, but I have no idea yet what that would look like. Tom wants someone to love and give him children. Am I ready for that? What about my career?"

"Suzi, I hate to point this out, but at the moment, your career is kind of stalled."

"I know. And I don't know if I really want to restart that career. Ultimately, if Tom decides he loves me and wants to marry me, I don't know if I can walk away from him. But here's the thing: the physical attraction we feel for each other is like magic, but I'm pretty sure true love is something more... something much more important. I'm fine as long as he's with me, but as soon as I'm alone, doubts begin to creep in. Is it shades of Jay all over again? I have no idea if what I feel for him is true love. I don't know if I will ever be able to trust a man completely again."

Ellen tried to reassure me on that score, but my doubts were not that easily set aside. We talked about other things until I began to feel sleepy. She was still planning to come visit me after her mini-honeymoon with Jon. I could hardly wait.

During the night, I dreamed Colleen was chasing me across an arid desert. I woke up panting and sweaty, tangled in my sheets. Tom, drat the man, had not appeared on the scene to rescue me. It took me a long time to cool off and go back to sleep.

# CHAPTER 17

SATURDAY DAWNED AS USUAL, BUT I slept through the sunrise. The disappointments and anxieties of the past two weeks had taken their toll on me, and when I finally woke at mid-morning, I felt as exhausted as if I had lain awake all night.

Coffee and a shower helped, and by noon I was feeling somewhat better. I checked my wardrobe for something to wear to a square dance, and laid out jeans, a light green V-necked T-shirt and a brown, tooled leather belt. My loafers would have to do as footwear. Maybe, if I became a good square dancer, I could justify buying a pair of cowboy boots.

I puttered around the herb garden, and checked my tomato plants. They were still alive, and to my amazement, they were actually beginning to grow. Immersed in my research at the library yesterday, I had forgotten to buy tomato cages. I decided now was as good a time as any, so I drove to a garden center I had noticed on the road to Ellijay. I thought an employee there probably could answer my questions better than someone at the big box store.

Sure enough, the teenaged boy who waited on me showed me exactly what to do with the cages as the plants grew taller, how to prune off shoots that might not bear the best fruit, and how to tie up the vines as the tomatoes grew heavier.

I took my purchases back to Margaret's and installed a tomato cage over each of my two baby plants. Satisfied that they were safe for now, I headed back inside to shower, eat a light supper, and get ready for the square dance.

❧

Dan arrived exactly at six-forty-five. He was dapper in pressed blue jeans, a blue chambray western-style shirt, a brown leather vest, and fancy brown and tan cowboy boots. His white cowboy hat, which he swept off and placed over his heart in a dramatic bow when I answered the door, completed the picture. He looked me over critically.

"Hi, Suzanna. You look terrific."

"You do too, Dan. Do you square dance often?"

"There's one each month at the Veterans Hall where we'll be goin' tonight, but there's others from time to time. I don't go to all of 'em."

"Do you have a regular partner?"

"Nah, I don't have a steady girl right now. Like most of the folks who come, I usually dance with a lot of different partners. You'll see. I hope you'll have a good time."

He led me to his pick-up. It was newly washed, I saw. Yesterday, it had been practically covered in mud. He handed me up, and went around to the driver's side to get in. Maybe all southern men were trained to treat women like precious objects. I easily could have climbed into the cab on my own. I could open the passenger door on Tom's sports car on my own, too.

I decided to banish Tom from my thoughts for tonight. If I could.

"So, Dan. How did Linda do yesterday after I left? I hope Harold didn't give you, or her, too much trouble."

"She'll be fine with a little more practice. Harold stopped grumblin' finally, when he saw she was beginnin' to get the hang of it. Castin' isn't easy for some people. You're a natural. Maybe we can go fishin' together sometime?"

That was a question I wanted to avoid. I was still hoping to go fishing, regularly, with Tom.

"I don't know, Dan. Maybe. I'm pretty wrapped up in family history right now. I'm spending most of my time in the library."

"Well, you have to come out sometimes, right? I'll give you a call next Friday. Okay?"

"Sure," I said. Maybe by the end of next week, I would have a clearer picture of where, if anywhere, Tom and I were headed.

It was only a few minutes' drive to the Veterans Hall. According to Dan, the building was used for all sorts of different events besides dances. It was the most popular place to hold wedding and birthday parties, and the Veterans group was happy to rent it to almost anyone who approached them.

Inside, the building was brilliantly lit. There was a large stage at one end of the room, where a six-piece band was playing country music. An older man was holding a microphone and calling the steps to a dance already in progress. Couples whirled around in time to the music and the caller's commands.

"Okay, what's 'all-a-man-left' and doe-see-doe?" I had never heard those terms before.

"Why don't you just watch for a few minutes? You'll soon see how to do those steps, and when the next dance starts, we can try it. There's always new folks at these dances. Nobody minds mistakes. In fact, if you get started off in the wrong direction, somebody will just turn you back around. Don't worry."

I looked at him skeptically. He seemed to have a lot more faith in my abilities than I did.

When I turned back to watch the dancers, however, I began to see the patterns. The music was lively, and soon my feet were tapping to the beat.

Finally, the music ended. The caller took a drink from a bottle of water at his feet, and announced that the next dance would be especially for newbies. Everybody could join in, but it would be only half as fast as normal.

The music started, and the caller began to sing-song the steps. Dan took my hand and suddenly, we were part of a square.

"Don't worry, Suzanna. Just follow my lead."

I nodded, and then, we began to move. It was a new sensation, and it took me a few beats to understand how to listen to the caller and follow his instructions at the same time. By the third number, this one at regular speed, emphasis on speed, I was doing well. I had only gotten turned around once, and I had neither tripped anyone nor stepped on anybody's toes. Though I was beginning to feel quite warm, I was having a wonderful time. Dan was a considerate partner, solicitously trying to make sure I was facing the right direction and nudging me gently when I was slow to follow.

The next dance was a Texas Two-Step, danced only with one's partner, instead of in a square. The caller asked three experienced couples to join him on stage to demonstrate the steps. They seemed simple enough, and I was looking forward to trying them.

At one point during the demonstration, I caught a glimpse of Tom. He was standing across the room, and as I assumed Colleen was with him, I tried to turn my attention back to Dan and the caller. I was shocked, wondering what they were doing here when Colleen's mother was so sick.

Dan and I faced each other and began to dance when, suddenly, Tom appeared at my side.

His hair was loose and tousled, his clothes rumpled, and it was obvious he had been drinking heavily. Swaying slightly, he pushed Dan aside. Dan pushed back, and Tom went down on one knee. He managed to regain his footing, and came up shaking his head. He raised his arm to push Dan again, but his aim was slightly off. He missed Dan, and almost fell again. So far, neither man had said a word. That changed quickly.

"Now, Tom," Dan was trying to be discreet, holding Tom away with a strong, steady arm, and trying to shield me. "Let's not fight in here. Why don't we take this outside?"

"Get away from her, Dan. She's mine tonight." Tom's voice was loud.

"Tom! Let's go outside." Dan turned Tom around and pushed him forward. Couples moved apart to make a pathway as Tom stumbled toward the door.

I was stunned. Our acquaintance was short, I realized, but Tom had shown no evidence of hard drinking before tonight. He drank only one beer at Billy's Barbeque in April. The wine we shared during our recent grilled chicken and salad dinner at Margaret's had been followed by large mugs of coffee. What was going on?

I ran to the door and held it open for the two men, as Dan struggled to keep Tom moving forward.

When we emerged outside, several smokers shifted away as Dan deposited Tom on the top step of the wide porch. Tom, quiet now, was sitting with his forehead resting on his knees, hands hanging loosely by his feet. I looked at Dan. He shrugged.

"Look, Dan. We have to get him home so he can sleep this off."

"Well, I don't think he's our responsibility. I saw his sister-in-law in there with her boyfriend. Stay here with him, and I'll go get 'em and bring 'em out here."

I sat down on the step next to Tom and touched his shoulder. "Are you all right?"

He groaned. "No. Look, I'm sorry. I din't wanna make a scene. Okay?"

"No. It's not okay. You're drunk. What on earth

has happened?"

Before he could reply, Sheila and her friend, whose name I was not able to catch, came rushing out. Sheila took one look at Tom and told her friend to help him up.

"Come on Tom. Time to call it a night. We're takin' you home."

Tom groaned again and tried to wave them off, but Sheila and her friend, whatever his name was, he was a large, strong man, picked him up by his armpits and levered him to his feet. They half carried, half dragged him to a pickup truck parked nearby, bundled him inside, and a minute later, drove away.

Dan and I looked at each other.

"Well, Suzanna. What was that about? Are you seein' him?"

"No. He's been dating a woman named Colleen, as far as I know. He helped me find a place to rent for the summer and he's helping me with research into my family's history, but we are definitely not seeing each other socially. I don't know what made him behave like that."

Of course, I was not being completely honest with Dan. But, we were *not* seeing each other, at least not as long as Colleen was in the picture. What was Tom thinking to accost Dan and humiliate me like that? He had a lot to answer for.

"Dan, I think I've had enough for one evening. Please take me home."

He looked at me, sighed, and took my arm. "Okay, come on. My truck's over here."

Twenty minutes later, we were back at Margaret's. I got out before Dan could come around to open my door. We stood facing each other in the glare of the porch light.

"Dan, thank you for taking me to the dance. You were right. I was having a great time before…"

"Yeah, me too. Can I call you again?"

"To be truthful, I don't know. Let's let this ride for a while. Maybe in a week or two I'll feel differently."

He hesitated, looking at his feet, hat pushed back on his head. "I was hopin' for more…"

"I know. Please just go now. Call me in a week or two. Okay?"

He nodded and walked back to his truck. I watched as he backed down the driveway and drove away.

I was too upset to go inside just yet. I sat down on the porch swing and set it in motion while I played the evening's events over in my mind. Eventually, I got up and went inside to get ready for bed. It was only nine-thirty, but I was exhausted.

# CHAPTER 18

SOMETIME DURING THE NIGHT, I jerked awake, every sense on alert. Who, or what, had awakened me?

I heard shuffling and creaking noises, and they sounded like they were coming from the front porch. A bear? Tom had been trying to scare me when he mentioned bears and snakes in the area, but maybe he was right.

I stumbled out of bed and grabbed my robe from the bedside chair. Tiptoeing to the front door, I stubbed my toe on the low bookcase that held the flat screen TV. I stifled my shriek of pain, and hopped the rest of the way on the other foot. There was no peep hole, but if I moved the daisy-sprinkled curtain on the window next to the door, and craned my neck, I would be able to see who, or what, was on the porch.

I sighed in relief, or more truthfully, in apprehension and forgot all about my toe. It was Tom, slumped in the porch swing, clutching what might be coffee in a giant-sized paper cup. What was he doing here at this time of night?

I ran my hands through my tangled curls and

pulled the robe tighter around my body. I tried to take a deep breath to steady myself. I found deep breathing extremely difficult around Tom, but I gave it my all. Then I opened the door.

"Tom! What are you doing here? Do you know what time it is?" I had no idea, since I had neglected to check the glow-in-the-dark bedside clock, and my cell phone was on the night table next to the clock.

"Ahh, Suzanna. I'm sorry, I know it's late. But I'm beggin' you to forgive me for my behavior this evenin'. I don't know what came over me! Well, that's not right. I do, actually. Seein' you with another man made me crazy. I acted like a total fool."

He was no longer slurring his words, but his scruffy appearance was far different from his usual clean-cut style. His clothes were even more rumpled than before and his hair was snarled as if he had been pulling it and twisting it around his fingers. He sat slouched in the swing, elbows propped on his knees. He was having a hard time meeting my eyes. It was clear he had been using the past few hours to try to sober up. I had no idea what to say to him, except to state the truth.

"Look, Tom. You have no legitimate claim on me, and I was shocked to see you so drunk. Trying to start a fight with Dan over me was outrageous. Were you even aware that when you started the commotion, the band stopped playing and everyone stopped dancing to see what was happening? You upset Dan, and humiliated me, in front of all those people.

"That made me angry, as you can imagine.

But, I was even more upset that you interrupted Sheila's evening. She works so hard, and she had a right to a nice evening out. Instead, she and her friend left the dance to take care of you without a word of complaint. It was unfair to her, and her friend, to ruin their evening like that.

"Of course, my evening was ruined, and Dan's was too. He brought me home, and drove away. We were both angry with you, of course, but he was disappointed as well. He had wanted to take me for coffee after the dance. Tom, Dan was completely professional during our fishing lessons, and he behaved like a gentleman this evening.

"Then, you barged in. Dan was still acting like a gentleman when he left me on this doorstep tonight. No touching. No kissing. Now, are you satisfied?" My voice had gradually escalated from a reasonable tone to a tearful squeak.

He came off the swing abruptly and started toward me. Realizing that he still carried his coffee cup, he stooped to set it out of the way and reached out to me. I stepped back, beyond his reach, and he stopped.

"Suzanna, I'm so sorry. If I could go back and not do any of what happened, I would. But I can't. Please, believe me. I'm not a drinker. I can't remember the last time I had too much to drink." He rubbed his eyes and dragged his fingers through his hair in frustration.

"I have no excuse. True, the past couple of weeks have been terrible. Just awful. But that's not really an excuse. All I can say is, I'm sorry." He finally raised his eyes to mine. They were bloodshot, and very tired. He looked like he was about to cry.

"You know how I feel about you. I can't believe I acted so stupidly."

Despite my earlier outburst, my heart was beginning to melt, and my stomach was doing its usual crazy flip-flops. He was waiting for me to say something, to yell, cry, slam the door in his face. Or, to forgive him. I was not yet ready to do that, but I was finished yelling.

"Tom, I don't know what else to say to you right now. Why did you start drinking, especially if, as you just said, you never do that?"

"Well, when I left the hospital this evenin', after another of Colleen's embarrassin' public scenes, I ran into an old friend I hadn't seen since college. He was in town to sell a real-estate plan to our city council, and it didn't go the way he'd hoped. He invited me to join him at the bar in his hotel, to catch up on old times, he said. So, I went. He told me about his day, which had started out well, at least. Then, he asked me what I was doin' these days, and when I told him, he slapped his forehead. I don't know if it would have helped or not, but he realized that if he'd talked to me first and got my advice, his sales pitch to the council might have been more successful.

"He left soon afterwards. He said he had to get an early start tomorrow morning. So, there I was. I'd already had two drinks, and I was feeling pretty low. Soon, two drinks became four, then five. I finally dragged myself out of the bar and headed home.

"I don't know what possessed me to drop in at the dance. I'd taken Colleen there several times, but I certainly wasn't plannin' to take her there tonight, or anywhere else, ever again! I was just goin' to stay for a little while, but when I saw you dancin' with Dan, who by the way, has never been my best friend, I saw red. I didn't expect to see you there."

I raised an eyebrow.

"I can only keep repeatin' how sorry I am. I understand how you must have felt. It was certainly not my finest hour."

He was staring at the floor again, and looking so dejected, my heart melted a little more.

"Tom, sit down." He backed up and sat in the swing again while I sat in one of the rocking chairs on the other side of the door. "So, tell me what's happening at the hospital? How is Mrs. Jenkins doing?"

"Lord, I don't know. She's hangin' in there, in and out of consciousness. Not speakin', not eatin'. The doctors keep sayin' it won't be long now. They're keepin' her comfortable, which is a blessin', but that's all they can do for her now. It really is just a matter of time."

"And when her time comes, what then?"

"Sheila told you that Colleen's claimin' to be pregnant, right?"

I nodded.

"Sheila told me tonight about that conversation. I just can't believe Colleen. We were only intimate twice, and we used double protection both times. Ironically, that was because she didn't want to become pregnant before the weddin'! That's, actually, quite funny, because I hadn't asked her to marry me yet."

"Okay. So, what will you do when Mrs. Jenkins

is gone? Sheila said something about you taking her to see a doctor?"

"Yep, Sheila's given me the name of her OB/GYN doctor, and as soon as it's the right time, I'll make an appointment. If it's a mistake, or a lie, then we'll know for sure. I'll have to give it a day or two after the funeral. But, I can't wait for this to be over. I feel like a prisoner."

"Will you marry her if she's really pregnant, and a DNA test proves the baby's yours?"

I wanted him to say no, but all kinds of physical and emotional consequences for him came with either a yes or a no. And, for me too. How could I mutely stand by and watch him throw away his future happiness? Of course, marriage might work out for them, if Colleen were willing to change.

"No, Suzanna. I'm not goin' to marry her. I'd take care of the baby financially, of course, but I won't marry her."

I shook my head. "There are two other options I can think of. One, she might opt to have an abortion. Two, you may decide you want custody of the baby."

I waited. He looked away, out toward the forest. Finally, he rose again to his feet, and turned back to me.

"If she decides to have an abortion, that's on her. But, I will never marry her."

He looked pleadingly into my eyes. "I think you have an idea of how I feel about you. I sure hope so, even though I haven't been able to court you the way I wanted to. I'm sorry about that too. But, I want you to understand. It's you I want to marry, if you'll have me. It's our children I want.

I have no right to ask you now. But, please, say you'll forgive me, and take my hand in pledge of that."

I stood as well, and took a step closer to him. "That's very old fashioned and proper."

"I couldn't have acted less like your 'knight in shinin' armor' tonight, but that's the way I wish you could see me, ready to do honorable battle for you, to love and protect you always."

He stood perfectly straight, his height making me feel small, his right hand extended toward me. There was no trace of his earlier drunkenness. I took another step forward and placed my right hand in his.

"Sheila says you and I belong together. She seems very sure of that. So, I guess I'll have to forgive you."

Tom's smile this time was his sweet one, and my heart melted completely. He gently pulled me into his arms and softly kissed my lips. His arms tightened around me and I slipped mine around his waist. My ear, pressed against his shoulder, heard the echo of his steady heartbeat. We stood like that for several minutes, swaying slightly to music only we could sense.

Finally, he stepped back. "I'm goin' home now. I need to sleep and I'm sure you do too. I'm goin' to call you each day after I leave the hospital. I won't come by again until this is over, but I need to hear your voice. Otherwise, I may go completely nuts. Okay?"

I nodded. I was fighting to keep from begging him to stay. But, I knew he was doing the right thing by leaving. I watched him as he trotted down the porch steps and out to his car. We waved as he backed down the driveway and drove away.

I finally turned back to the front door, and spotted his empty coffee cup on the floor near the swing. I picked it up, and carried it inside.

# CHAPTER 19

᷃

ANOTHER WEEK PASSED. LOOKING FOR something distracting to do, I began to sort through my research notes. I needed to get them organized before I could begin to write my family's story. I had decided to start with the childhood my brother and I had shared. I would write about our memories of our home and our parents, describe their fatal accident, and tell what it was like suddenly to become orphans and be forced to move to Grandma and Grandpa Kelly's big Long Island house. I already knew quite a lot about our Kelly grandparents' lives after they brought Ron and me to live with them, so that part would be easy.

Without active help from Tom, though, I was not going to get much further with Grandma Rose's family history. As genealogical details became more challenging to find, I was beginning to focus my research on what life was like in Fannin County during the 20th Century, and back into the 1800s.

Tom usually scheduled his meetings with clients from nine o'clock in the morning until around four in the afternoon. Taking care of his horses and doing other chores at home took up his early mornings and late afternoons. His continuing vigil at the hospital filled his evenings.

Discreetly observing them at the hospital, Sheila reported a distinct chill between Tom and Colleen. Lately, Colleen's face wore a hard and determined look, and Sheila was sure she had some other desperate ploy in mind if being pregnant were not enough to bring Tom to the altar.

As promised, Tom called me each evening after he returned home. Mrs. Jenkins had sunk lower into her coma, and her doctors had stopped predicting how much longer she had to live. Without an end in sight, Tom was depressed and increasingly moody.

We made and remade plans for our future courtship, once we had the opportunity to have one. It was difficult, but we tried to keep our conversations as light as possible. I would bring him up to date with any genealogical discoveries I had made that day, and he would promise to run a search online for tidbits I might have missed, or to open other channels of research. He sometimes had discoveries of his own to report, though not often. I told him about the books I was reading, and filled him in on the details of my daily activities. It all would have been too boring in other circumstances, but I knew how much he depended on these conversations to keep his spirits up. I simply loved to hear his voice.

One safe topic was Margaret's herb garden. I also kept him up to date with the growth of my tomato plants. He was glad to hear that they were thriving. He wanted to be there when it was time to prune the vines to produce more tomatoes, so he could show me how. I told him that I had gotten advice from the teenager in the garden center, but he assured me that it would be better to get a hands-on demonstration. Inwardly, I sighed. I wanted his hands on me.

We both longed to be together physically, but we rarely mentioned that. It was much too difficult. We always ended our conversations with the promise of love.

In bed, I lay awake thinking about Tom. I did love him. I was sure of that, now. Oddly enough, I could trace my growing certainty of that to his night of drunkenness. Over the time of our acquaintance, he had become a sort of god-like figure in my imagination. Seeing him at his worst, made him human, and his humility made me open my heart to him.

But, to marry him… Could I make such an enormous change in my life and remain happy? I was wise enough to know that loving Tom was not going to be enough for me, thrilling though our life together might prove to be. I was going to have to find something to do in addition to being Mrs. Wolf someday, and the mother of our children.

❦

Finally, early that Friday evening, Sheila called. I could hear from her excited voice that something had happened.

"Suzanna, put on somethin' sexy! Tom's on his way over to see you."

"What? Has something happened? Did Mrs. Jenkins die?"

"I can't go into it now. Let Tom tell you what's happened. Oops, got to go!" She hung up.

I ran into the bedroom and surveyed my outfit in the dresser's mirror. Not sexy enough, I judged. I whipped off my top and put on a low-cut tank top in a medium olive green. It coordinated nicely with my khaki shorts. I gave my hair a quick pass with my hairbrush, pinned it off my face with a clip, and swiped my mouth with a pale lipstick. My mascara was fine, and I was about to brush a little blush on my cheeks when I heard a car screech into the driveway. Tom!

I ran to open the door, and there he was. He was beaming. He rushed in and pulled me into his arms. He was laughing and dancing me around the room, while I tried not to trip and fall at his feet.

"I'm free, I'm free!" I covered the ear he was shouting into with one hand before he deafened me. "I'm free! Will you marry me? Please?" He stopped shouting and dropped to one knee, holding both my hands in his. "I don't have a ring yet. I want you to pick it out, but will you?"

He stopped talking suddenly, and looked pleadingly up at me, his eyes searching mine.

"Tom, what's happened? You're moving too fast! I need time to get to know you better. You don't know me either. Yes, we have this amazing physical connection. It's electrifying, but I don't think that's enough to base a marriage on."

He climbed to his feet and stood looking at the floor, suddenly deflated. He still held my hands, loosely now, and I gently tugged him over to the sofa.

"Why don't we sit down and you tell me what's happened! Please!"

He sat. I sat next to him, still with our hands clasped. He took a deep breath, and let it out slowly. He looked directly at me now, and shook his head.

"Suzanna, darlin', I'm sorry. I don't mean to rush you. I'm just so happy, finally, to be free of Colleen and her lies."

"She was lying to you?" My voice rose in frustration. "What has happened?" I was beginning to sound like a broken record. If he would just tell me what had happened…

"Okay. So, I was at the hospital and found her sittin' on a couch in the waitin' room. Not the main waitin' room, the one for the families of cancer patients. It's much smaller. Mrs. Jenkins has been goin' downhill for the past week, as I've been tellin' you. Tonight, one of her doctors came into the room to find Colleen. He said, 'If you want to see your mother alive one more time, you'd better come now.'

"Colleen jumped up to follow the doctor, and she knocked her purse off the edge of the couch. It fell open on the floor. Colleen noticed it, but didn't want to stop. She told me to pick it up as she ran out of the room.

"I was sittin' on the other end of the couch. I said, 'Okay,' but when I leaned over to get it, I saw that an open package of tampons and a partially used pack of birth control pills had spilled out of it. I thought that was odd. Why would a pregnant woman be carryin' birth control pills and tampons in her purse?

"When she came back, she looked shattered. Her mom had finally died. She slumped down on the couch, expectin' me to comfort her.

"Instead, I held up the tampons and birth control pills. All of a sudden, she turned bright red and started makin' excuses: They weren't hers, she was holdin' them for one of her friends, they were old, she hadn't used them in months. Her excuses just weren't plausible. Especially since she'd told me she had *never* used birth control pills. That was, supposedly, why we had to use double protection, a spermicidal gel *and* a condom, durin' the only two times I convinced her to go to bed with me.

"Finally, she confessed. She wasn't pregnant, had never been pregnant, and had been usin' the birth control pills the whole time we were datin', 'just in case'." His voice grew louder in indignation. "In case of what, I wondered. Did she think I might rape her?"

"I told her, again, that she and I were through, and she started swearin' at me, usin' some language I've never even heard before, and believe me, I've heard a lot.

"I let her carry on for a little while and then I went to get a doctor. I told him she was hysterical over the death of her mother. So, he gave her a sedative, and I left."

"So, you see, she has nuthin' to hold me with now. I'm sorry it's ended this way but, what really gets me, is that I didn't know her at all. I just saw her pretty face and body, and never looked beneath the surface."

He shook his head sadly. "So, I have to admit it. You're right, Suzanna. We can't get married right away. I can't even ask you to marry me right now. We do have to get to know each other first. I've just had a lucky escape and it's a lesson to learn, isn't it? Too bad it took me all this time and so much emotional upheaval to learn it."

Looking at me intently, he tucked a stray lock of hair behind my ear. "Can you forgive me for actin' like an idiot twice in one week?"

"I guess so, though I've had almost as much emotional upheaval as you've had. I think you're going to have to make it up to me."

"How?"

"Well, you can start by kissing me."

"Oh? Okay! I think I can handle that." And, he did.

I reached up and untied his hair. I finally could run my fingers through it as I had been longing to do ever since I had met him. Cradling my face in his beautiful hands, his sweet kisses turned hot as I met him kiss for kiss, his need meeting mine.

Moments later, he pulled my tank top over my head, and I felt the exquisite touch of his hands and mouth when he removed my bra. Craving the feeling of his skin on mine, I fumbled with his shirt buttons, loosened his belt, and unzipped his fly. He pulled away just long enough to kick off his boots and strip off the rest of his clothes before repossessing my mouth and attempting to undo the button at the waist of my shorts. He was having trouble with it, probably because I was busy exploring the muscles of his chest and arms, and trying to push his underwear below his waist.

Breathlessly, I struggled to find my voice. "Tom."

He finally conquered the button, and was in the process of unzipping my shorts.

"Tom!"

Dazed, he looked up at me. "What, darlin'?"

"I've been married before. I need to tell you about it."

"Now? I already know you've been married before. I did a background check on you, remember?" His breathing was as ragged as mine.

"Don't you want to know more about it?"

"Yep, but do you have to tell me about it now?"

He had my shorts and underwear down to my ankles, and he was touching me in a way that drove my good intentions completely from my mind. My center was melting. I arched my back and writhed in delight.

"No, I guess not." I reached to touch him. He was much larger than I had expected. I gasped in astonished anticipation.

"Good. Stop talkin'. *Ahhh*, Suzanna!" He groaned with pleasure as I grasped him in both hands. "Oh, wait. *Ahhh*! I have a condom. It's in my, *ahhhh*, jeans pocket."

"Can you reach your pocket?"

"*Ahhhh*, Suzanna, darlin'! Yep, but you'll have to let go of me for a minute."

"Okay, but hurry!"

He pulled away, and I heard the sound of a package ripping.

A minute later, he was back, kissing and touching me as I kissed and touched him. At last, the tension built until I thought I would shatter.

He entered me then, and we sailed off into an astonishing world of our own making.

❦

Neither of us could imagine making love in Margaret's bed. It was bad enough to have done it on her couch, but when our kisses ignited, there was no stopping the inevitable conclusion.

Later, after we had made love again, more slowly, this time, but no less passionately, Tom got up to rebuild the dying fire. While he stacked more logs in the fireplace and set them ablaze, I brought thick towels from the bathroom and spread them over the big hooked rug in front of the fireplace. Tom watched the firelight play over my body and then pulled me down to sit beside him on the towels. He held me close as we gazed silently into the fire, still caressing each other. The electricity between us sizzled and popped like the logs in the fireplace.

He seemed as fascinated with my hair as I was with his. He buried his face in it and wrapped tendrils of my curls around his fingers. I loved to have someone's hands smoothing and playing with my hair, a specialty of my Grandma Rose. She often soothed teenaged tears and hurt feelings in just that way. I had missed her magic fingers. Tom's, I was delighted to discover, were just as talented.

"Ummm. I love when you do that. Tom, do you like it too?"

I felt him nod, and reached up to run my hands through his thick mane. It was coarser than mine, but it sifted through my fingers as if alive. He groaned with pleasure, kissed my temple, and rested his cheek on the top of my head.

After a time, Tom leaned back against the couch and, stroking my nipples rhythmically with his thumbs, he reminded me to tell him about my aborted marriage. I took both his hands in mine to still the distracting sensations he was arousing in me.

When I finished my sad tale, he shook his head in amazement. "What a fool he was. I can't believe he treated you like that. There are words for men like him, but I won't repeat 'em to you. Suzanna, look. None of that was your fault, you know."

"Oh, but I think it was. I was too stupid and naïve to ask the most basic questions. He led and I followed blindly."

"Don't be so hard on yourself."

Tom kissed away my next protest, and we sailed away yet again.

Much later, Tom helped me pack a suitcase, and we drove to his house. At first, I had refused to go with him. I was worried about what Margaret might say.

"Margaret will be happy for us. Please, Suzanna. You have to come with me. I *need* you. I need to wake up with you at my side ever' mornin' for the rest of my life."

How could I say no?

# CHAPTER 20

W HEN I OPENED MY EYES the following
morning, I was alone in Tom's bed. I
fumbled for my cell phone, and discovered it was
only five-thirty in the morning. I wondered where
Tom was, but I was too sleepy to wonder for long. I
fell back into a dreamless sleep.

When I woke again, I could smell the delectable
aroma of coffee. Seconds later, Tom appeared
carrying two steaming mugs. He set them down
on the bedside table and gathered me into his
arms.

"Ah, you're awake at last. I thought you'd sleep
away the whole day."

"I woke up at five-thirty, but you were gone.
Where were you?"

"I had to feed and water the animals and do
a few other outside chores. When I came back
inside you were dead to the world, and I didn't
want to wake you. So, I showered and dressed,
and started brewin' some coffee. Want some?"

"Yes, but not until you kiss me!"

"Happy to oblige." And he did.

Soon, his clothes were off again, and we were

tangled in his sheets. Much later, he rose and left the room to reheat our cold coffee in the microwave. I sat up and watched his retreating back with awe. He was so beautiful, his muscles long and strong. I lay back down, and savored the perfection of our physical union. In that way, at least, Sheila was right. We did belong together.

Tom soon reappeared with more hot coffee. He pulled me up beside him against the headboard, and we sipped in silence. I was tucked under one muscular arm.

Finally, our mugs empty, Tom turned to me. "You want to shower first? I'll cook breakfast in the meantime. Then, after we eat, it'll be my turn in the shower. I have to be in Blue Ridge in two hours, unless you keep me in bed all day. I could cancel my appointments..."

"Then, what would we live on?"

"Oh, you're some kind of slave driver, are you?"

He was kissing me again, pursuing me across the wide bed. We were laughing as I pretended to push him away. But, reluctantly, we knew we needed to stop.

"I sure hope this wasn't some sort of fantasy I dreamed up. Will you promise me you won't vanish while I'm at work today?"

I took his large, beautiful hand and pressed its palm to my lips. "See, I'm promising, and sealing it with a kiss."

His embrace nearly crushed me. But, I was holding him just as tightly.

❦

When I appeared in the kitchen, washed and dressed, breakfast was almost ready. He had made scrambled eggs and his signature rolls were there, too. We sat side by side on the red-upholstered stools at the kitchen island, while our food disappeared in record time. We had missed dinner last night, and our recent strenuous physical activities ensured that we both had good appetites. As usual, Tom's food was delicious.

"I wasn't sure what you'd want to eat this mornin', so I kept it simple. Write me a list of things you like, and if I don't already know how to make somethin' on the list, I'll check the internet for it and learn."

"Tom, everything you make is so good. If I just put myself in your hands, I'll love whatever you cook. But, wait! I've already put myself in your hands, haven't I?"

"You look good in my hands. Have I told you yet today how beautiful you are? Now that I have a mental picture of you in my bed with your gorgeous red hair spread out over the pillow, I'm not sure if I'll be able to concentrate on business today." His hand lightly brushed my cheek, his fingertips gently raising my face to his. He gazed intently into my eyes until I felt as if he could see into my very soul.

"I love you, Suzanna." He kissed me softly, and rose to carry our plates to the sink.

My insides, as well as my brain, had turned to jelly. When he looked at me like that, I lost the ability to think. It took a few seconds for me to come back to full consciousness.

"Oh! Tom, leave those. I'll rinse them and put

them into the dishwasher. And, if you don't mind, I'll poke around a little in your kitchen so I can see where you keep things. Okay?"

"Sure. This is your home now. If you want to make changes, I'll at least hear you out."

Now was my chance. "Okay, Tom, who decorated this house? I've been wanting to ask you ever since we first met. It's a showplace, but it's also very comfortable. Sort of like you. Gorgeous, but easy to be with."

"Why, Suzanna, darlin'. You'll make me blush! It was me. I fell in love with Tiffany lamps years ago, and I'm too big to sit on spindly furniture. I need some mass. I'm glad you like it."

He showered quickly and was soon standing at the door, ready to leave. "I don't want to leave you, but you said it. What will we live on if I don't go to work? This is a conversation we'll need to have, but not this minute. Come here and kiss me good-bye, woman."

And I did.

$$\mathbb{C}$$

During our first few weeks together, Tom shortened his work hours as much as he could, making later morning appointments and scheduling his afternoon ones to end earlier than usual. We brought the rest of my clothing and personal items to his house, and I began to find my way around the kitchen. He had a housekeeper who came in to clean twice a week, and I kept things tidy the rest of the time. Not that Tom needed much tidying up after. He was not one to leave his socks on the floor.

Incorporating my preferred food list, we began to cook together. After our first week, I begged Tom to let me help him with the animals, and he taught me how to take care of his three horses and his two goats, 'slop' his pigs, and feed his chickens and gather their eggs. In the late afternoons, I helped him finish the chores for the day. He also had close replicas of Margaret's vegetable and herb gardens that needed to be planted, weeded, watered, and nurtured. There was always something to do.

I found I loved the work, especially caring for Tom's horses. I had been intimidated by them when I had seen them on my first visit to the house to meet Tom. Now, I slowly began to form a bond of trust with Beauty, his big black stallion, and the other two horses.

I had gone horseback riding twice before in New York City, but that was a long time ago. Tom put me up on either of his two mares, a chestnut named Lady, or Blondie, a light tan. With Tom at my side on Beauty, I re-learned how to ride and, in a few days, my sore muscles eased. Our early morning and late afternoon rides became fixtures of our days.

Our evenings were our own. No friends or family intruded on us at first. We talked about our dreams, and discussed every topic we found interesting. Tom had strong religious and political views, but they were his own considered opinions. He hated political rhetoric and religious dogma, and avoided them. We often agreed, but not always, and when we disagreed, we listened carefully to each other. Strongly held views were non-negotiable, and we respected that and each other.

There were all kinds of books on his shelves, everything from travelogues to philosophy, classic fiction to thrillers. Though our tastes were different, we both found magazine articles and passages in books to share, often taking turns reading aloud to each other. We watched TV and movies occasionally too, though we usually found ourselves making love before the final credits rolled.

To my continuing delight, we shared a wry sense of humor, and laughed together often. The deep, musical sound of Tom's laughter was as sexy as his speaking voice. I loved to hear him laugh.

When we were tired, we slept tangled together, always touching.

𝕮

There was a trailhead in the forest near Tom's house and, when the weather cooperated, he showed me his favorite hikes. He took me fishing, finally, and helped me perfect my casting technique, and broaden my knowledge of flies. We found the picnic area along the Toccoa River in Dial that we had had to turn back from in April, and using Margaret's Jeep, we visited it several times. Also, as he had promised, Tom took me on the scenic railroad tour, and we ate lunch in a picturesque tavern in the town of Copperhill, just over the Georgia border in Tennessee.

Every other day, I drove to Margaret's to check

on the cabin and keep up her herb garden, and once a week, Tom went with me to mow her grass. Tom had called her to tell her I was living with him in his house. He told me she was happy for us. I hoped we would like each other when she finally came home in the fall.

It was an idyllic time… almost like a honeymoon. The payoff for all our time together was a deepening respect and love for each other. There was no doubt, not after those first several weeks together, that we were indeed meant for each other.

☾

So much lovemaking, so much contentment. But, inevitably, even as we planned our future together, I continued to be troubled by doubts. At last, I found the courage to tell Tom about them.

"I keep remembering how easy it was for my first husband to make a fool of me. What if what you and I share is also only an illusion, and a short one, at that? Much as I love this life we're living together right now, I can't believe it will last."

Tom frowned. "What do you mean? Why do you think that what we have won't last?"

I took his hands in mine. "All kinds of problems will crop up. They're inevitable: illness, financial worries, angry disagreements, boredom, and there are probably others that haven't crossed my mind yet. There are lots of possibilities."

"Suzanna, darlin', you're right, of course. Life isn't all joy and sex, but we can face anythin' if we're together."

"How can you be so sure? I guess we could probably weather illness and financial problems, and anger can be resolved, but what about boredom? I'm used to working, paying my own way, and depending on my own efforts to achieve success."

"I know."

"So, what if I became bored with our life together? I don't know if helping you with your chores, and raising our children will be enough for me. And then there's you. What if you become bored?"

"With you? No way! I'll never be bored with you. I'll just have to work hard to keep you happy!"

He kissed away my doubts and fears, and promised to help me find something I could do in Blue Ridge that would be fulfilling. He was as anxious as I was for me to achieve a satisfying balance between the family life we were hoping to create and the kind of work that would allow me to believe I was contributing something to the broader world.

<br>

&

<br>

The next morning, after our chores were done and we had eaten breakfast, Tom told me he had a surprise for me. He took my hand and led me to his car.

"A surprise? What do you mean?"

"We're goin' for a short drive, and then we're goin' to visit some special people. I know you like one of 'em, but you've never met the other one."

"Are you talking about Sheila and her son, Matt?"

"You're so smart! I won't be able to keep anythin' secret from you!" He pulled me into his arms and held me tightly before opening the car door and helping me inside.

He got in and started the car. "Yep, you guessed it. Before I convinced you to move in with me, I used to spend an hour there several mornin's a week, before goin' to work, to play with Matt, and check that Sheila was okay. I've been missin' 'em and feelin' kind of guilty for neglectin' 'em."

"Why on earth didn't you say something sooner? I would have been happy to do this weeks ago!"

"But, I wanted to spend all my time with you." He reached over and took my hand, kissing my palm before concentrating again on the road.

There was that jolt of electricity again. I gazed at him, counting my blessings to be here with him.

When we pulled into Sheila's driveway, her front door popped open and an excited little boy began to shout and wave.

"Uncle Tommy! Uncle Tommy!"

As soon as we got out of the car, Matt ran to Tom and hugged his legs. Tom picked him up and held him over his head while Matt squirmed and giggled in delight. Tom hugged him, and murmured something in Matt's ear. The little boy pulled back and looked over at me.

Still holding Matt in his arms, Tom grinned at me. "Matt, this is Suzanna. She's come to live with me, and I like her very much. I hope you'll like her too. Want to say 'Hey' to her?"

Matt, stared at me for a moment, looked back at

Tom, and then stared at me some more.

"Hi, Matt. I'm happy to meet you. I hope we'll be good friends. My brother has two boys not much older than you, but they live in Texas, a long way from here. I miss them very much. Would you like to see a photo of them?"

He nodded, and I pulled out my cell phone. Quickly pulling up a photo Ron had sent me recently, I showed it to him.

Tom nudged him. "Matt, say 'Hi, Suzanna.' Go on."

"Hi, Suzi..." He buried his head in Tom's shoulder.

"Maybe the boys in this picture will visit us someday and you can play together. But, you probably have lots of friends at pre-school, right?"

He picked up his head and nodded.

As Tom put him back down, I said, "I bet you have lots of pictures and things you've made at school to show your Uncle Tom. Is it all right if I come inside and see them too?"

The little boy took Tom's hand and then reached up for mine. He led us, hand in hand, inside the house. Sheila had been watching and listening from the door. With tears in her eyes she hugged Tom and then me.

Meanwhile, Matt was waiting impatiently by the refrigerator for the adults to stop hugging each other. The fridge was covered with colorful drawings and collages, obviously done with a small, exuberant hand.

Matt proudly pointed to each one, explaining what they represented. Finally, he pointed to the last one. "This one's for you, Uncle Tommy. I made it yesterday. It's a picture of Beauty."

"Why Matt, that looks almost exactly like him. Can I take it home with me? And can Suzanna see it too?"

Matt nodded, and Tom and he stepped aside so I could get a better view.

"Oh, Matt. That's really nice. You're going to be quite a good artist when you get bigger."

"Say, 'Thank you,' Matt." Sheila was trying to teach Matt good manners. I knew how hard that was from observing my own nephews. They meant to say please and thank you, but they often forgot, especially when they were excited.

Sheila shooed Tom and Matt outside, and offered me coffee. We sat down in her cheerful kitchen.

"Suzanna, I'm so glad you came with Tom today. Matt was startin' to get antsy. He kept askin' why Uncle Tommy hadn't come, when was Uncle Tommy comin', and is Uncle Tommy comin' today?"

"Oh, Sheila. I'm so sorry. We were so wrapped up in each other, and the time just passed. I'm so happy we came today. I've been looking forward to meeting Matt. Tom speaks so highly of him and the way you've been raising him. He's adorable. And smart too, I understand."

"Thanks, Suzanna. Yes, he's pretty smart. He's scored really high on the tests they gave him at the beginnin' of pre-school. I had no idea they started testin' intelligence so young these days, but I guess they have their reasons. As long as he's happy and not bored, I'm happy."

"I know, from my nephews' experiences, that they try to identify gifted children early so they can avoid having them so bored that they don't do well in school. My older nephew is in a special class for smart kids. I'm hoping the younger one also will be given that chance."

"I think that's what happened to Mike. He did start school, but he dropped out even before he ran away. Somehow, the school officials never sent a truant officer to check on him. They just let him disappear."

"That's terrible."

"Water under the bridge. Well, the boys are just roughhousing out there. But, if you're serious about gettin' to know Matt, he loves stories. Especially stories about boys his age. Maybe you could read to him."

"I'd love that. I'll check with the librarian for suggestions next time I'm in the library. The computer should show what you've already checked out so I don't duplicate anything."

"Perfect."

We sipped our coffee and gossiped until Tom and Matt came back inside.

"Matt and I had a heart to heart talk just now, and he thinks maybe you're okay, Suzanna." Tom was grinning, clearly happy with the time spent with his nephew.

Matt went to the refrigerator and took down his drawing of Beauty. He shyly approached me and laid it in my lap. "This is for you. Uncle Tommy said it would be okay for you to take it home to put on his fridge."

He looked up at me, waiting. "Thank you, Matt. I'll put it on our refrigerator as soon as we get back home."

He seemed satisfied.

Tom squatted on his heels. I watched as Matt said good-bye to him, solemnly shaking his large right hand with his little one before throwing both arms around Tom's neck. Tom hugged him for a long moment before whispering again in Matt's ear.

Matt turned to me. "I'm supposed to kiss you good-bye."

"You don't have to, but I'd be really happy if you would." I waited while he considered that.

I leaned forward, and Matt planted a big, wet kiss on my cheek. I was thrilled. "Thank you, Matt. It is a pleasure to know you. Is it okay if I kiss you, too?"

Matt's face turned red, but he nodded. He even allowed me to give him a small hug. I hoped for more when we got to know each other better.

☾

After that, we began going to see Matt and Sheila twice a week after our morning chores were done. Also, I resumed my afternoon drives into Blue Ridge to continue my library research, take out books to read to Matt, and meet Sheila, Janet, and Katie at The Elms. Sometimes while I was there, friends of Tom's would come up to me to introduce themselves and tell me how much they liked and admired him. Janet and Katie seemed happy for us, but Sheila was thrilled, and kept me up to date on the gossip.

One day, Sheila waited until the others had gone before telling me the latest. "Colleen hasn't been seen since her mother's funeral, and there's been quite a bit of talk about her. Ever'body at the hospital either overheard some of the earlier scenes she made, or soon heard about them, especially the one after her mother died. She wasn't well liked anyway, and her behavior that day was dreadful. Pretty soon, the word got around that she had been tryin' to blackmail Tom into marryin' her, and after that a lot of people said they wouldn't have anythin' more to do with her.

"By the way, very few people came to her mother's funeral, though that's not really surprisin'. She wasn't very well liked either."

It was strange that no one had seen Colleen for so long. By then, it was three weeks or so since her mother's funeral.

"That's weird. So, where is she? If she hasn't been seen anywhere around town, did she move away? What's happened with her job at the hotel?"

"I'm pretty sure she hasn't come to work at all since the funeral. And since nobody's seen her, and there's no new information about her, there's a lot of speculation about where she could be."

"Tom and I are just relieved not to have to worry about her any more. But, isn't it odd that she's just disappeared?"

"I'm not sure whether anyone official has investigated that. Somebody needs to report her missin', I think, before Bobby James, our Police Chief, will investigate. He'd look pretty silly if he barged into her house and found her watchin' TV and pettin' her cat."

We both laughed at that picture, but I wondered whether there was a real reason to worry about her. Neither Tom nor I would miss her if she moved away from Blue Ridge. But, regardless of all the reasons we had to dislike Colleen, I wanted nothing bad to happen to her.

# CHAPTER 21

ℭ

ONE MORNING, A FEW DAYS later, Tom and I were walking back to his house after taking care of our morning chores when the Blue Ridge Police Department Chief's car pulled into the driveway.

Tom and I looked at each other in surprise as the Chief got out of his car. "Hey, Bobby. What brings you out this way so early in the mornin'? Can we get you some coffee? Come on inside." Tom turned to lead the way, but the Chief stood by his car.

"Tom, Ma'am, I'm here on official business."

Tom and I looked at each other again. "What official business?"

"What do you know about the fire at your former girlfriend's house last night?" The Chief's voice was harsh and loud.

Dumbstruck, Tom took my hand. "Fire? At Colleen's?"

"Yep. You want to tell me why you did it?"

"Did it? Are you jokin'? Why would I ever do such a thing? How long have you known me, Bobby?" Tom started walking toward the Chief, both hands out-flung in disbelief.

"Stay right where you are, Tom. I need to bring you and your, er, friend, Ms. Smith, with me back to the station for questionin'. Are you willin', or do I have to call for backup?"

"Am I… Are we under arrest?" Tom was shocked. He backed up and took my hand again.

"Not yet. I could have arrested you for public drunkenness after you made that scene at the square dance a few weeks ago, but I gave you a pass, especially since Dan Saunders didn't press charges. You were lucky then, but not today. You need to come with me now."

Chief Bobby James was a short, middle-aged man with a stomach that strained the buttons on his uniform shirt. He had a full gray beard, and was known as a 'good ole boy.' Sheila had mentioned his name, and I had seen him at The Elms a few times, eating a late lunch with one of his deputies and joking with the waitresses. I had never had reason to have a conversation with him.

In disbelief, I opened my mouth to tell him that Tom had nothing to do with a fire at Colleen's. He had been here with me every moment since he came home from work yesterday afternoon.

Tom squeezed my hand and shook his head at me. I closed my mouth, but my thoughts were in turmoil. What on earth had happened?

"Look, Bobby," Tom was clearly frustrated and angry, but he was trying to remain reasonable. "I'll come with you, but surely we can clear this up without involving Ms. Smith."

"Nope!" The Chief's red face was getting redder, and he was clearly about to explode with anger. "You'd better cooperate! Get in the car right now!"

In shocked silence, Tom put his arm around me, and we got into the back of the Chief's car. There was a metal grill between us and the front seats. I had seen such cars in TV police dramas, but never expected to be riding in one in real life. Tom pulled me against his side, kissed me on my temple, and laced his fingers with mine.

"Don't worry, Suzanna, this will be over as soon as we can get 'em to listen to us."

I *was* worried, and frightened. I rested my head on his shoulder, taking at least partial comfort in his nearness. He put both arms around me then, and held me tightly all the way to the Police Station.

Two deputies came out to meet the Chief. At his instruction, one took my arm and the other took Tom's to escort us into the station. They led us past the front desk, a room containing the deputies' desks, and down a narrow hallway lined with closed doors. The deputies stopped outside two separate rooms.

They were splitting us up, I realized, panicking. "Do we need to call our lawyers?" I had no lawyer, not in Blue Ridge, at least, but I hoped Tom would know someone who could help us.

"Suzanna, I'm goin' to call mine, whether we need him or not. He has a colleague, a woman, who can help you." He glanced at the Chief, who had followed us down the hall. "Okay?"

"If you think you need one, go ahead, but make it snappy." The Chief seemed unwilling to give us any benefit of a doubt. He appeared to have made up his mind that we were guilty of setting a fire at Colleen's house, and were playing innocent.

I could understand the Chief's confidence. If Colleen had died inside the house, the charges against us would be arson… and, maybe, murder. Who else would have a motive if Tom, or Tom and I, were innocent? We were the Chief's most logical suspects for whatever had happened. Everyone knew, or would assume, that neither of us had any love for Colleen.

I had one last glimpse of Tom as he was escorted into an interview room. The deputy immediately came back into the hallway, and locked the door from the outside.

My deputy led me inside another room. As soon as he closed the door and locked it, I looked around. The room was stuffy and almost bare of furnishings. There was only a six-foot-long scratched and scarred wooden table and several mismatched metal folding chairs. A camera was affixed to the ceiling in one corner, with its lens pointed toward the table. A large window with black glass took up part of one wall, and I assumed it was two-way, as in those TV dramas. There were probably a microphone and recording equipment too, though they were out of sight.

I sat down, put my elbows on the table, and tried to look patient. I was not. I pulled my cellphone out of my vest pocket. Who could I call? Ellen, who was in South America right now? Sure, that would help. There was Ron, of course, but he was in Texas, probably at work.

And, there was Sheila, but she belonged in Tom's corner. All she knew of me, really, was what he had told her about me, and what more she had learned during our short acquaintance. All at once, I felt very alone.

Time passed slowly. In the movies, or on TV, the police sometimes offered their suspects coffee, a cup of water, a can of soda pop... something. This was not a movie or TV show, unfortunately. I was hungry. We had not yet had breakfast when the Chief arrived. My only cup of coffee, sipped in bed before we got up to take care of the animals, seemed ages ago.

℅

More than an hour later, the door to my room opened and a woman stepped in. She looked young, late twenties, I thought, and tall. She wore a gray suit, the skirt ending discreetly below her knees, and black pumps. Her white blouse was plain, and her jewelry consisted of a large silver wristwatch and pearl stud earrings. Her skin was very black.

"Hello, Ms. Smith. I'm Delores Watkins." She came forward to shake hands, and sat down beside me. "I work with Tom's lawyer, Kyle Berry. I'm sorry it took us so long to get here. We were in court, and it just recessed a few minutes ago. When Tom called, he left a message that gave Kyle an idea of what happened this morning. I'd like to hear your version. Okay?"

I nodded. "Ms. Watkins. I'm very happy to meet you. As you can imagine, I've been feeling pretty low. I hope you and your partner can help us. We really have very little idea what has actually happened, and why we are here. Chief James said there had been a fire at Colleen Jenkin's house. Then, he told us to get into his car and he drove us here. The deputies put Tom in a different room." The lawyer spoke with a Boston accent. I wondered how she wound up working in Fannin County.

"Yes, divide and conquer. That's a technique the police like to use, and sometimes it works. Did anyone come in here to question you?"

"No."

"Didn't they offer you something to drink? No coffee, or water?"

"No, and I'm starving. I'm sure Tom is too. We had just finished taking care of the animals and were heading back into the house to shower and have breakfast when the Chief arrived. Please, can't you tell me what's going on? My imagination is running wild. Some solid facts would be good."

"Let's wait a few minutes. Kyle's getting the paperwork done to get you both released. They can't hold you indefinitely without charging you, and it's way too early for that. There's no evidence, so far as we know, linking either of you to the fire."

"Well, there won't be any. The first we heard of any fire was when the Chief showed up this morning."

"There's been quite a bit of TV coverage."

"We didn't have the TV on. Not last night, and not this morning either. We probably would have turned it on while we were eating breakfast, but as I said before, we didn't get a chance even to go inside."

"Okay. Sit tight while I go see how Kyle's doing. I'll be right back."

It was another fifteen minutes before she reappeared.

"Okay. You're free to go, but we want you to come back to our offices so we can talk about what's happened and what may be the next steps you'll want to consider. Ready?" She stood at the door. "Okay if I call you Suzanna?"

I nodded.

"Good. Please call me Delores. We've got a car outside. When we get back to our offices, we'll order in whatever you'd like to eat."

We walked together down the hall, past the deputies' desks and, finally, outside. I felt as if I had been rescued from a dungeon, though I knew there still might be dragons awaiting us.

Tom was standing next to the lawyer's black sedan. He took my hands, helped me into the car and pulled me into a fierce embrace as soon as he joined me. A man, whom I guessed was Mr. Berry, was behind the steering wheel. Delores sat in the front passenger seat.

Our driver glanced back at me. "Hello, Ms. Smith. I'm Kyle Berry. I'll shake hands with you when we get you back to our offices."

I murmured a response, but I was busy hugging Tom. As the car pulled away from the curb, I pulled back slightly and looked up at Tom. I kept my voice low. "Tom, did an officer question you?"

He whispered back, "No. You?"

I shook my head.

Frowning, he pulled me more tightly against his side, and in only a few minutes we arrived at the rear entrance to Berry, Jones, Watkins, Attys. at Law.

"We're goin' in the back way to avoid the reporters who may already be camped out at our front door. We were lucky to escape them at the police station, but now the word is officially out that you two were detained by the police. It was broadcast on our local TV and radio stations just before we left the station. That means the state media probably will pick it up soon. Naturally, just about everyone will be eager to learn more." Kyle got out of the car, belatedly shook my hand, and led us quickly inside.

"Okay, let's get you fed and then we'll get down to business. Here's a bunch of takeout menus. Order whatever you want. It's on us, since you don't have any money or credit cards on you. But, don't worry," Kyle joked. "It'll to be reflected in our hourly fees!"

Seeing the worried expression on my face, he turned to Delores. "Why don't you get them settled in the conference room while I catch up on what the reporters are sayin' now."

Delores led us into a spacious conference room. A large walnut table with matching chairs, comfortably upholstered in well-padded black leather, sat in the middle. Along the walls there were several bookshelves, crammed with legal volumes, and a large crystal award from the Georgia Bar Association sat on a credenza. The room was brightly lit, its high windows sparkling in the late morning sunshine.

Tom pulled a takeout menu from The Elms from the stack, and we pored over it. Delores wrote our choices on a legal pad and hurried out of the room to place our order.

Though we tried to make light of our predicament, Tom looked as grim as I felt. Making the most of our brief privacy, we held each other tightly as we kissed and assured each other that everything would be all right.

But, would it?

# CHAPTER 22

When the food came, we devoured every morsel in record time. Egg sandwiches, fries, and coleslaw had never tasted so delicious. The office's receptionist supplied us with a pot of coffee and a pitcher of ice water. Satisfied at last, we waited for Kyle to come back with the most up-to-date reported developments.

He finally returned, and keeping his face carefully blank, he filled us in on the details the Police Chief had refused to share with us.

"The fire seems to have started sometime late last night. The Jenkins home is rather isolated, near the edge of town, set in several acres of mostly wooded land." Tom already knew that, of course, but this description was for my benefit.

"The fire wasn't discovered until early this mornin', when a neighbor, drivin' past the property on his way to work, around six o'clock, or so, smelled smoke and decided to investigate. Since it looked like it was too late for the fire department to save the house, he called the police. In his statement, he told them that the house had burned almost to the ground by the time he arrived, and a car, parked nearby, looked like it had exploded."

I gasped, and Tom squeezed my hand.

"The Chief and two deputies answered the call immediately. The house, what was left of it at least, was still smolderin'. They looked for a body, but could only do a cursory check. They called Atlanta for both an Arson Squad and a CSI Unit, and they arrived quickly, just before seven-thirty.

"Both teams got to work, and the preliminary report, still to be rechecked and verified with tests and what-not, was that the fire had been set on purpose. In their view, it was arson.

"Chief James, of course, knew all about the ruckus Colleen had put up when you tried to break off your relationship with her, Tom, and her attempt at blackmailing you to marry her. Just about ever'body knows." He shook his head in wonder at the crazy things people do.

"So, naturally, the Chief decided you had motive, and certainly opportunity, since the house is so isolated. And maybe, just maybe, the two of you had worked together. Hence your early mornin' visit from him and your excitin' sojourn in our police station's finest interview rooms."

"Here's the situation. If Colleen turns up safe and sound and blames you for the fire, you might only be charged with second degree arson. If she doesn't, and a body is found, you may be lookin' at first degree arson, a much more serious charge. The media will call it murder."

Tom and I looked at each other in dismay. I shivered. I hugged myself and began to rub my upper arms. *I* knew Tom had done nothing. But, where was Colleen?

Tom looked up at Kyle. "And if she says she started the fire by accident, or somethin' else happened, then Suzanna and I would be declared innocent. Right?"

"Do you really think she'd say that?"

"I don't know. I'd like to think she'd tell the truth. But, I just don't know."

"Well, I'd like to think Colleen will turn up healthy and wonderin' what happened to her house and car. However, I think it's possible Chief James has somethin' he hasn't shared with us yet. He looks too smug."

Tom looked at Kyle with shock. "What?"

"Now, don't get too excited. I could be wrong. He may just be posturin'. Just go about your normal business, and try not to worry too much."

# CHAPTER 23

❧

DELORES DROVE US HOME AFTER our meeting was over, taking a roundabout route in case the reporters clustered around their building's front entrance had seen us leave and were tailing us. To our relief, there were none already waiting for us at Tom's house, though we realized that would soon change.

It was late, almost time to do our afternoon chores. We decided to start early and take our time. Brushing, feeding and watering the horses and taking care of the other animals helped to temporarily raise our spirits. Of course, we were both deeply uneasy, but there was nothing we could do but wait to see what would happen next. Maybe Colleen would return from wherever she had gone, or her body would be found. I hated to dwell on that possibility, but my thoughts returned to it over and over.

❧

Kyle called while we were eating supper. "Tom, Chief James has just announced to the media that a belt buckle with your initials on it was found near the car. Apparently, the Arson squad found it this mornin'. I guess that's why the Chief was lookin' smug. He thinks he's got y'all."

Tom groaned. "I remember that buckle goin' missin'. But it was months ago, not last night. Someone, maybe Colleen, is tryin' to frame me."

By evening, reporters from local and state media were camped out, as close as possible, to Tom's doorstep.

Tom cancelled all his appointments for the next few days and we stayed home, quietly declining to answer questions from busybodies and reporters. We refused to be drawn into answering the hateful messages we received, and when Tom's house and business phone lines continued to ring non-stop, we unplugged them. Some of the voicemail messages threatened our lives. Others demanded to know why we "did it."

Until this ordeal was finished, all communication with our lawyers and our friends would have to be through our cell phones. We put them on vibrate. We were tired of hearing phones ringing.

Neither of us was particularly active on social media. We posted brief denials of any wrongdoing and let it go at that. Only a few hours later, we closed all our social accounts. Trolls had taken them hostage.

Our only visitors were Sheila and Matt, and a few trusted friends. We were grateful they came, since they had to get past journalists shouting questions and shoving microphones in their faces, just to get to our door. Even after several days of inactivity from us and no additional news, they refused to give up and go away. Luckily, Tom's freezer was full and there was enough fodder for the animals for the foreseeable future. We had no need to leave his property for quite some time.

There were, however, a few things we were unable to do for ourselves, and Sheila and Tom's friends quietly stepped in to help. Margaret's herb garden had to be watered, and her journal had to be kept up. It was now high summer, and the plants would die without regular watering. Much to our relief, Margaret's closest neighbor and good friend, Betty Jordan, volunteered to maintain all her garden beds. Her husband, Bill, agreed to mow the grass.

Also, Tom's three horses needed to be exercised every day, and that meant riding them away from Tom's property. He owned several mostly forested acres, and his only pasture was the relatively small one near his barn. The horses needed wide open country to gallop full out.

Shep Harris, Tom's nearest neighbor, took over exercising Beauty, Tom's black stallion. Sheila and her friend Joe Shelby, whom I had met the night of the ill-fated square dance, began working with Lady and Blondie. It was hard to watch them riding away without us, but we were more than grateful for their help.

Sheila also took on the task of keeping us in milk, other perishables, and personal items as we ran out. I had no idea what we would have done without these generous and helpful people.

Tom and I were aware of Chief James' continued suspicion of us. Several times a day, a police cruiser coasted slowly past Tom's driveway, the driver pausing long enough to make sure we had seen the car. Though we tried to keep busy taking care of the animals, cooking, cleaning, reading, watching old movies on TV, etc., we felt trapped… watched… the butt of speculation.

We were unhappily aware of how perilously close we were to being charged, tried, and sent to prison for crimes we had not committed. Tom's professional reputation was in danger of being irreparably harmed, and our passionate love story brought to an abrupt end.

We made love feverishly, praying each time that it would not be our last opportunity. I knew now, beyond all doubt, that I loved Tom completely. He was everything I wanted and needed. My heart lifted when I remembered the wish list of traits I had hoped my dream husband would possess. Tom satisfied every single wish on it. That he was an exciting, caring, and inventive lover, who always made sure my sexual needs were fulfilled before his own, flooded me with a happiness I had almost despaired of ever experiencing.

I no longer considered the possibility of returning to Manhattan to look for another job. I would be staying here in Fannin County with Tom. I dreamed of our future life together and knew it would be right. I trusted him utterly with my heart, as he trusted me with his. We only had to make it through this crisis.

❧

Seven endless days after our initial confrontation with Chief James, Sheila called Tom with news.

"Hey, Sheila. Hey, slow down. What? Could

you repeat that?" He was pacing in front of the empty fireplace as I watched anxiously.

"Really? Thanks, Sheila. I'll call you back later." He hung up and turned to me, a sorrowful expression on his face.

"What? Tom, what's happened?"

"Colleen's body has been reported found. Sheila said to put on the TV."

He was already doing so. We watched avidly as local reporters told and re-told the story, along with breathless and provocative speculation. The facts so far were sparse: A tourist, fishing off his rented rowboat as it floated down the Toccoa River, had spotted a body lying on the rocks under the Dial Bridge, and called 911 from his cell phone. Police tentatively identified the body as Colleen's. They secured the scene, and a new CSI Unit arrived from Atlanta to investigate.

We kept the TV on, with its volume low, in the hope that more news would surface. Late that afternoon, there was another news bulletin. An older model car had been reported abandoned in the parking lot at the Dial General Store and Luncheonette. Police and others were investigating, and viewers were urged to stay tuned for further news.

# CHAPTER 24

F OUR DAYS LATER, WE WERE just finishing breakfast when Tom's lawyer, Kyle Berry, called with some real news. Tom put his phone on speaker so I could hear too.

"Okay, Tom. Listen up. Chief James is scheduled to hold a news conference at noon. But, before that, he's comin' in person to apologize to you. You and Suzanna are to be completely exonerated."

Tom and I listened with amazement, hugging each other tightly. I could hardly believe we were no longer under suspicion. Tears of relief flooded my eyes and Tom kissed them away before remembering Kyle was still on the line.

"Kyle, I can't thank you enough for callin' with this news. We are, as you can imagine, thrilled to hear it. Thanks so much for your assistance through this. I can't tell you how much we appreciate it."

"Think nuthin' of it. Just pay my bill. Though I don't think it'll hurt you too much, even though you've probably lost quite a lot of business during all this. But, I have to tell you, you have some pretty loyal friends. They've taken it upon themselves to raise money for your legal fees.

"What? Kyle, what do you mean?" We gazed at each other in amazement.

There's goin' to be a fund-raiser this Saturday, a 5K run in your name, Tom. They've already raised a good sum, and our fee will probably amount to something quite a bit less that the final total they'll raise."

"Kyle, you can't mean that."

"Well, yes I can. It's gratifyin' to represent people who are actually *not* guilty of the crimes they're accused of, instead of them just *sayin'* they're innocent. It's good for the soul, if not necessarily the pocketbook. Though in this case, our pocketbooks will be satisfied too. So, accept Chief James's apology and get on with your lives. Is it possible that there's a weddin' in your future?"

"Well, I sure hope so. If she'll have me, that is."

"From what I've seen, I think she will. Give her our regards, okay? She's got guts."

"Thanks, Kyle. And, please thank Delores, too. You guys are the best. Oops, got to go. Looks like the Chief has arrived. Thanks again for everythin'."

Tom disconnected and grabbed my hand. We watched from the front door as newspaper and TV reporters, plus their cameras and crews, followed Chief James's police vehicle in a long cavalcade. He pulled into Tom's driveway behind Margaret's Jeep, while the other cars and trucks blocked the road.

James got out of his car, and tried to reach our front door before he was mobbed. It was a tie, but we pulled him inside and slammed the door shut without injuring him or any members of the press.

Tom invited him into the great room and told him to take a seat. To his credit, Chief James's behavior was subdued and carefully polite, a welcome change from his recent arrogant rudeness.

"Tom, Ms. Smith, I'm here to apologize to you for the ordeal you've just had to suffer through. I'm truly sorry. You've never given me any reason to suspect you of anythin' like this before, Tom, and I let circumstantial evidence, admittedly pretty thin, convince me that you, either alone or with Ms. Smith here, were guilty."

"Chief, we've always understood *why* you suspected us. We were the perfect suspects. It was the way you treated us from the beginnin' that upset me the most. I felt we had a right to a little more respect. Nuthin' had been proven against us."

The chief was turning his hat in his hands and looking at the floor. He nodded. "Well, that's why I'm here. As you can imagine, I don't go around apologizin' for my professional conduct very often. But, in your case, I was wrong, and I wanted you to hear it from me in person, not on TV. Though of course, I'll repeat this for the cameras. I want ever'body who has followed this story as it unfolded to know that you both are innocent of any wrongdoin'."

"Thank you, Chief," I said. I looked at Tom.

He hesitated, clearly not ready to accept James's apology quite yet. "I'd like to think this county's officials still believe the people who live here are innocent until proven guilty. We're your neighbors."

"Well, I certainly can't deny that I slipped up here, but I sincerely promise to try to do better in the future. I mean it when I say I'm sorry. Will you shake my hand?"

Tom hesitated, staring hard at James. Finally, he put out his hand and they shook. We watched the Chief and his parade of reporters drive away, on their way to the press briefing at the Court House.

**☙**

Just before noon, we turned on the TV.

True to his word, Chief James stepped to the podium, temporarily set up at the foot of the steps to the Court House, exactly at noon. Some two dozen reporters greeted his appearance with shouted questions. He raised his hands to quiet the crowd, which in addition to reporters, also included business owners and other people who had heard about the news conference. Standing nearby were the police detectives who handled the investigation, and representatives of both the Arson Squad and the two CSI Units.

"Okay, let's get started. I'm Chief of Blue Ridge Police, Robert James. Before I lay out the facts in this investigation, I have a preliminary statement to make." He cleared his throat and squinted at the paper he held in his hand.

"When it was discovered that the house Ms. Colleen Jenkins had shared with her widowed and recently deceased mother, Mrs. Clara Jenkins, had been destroyed by fire, along with Ms. Colleen

Jenkins' car, we immediately suspected arson. Ms. Jenkins had not been seen since her mother's funeral, now more than a month ago, and there was speculation that she might have been killed in the fire. In a classic case of 'rushin' to judgment,' I brought local realtor Mr. Thomas Wolf and his friend, Ms. Suzanna Smith, into the police station for questionin'. In my defense, they were the best and most logical suspects to have set the fire and murdered Ms. Jenkins, for reasons that have been repeatedly hashed over in the media. I'm not goin' to repeat those reasons now. Enough has been said.

"I state now, and will continue to state: Mr. Wolf and Ms. Smith are *not* suspects in this case. In fact, they are completely innocent of *any* wrongdoin' havin' to do with this case. I have met with 'em personally, in Mr. Wolf's home, to apologize for jumpin' to the incorrect conclusion that they were guilty of arson and possibly, murder. I gave 'em quite a few very difficult days, and I am truly sorry.

"That is the end of my preliminary statement."

Looking up, Chief James thanked an assistant who handed him a folder containing other papers. He took a deep breath and continued. "So, who's responsible for all this? Who set the fire that destroyed Ms. Colleen Jenkins' house and car? And, was Ms. Colleen Jenkins actually murdered?

"Accordin' to all the evidence uncovered by the Arson Squad, CSI Units, and police detectives, with the assistance of the FBI and the Governor's Office, we are confident that *she*, Ms. Colleen Jenkins, set the fire that destroyed her house and car, and that she died either in an accidental fall, or committed suicide."

Chief James paused as the reporters and others in the crowd began to shout questions. He raised his hands and his voice, and the crowd quieted to a muted buzz.

"Here are the facts. An investigation of Mrs. Clara Jenkins' financial situation shows that she was virtually bankrupt. Her long illness and death left her daughter and only heir, Ms. Colleen Jenkins, deeply in debt. Workin' at a minimum wage job, she had no ability to pay bills, maintain the house, or repay her mother's debts.

"Our detectives have discovered that after her mother's funeral, Ms. Jenkins hitchhiked away from Blue Ridge, leavin' her car in her driveway to make it look as if she was at home. She rode first with a trucker travelin' to Atlanta, and when he pulled into a truck stop halfway there to have a meal and take a nap, she traveled on to Atlanta with another trucker. We have spoken with both drivers.

"Usin' her credit card statements and cell phone records, we've traced most of her movements in Atlanta. First, she checked into an inexpensive motel, and set out to pick up affluent men in various upscale bars. Accordin' to several bartenders, she was unsuccessful and began drinkin' heavily. We've heard evidence that she was thrown out of at least one bar.

"She had a back-up plan, however. Ms. Jenkins was angry with Mr. Wolf for breakin' off their relationship, so she apparently decided to take revenge on him and his friend, Ms. Suzanna

Smith. Before maxin' out her credit cards, she bought an older model used car from an Atlanta dealer. She then bought a gas can, and filled it when she gassed up the car. She also bought several bottles of bourbon. She drove back to her house in Blue Ridge, appropriated her mother's bottle of prescription sedatives, and emptied the gas can in the house. She then set the house on fire, and sparks from the flames set her car on fire as well.

"A belt buckle engraved with Mr. Wolf's initials was found at the scene of the fire, apparently part of Ms. Jenkins revenge scheme. Two witnesses have come forward statin' that he told 'em back in March of this year how upset he was that he'd lost that buckle.

"The arson squad found a gas can cap several feet from Ms. Jenkins' burned house. It has her fingerprints on it. Also at the fire scene, tossed into the bushes that lined the driveway, they found a partially used book of matches from an upscale Atlanta bar that she was known to have visited during her recent trip to Atlanta. These facts help confirm that Ms. Jenkins was the person who set the fire that destroyed her home and car.

"The next several days are a puzzle. No one has come forward who saw her durin' that time. Where was she hidin'? All we know is that at some point, she drove her older model used car to Dial's General Store, which is next to the bridge over the Toccoa River, and parked it in the store's lot. The proprietor of the General Store reported it abandoned, but hadn't noticed when it first appeared.

"We've thoroughly searched the area surroundin' the General Store. An empty bottle of bourbon of the same brand she purchased in Atlanta was found in the forest nearby, and we are testin' it for DNA, but no other evidence that links her to any particular spot has turned up.

"In examinin' the car, the CSI Unit found an uncapped empty gas can that exactly fits the gas cap found at the scene of Ms. Jenkins' house fire. Her fingerprints are on the gas can. Also in the car were two other empty bottles of bourbon of the same brand as the one found in the forest, and an empty bottle of Mrs. Clara Jenkin's prescription sedatives, along with a ramblin', accusatory letter addressed to Mr. Wolf. Handwritin' experts confirm that the letter was written by Ms. Colleen Jenkins.

"The CSI Unit also found Ms. Jenkins' cell phone under the front seat of her car. As I mentioned before, her phone records helped verify her movements and much of the other evidence our detectives, the FBI, the arson squad, and the CSI Units found in their investigations.

"Ms. Jenkins suffered massive head trauma when her body fell into the Toccoa River. We know she was still alive, when she fell. We found blood traces on one of the larger rocks in the river. The blood is hers, so she must have struck her head on it. But, because river water was found in her lungs, the actual cause of Ms. Colleen Jenkin's death was by drownin'.

"Here's what we don't know. Did she mean to commit suicide? The empty bottles of bourbon and the empty bottle of prescription sedatives point to the possibility that she chose to end her life while inebriated. Or, with her faculties impaired, she might just have slipped and fallen. The toxicology report was expedited, and shows an extremely high level of both substances in her body."

"I want to thank the Governors' office, the FBI, the state and local police investigators and technical personnel, and everyone else who helped facilitate this investigation. I also want to thank the media for your cooperation. Your technical questions will be answered by the various experts here with me, and my deputy here will hand out a bulleted list of the points of evidence."

Chief James stepped back from the podium. The lead police detective took the microphone, introduced himself, and asked for questions.

☾

Tom flicked off the TV and we sat looking at each other, both of us stunned.

"I can't believe it's really over." I shook my head in amazement. "I'm having a very hard time taking it all in."

We stood facing each other, Tom's hands gently holding my tingling upper arms. "There's nothin' to stop us now, Suzanna. I'm goin' to ask you again. Please, will you marry me, darlin'?"

I tilted my head, looked up at him, and hesitated, considering. "Well… I don't know. I haven't known you very long, and you seem to make really bad choices."

Tom's face darkened. "What do you mean?"

"Well, Colleen?"

"Aw, Suzanna. You can't hold that against me. As soon as I was sure about you, I tried to break it off with her."

"Yeah? It sure took you long enough!"

"*What?*" He looked devastated.

"Tom! I'm kidding. Of course, I'll marry you."

He picked me up, slung me over one broad shoulder, and headed for our bedroom. I was shrieking and laughing, and pounding his back with my fists.

"Hah! Serves you right." He lowered me to the wide bed and followed me down. Our clothes slowed us only momentarily. We were adept by now at rapid disrobing. Skin to skin, hip to hip, our lips and hands and tongues met and moved lower, finding their match again and again as the tension built. And, at last, we came as close to heaven as mortals can.

# CHAPTER 25

ⵣ

THE 5K RUN/WALK FUNDRAISER WAS a resounding success. Tom and I were surrounded by well-wishers. A DJ from a local country radio station was playing music and announcing the names of each supporter as they completed the run/walk. When the last walker crossed the finish line, he offered to let Tom address the crowd to thank them. Tom nodded, holding the microphone in one hand, while clutching both my hands in his other.

"Friends, I want to thank y'all for comin' out today. Your support means so much to me, and to my fiancée, Ms. Suzanna Smith. We are very relieved that we are no longer under suspicion of settin' the fire that destroyed Ms. Colleen Jenkins' house and car, and of takin' her life.

"No one should die the way she did, and I'm very sorry about that. I had no idea of the depth of her mental problems and her despair."

He paused for a moment, looking deep into my eyes. "Suzanna and I have talked about what we could do to help others who are dealin' with mental issues. With my lawyer's permission, since the money raised today was originally earmarked for our legal fees, we would like to use the money instead to start a scholarship fund in Colleen's name for Blue Ridge High School graduates interested in enterin' the mental health professions. We believe anyone who needs help with mental problems should be able to find competent psychologists and psychiatrists. Educatin' those competent doctors should be a high priority. If we can help with that, Colleen will not have died in vain."

Applause broke out here and there among the crowd, and slowly built until the noise was deafening. There were some whistles and hollering too. Tom and I grinned at each other. It looked like the scholarship idea, which we had thought of only last night before falling asleep, was a winner.

When the clamor died down a bit, Tom spoke again. "I did lose some business durin' the past couple of weeks, but I can still pay our legal fees, Kyle, in case I've got you worryin'."

Kyle, grinning and nodding, waved and yelled, "Okay by me! That scholarship fund is a great idea."

"Suzanna and I want to thank y'all again for your good wishes and support. We are very grateful. And now, I'm thrilled to announce that we will be gettin' married this summer. We haven't set a firm date, but it will be as soon as I can drag her to the altar."

He handed the microphone back to the DJ and pulled me into his arms. As we kissed, the whistling, hooting, and general pandemonium was even louder than before. We never noticed.

❧

Later, when we were at home, Sheila called to tell us that more than $5,000 had been raised. We were amazed.

"Who's holdin' the money? Oh, Kyle? Perfect. Thanks, Sheila, for callin'. Suzanna and I will go see him on Monday. We'll need his help to set up the scholarship fund and get his advice on how to administer it."

He looked at me for agreement, and I nodded, grinning. He said good-bye, and disconnected.

"Suzanna, I'm thinkin' this might be part of what you've been lookin' for. Do you think so?" He was smiling his sweet, sweet smile and looking deep into my eyes. "Let's see what Kyle says."

"Ah, Tom. Have I told you yet today how much I love you?

"Um, no. Want to show me?"

And I did.

❧

Our meeting with Kyle went well. I had no prior knowledge of how to run a not-for-profit scholarship fund, but the information Kyle supplied made it seem less daunting than I had feared. In fact, I was excited. We decided I would indeed be the administrator of the fund, and Kyle agreed to handle the paperwork to get it set up and ready to function. Our target date for announcing the name of our first scholarship recipient was at next year's high school graduation ceremony.

The $5,000 raised was just the beginning. I envisioned raising much more as time went on. Kyle encouraged me to think big, and with his advice I set up an advisory board consisting of Kyle, Delores, Tom, Sheila, the high school principal, and the head of the science department. I could add others as time went on, but I thought for now, these people were my best choices. I needed to meet with the principal and the science teacher to discuss our goals, but I would have to wait until they both returned to Blue Ridge from their summer vacations.

❦

In the meantime, Tom and I gratefully fell back into our former routine. It was comforting to know that we were free to exercise our own horses, water and weed Margaret's garden ourselves, and go to and from Blue Ridge whenever we needed to, without media attention.

We invited all the people who helped us during our ordeal to Tom's house for a "thank you" dinner on the Saturday evening following the 5-K Run/Walk fundraiser. The weather was glorious, and not too humid. We served cocktails, beer, and appetizers on the patio behind the house, and a buffet style oven fried chicken dinner with roasted potatoes and grilled vegetables inside. Each diner was free to choose whether to eat inside or out.

Delores attended with her husband, Ted Watkins, who was also a lawyer in Kyle's practice. Her Boston accent had made me wonder why she was practicing here instead of in New England. They laughed and told me their story. Delores, who was from a small Massachusetts town on the

Atlantic coast, and Ted, who was born and raised in Fannin County, had met while they were both in law school in Boston. When they fell in love and she agreed to marry him, they moved to Blue Ridge and went to work for Kyle. I liked them both, and was delighted to have the mystery solved.

Everyone gathered around Tom's huge dining room table for dessert and coffee, which featured make-your-own ice cream sundaes and chocolate chip cookies from Margaret's recipe. At several points during the evening, Tom's eyes captured mine with an intimacy that heated my cheeks and made my stomach do its usual acrobatics.

❧

When Tom went back to work, he discovered that his real estate expertise was even more in demand than before. New clients, who might have gone to another realtor in the past, now chose to do business with him. It made him humble, but very proud, that so many people were ready to put their trust in him.

Interestingly, his brief notoriety brought him attention he might never have achieved otherwise. He was asked to be a local consultant to a large statewide real estate construction firm, and Georgia's Governor appointed him to a commission investigating real estate fraud. It meant more travel, including two-day stays in Atlanta twice a month, but the commission especially interested him, and he was glad to serve. We celebrated his homecomings with special dinners and passionate lovemaking.

❧

Now that we were free to make plans for our wedding, Tom and I began to talk about a date. We decided on the last Sunday in August. I wanted it to be outdoors, preferably in Margaret's rose garden, with her gorgeous mountain view as a backdrop. Tom agreed, and called her for permission. She not only agreed, but insisted on coming home early to help us celebrate. And, she informed us, she was going to bake our wedding cake.

Tom was thrilled. I was less so, but I hid my apprehension. I hoped she and I would get along well and, eventually, even have affection for each other. I knew Tom would be extremely unhappy if we were not able at least to be friends. I felt as if I were going to be meeting my future mother-in-law, with all the emotional baggage that entailed.

Neither Tom nor I were particularly religious, though Margaret had tried to instill some belief in him, and my Grandma Rose had tried to do the same in me. After discussing what to do, we decided to hire a justice of the peace, and to write our own vows.

Sheila took me shopping for a gown in Atlanta. Since I had been married before, my wedding gown needed to be simple, and in any soft color other than white. My final choice, endorsed enthusiastically by Sheila, was an ankle-length, form-fitting, strapless gown in a shimmering silk fabric, overlaid with lace in front and back.

It was in a gorgeous shade of pale blue-green that enhanced my complexion and, somehow, managed to subdue my red hair just enough to make it look more elegant. It was pricey, but I knew I could wear it again, maybe even at a future fundraising event for the Colleen Jenkins Foundation.

That practical thought was the only one I had that day. I found the sexiest, most impractical, teal-colored sandals that perfectly complimented my dress. They were not only expensive, but slightly uncomfortable. Naturally, I had to have them.

Fancy, sexy lingerie was next. There was a foundation shop next door to the boutique where I found the gown, and an hour later I had all the lacy lingerie I could possibly use. I knew I would be wearing them only briefly anyway, once Tom saw me in them.

We were unsure yet where we would go for our honeymoon, though we were leaning toward a Caribbean island, possibly Aruba. The truth was, it mattered very little where we went. It mattered only that we would be there, together, as husband and wife.

Ellen and Ron were up to date with all our plans. I had carefully kept our legal predicament a secret from Ellen, since she was out of the country anyway. Ron, however, had seen a reference to the case on the internet. He had called in a panic when he saw my name and Tom's listed as the prime suspects. I had reassured him even though, at the time, I was not at all certain we would be exonerated. He was as relieved as I was when we finally were cleared of suspicion.

( 

At last, Ellen was on her way back from South America and Mexico. Both of her projects were going well, finally, though there had been delays and other troubles with them. She was planning to visit us in early August, after she came back from her romantic holiday with her husband, Jon.

The day after she returned, she called me in tears. The romantic holiday was off. Her tears were not of sorrow, though. Instead, they were of rage. She had arrived home a little before she was expected and discovered Jon in bed with a recent client. And, not just any bed. They were in the bed Ellen had shared with Jon ever since she invited him to move in with her before they were married.

"Suzi, I was so shocked I couldn't say anything for at least a full minute. I just stood in the doorway gaping at them. They had the decency to cover up, but they couldn't talk their way out of that scene. I finally found my voice and told them both to get out.

"Of course, I'll never do business with that client ever again, though it might not have been her idea to get into our bed while I was out of town on business. Jon should have known better, but I'm beginning to wonder whether he actually wanted to be found out.

"Granted, things have been a little cool for quite a while between Jon and me. I've been gone quite a bit, and I guess he got lonely. I didn't get the impression that he and that woman had a real romance going. I think she was just a convenience, someone he could use."

"Oh, Ell. Do you really think he's that kind of sleaze ball?" I had met him a week before their wedding, and my impression of him at that time had been of a good guy, genuinely in love with Ellen. That was six years ago, however.

"Well, that's the thing. I don't know. But I do know one thing. His behavior is unacceptable. I've called my lawyers and started divorce proceedings. We have what I'm hoping is an iron-clad prenuptial agreement in effect. If it stands up, and I'm sure he'll try to break it, he won't be able to get his hands on either the firm or my house. I'll give him a generous settlement, but with the proviso that he stays far, far away from me and the firm forever. There are few things quite as shocking as coming home to find your husband in *your* bed with another woman. It's killed any love I might have had for him.

"Suzi, I have to be at work this week to show my face and keep the gossip to as low a volume as possible. I'll need to tie up a few loose ends. But, in a week or so, I could really use a few days away. Do you think I could come to visit you and Tom for a long weekend? But, I don't want to intrude on your idyll. Is there a good hotel in Blue Ridge? Maybe the one you stayed in last April?"

"I'll ask Tom, because we'd probably want to put you up in Margaret's cabin. I think he'll agree, but he'll want to call her to confirm. Just give me a day or two to get Margaret's answer. If that doesn't work out, a hotel's fine, but we'd really want you staying closer to us.

"Ell, I'm so sorry things have worked out the way they have with Jon. But, I'm really looking forward to seeing you. Just glad you can come to visit. We need to spend some time catching up. Sounds like we've got a lot to talk about."

"Thanks, Suzi. I can't wait to see you, too. Sorry it's under these circumstances. I keep checking to see if I'm heartbroken. The funny thing is, I'm not! There may be a very interesting reason for that, but I'll tell you more when I see you."

When we hung up, I sat for a while, thinking about our conversation. Going through a divorce is not a fun experience. And with Ellen and Jon, there were legal issues Jay and I had never had to work out. I was afraid it was going to be tough for Ellen to rid herself of her husband while keeping her house and her firm intact. I hoped she knew what she was doing.

C

When Tom came home from work that afternoon, we exercised the horses and finished the rest of our chores as usual. It was one of my favorite times of the day. I waited to tell Tom about my conversation with Ellen until we were almost finished eating our dinner, and he reacted just as I expected.

"Hey, I'll call Margaret and see if she'll give us permission for Ellen to stay at her place. I don't see why she'd object. I'm lookin' forward to meetin' Ellen and showin' off our tourist attractions. She sounds like an interestin' person, and if she really looks like you, I'll be seein' double. Don't worry though. I'll only really be lookin' at you!"

We had been eating outside on the patio, watching the sunset color the sky. He got up from the table, and came around to hug me. As usual, the moment turned passionate, and we headed inside, leaving the remnants of our dinner on the table. Let the squirrels have fun. We were.

# CHAPTER 26

❦

DURING THE PAST FEW WEEKS, as our emotions ricocheted between anger, anxiety, relief, and joy, neither of us had done any work on my family's history. I wanted to get back to it, but it would have to wait. Ellen was visiting soon, Margaret was returning home a week after Ellen left, and then, before we knew it, our wedding day would be here.

We knew the time between now and then would be hectic, but Tom had a plan. On the weekend after the thank-you dinner we hosted for our closest friends and supporters, he took me to Cherokee, North Carolina, for a romantic weekend with a theme.

Tom arranged for his animals to be taken care of while we were gone, and we left as soon as he came home from work on Friday. It was about 80 miles to Cherokee and we made it in less than two hours.

According to the literature Tom gave me to read on the way, the town of Cherokee is the Tribal cultural and governmental headquarters of the Eastern Band of Cherokee Indians. The

56,000-acre Qualla Boundary, the name of the Reservation, was set aside as their permanent home in 1865, and today, more than 60% of the more than 13,000 registered members of the Eastern Band live within its borders. Qualla Boundary is located next to the Great Smoky Mountains National Park and near the scenic Blue Ridge Parkway. The photos were gorgeous. I could hardly wait to arrive.

We checked into our hotel and ate dinner in the dining room. After a leisurely room service breakfast next morning, we headed to the Museum of the Cherokee Indian. Its modern architecture was attractive, and Tom told me it was considered one of the top cultural museums in the eastern United States. Its mission is to teach, promote and preserve Cherokee heritage, history and culture, and after viewing the extraordinary exhibits inside, I decided it was doing an outstanding job. The exhibits portrayed the colorful and dramatic history of the Cherokee people, from the first appearance of humans in the area, more than 11,000 years ago, to the present.

I was especially impressed with the way traditional beliefs were presented, in story form, as if parents were telling bedtime stories to their children. Of course, having Tom at my side, offering his own commentary, made my experience even richer and more fascinating. We spent more than three hours there, while I tried to absorb as much as I could.

When we left, we drove back to the main road to find a place for a quick lunch. Then, we headed to Oconaluftee Indian Village, a historically accurate reproduction of Cherokee life in the Eighteenth Century. As we walked along winding trails, our guide took us back to the 1760s.

We watched traditional Cherokee dances, a blowgun demonstration, preparations for war, saw typical period homes, and visited sacred ritual sites. We were able, encouraged even, to talk with the villagers, dressed in Cherokee clothing of 250 years ago, as they hulled canoes, carved masks, created pottery, wove baskets, and cooked on stone hearths. I learned that Cherokee men hunted deer, wild turkeys, and small game with bows and arrows and blowguns, and fished with poles, while women did most of the farm work, gathering herbs, digging root vegetables, and harvesting sunflower seeds and the three sisters (corn, beans, and squash). The sweet-tangy aroma of wood smoke followed us along the paths.

Back in the car, we checked the time. We wanted to visit the Qualla Arts and Crafts Mutual, a Cherokee artists' cooperative located across from the Museum. It was mid-afternoon. We decided to buy ice cream cones and come back in a half hour. It was a hot day, and the ice cream sounded perfect.

In the Arts cooperative, hand woven baskets, wood carvings, pottery, beadwork, and so much more, were attractively displayed. I lingered by shelves full of baskets and found one I loved, a beautiful white oak storage basket. I thought the price was much too high, but Tom insisted on buying it for me. The saleswoman remarked that the weaver was expected to come in with more baskets on Sunday. I glanced pleadingly at Tom and he promised to bring me back before he drove us home.

We said good-bye and went back to our hotel room to freshen up for dinner. Tom surprised me by taking me to a restaurant with Cherokee foods on the menu. I sampled a traditional stew made with venison and foraged root vegetables and herbs. I had never tasted venison before, and to my delight, the stew was delicious.

Then, Tom had another surprise for me. He had two tickets for the Cherokee drama, "Unto These Hills." I had seen several billboards advertising the play as we neared the town of Cherokee, but I had no real idea of what to expect.

We arrived at the outdoor amphitheater just as dusk was falling. Urgent drumbeats sounded as we descended the steps and found our seats. When the action began, I was captivated. The actors and dancers were dressed in native costumes, some wearing wooden clan masks like the ones I had seen in the Museum.

The narrator and the performers told the story of the Cherokee, beginning with their belief of how the earth was created, and leading us through their tribal history. They were essentially the same concepts as those portrayed in the Museum, but beautifully performed by talented Cherokee actors, dancers and drummers. The music was dramatic and emotional.

Tom kept his arm around my shoulders, and as the evening grew cooler, I snuggled closer. The performance was thrilling, and at the end, we joined the rest of the audience in giving them a well-deserved standing ovation.

❧

Later, as we prepared for bed, Tom watched me anxiously. He had been doing that all day, though he had tried not to be too obvious.

"Suzanna, darlin', I know I've thrown a lot at you today. How do you feel? Are you okay with all this?" He stood facing me, holding my hands, but not pulling me into his arms. Not yet, at least.

I understood his anxiety. He wanted very badly for me to understand what I was seeing and to accept him, as he was, but also, to embrace his rich heritage. For me, the whole experience had been fascinating, and eye-opening. I realized how little I had known about Cherokee culture, and how important it was to me to learn more.

"Tom, I know our backgrounds are very different, but that doesn't mean we can't bridge those differences. You've given me one of the most exciting and thought-provoking days of my life so far. I'm fascinated, and I think I'm beginning to understand a little about Cherokee culture and what happened here.

"But, I can't grasp it all in one day or one weekend. I'll need to do more reading, and I hope you'll help me choose some good books. But, for right now, promise me we'll come back here often, for special events, but also, so I can continue to learn and comprehend more. And later, when our children are old enough to realize what they're seeing, that we'll bring them here too. Okay?"

He nodded, slowly. "You're not bored, or frightened, by anythin' you've seen today?" He needed to be convinced.

"No, Tom, not at all. In fact, I'm honored that you wanted to share all this with me. And, if it's possible, I love you even more for doing that."

His sweetest smile lit his face. Reaching out to touch my cheek, he drew one finger down until he could tilt my face up to his. "Then, yes. I promise to come here often with you, and later with our children. I love you, Suzanna."

Now, he pulled me into his arms, and there was no more talking.

After breakfast next day, before leaving to drive home, we visited the cooperative again. The artist who had woven my basket was there, and I was able to speak with her. She smiled when I told her how much I loved my new storage basket. She said that her grandmother had taught her traditional Cherokee basket weaving. After she showed me a few of her other designs, I appreciated her talent even more. I would look for her work on future visits to the Cooperative.

# CHAPTER 27

❧

BACK HOME, THE DAYS PASSED quickly. Much to my relief, Margaret agreed for Ellen to stay in her cabin while she was visiting. The day before Ellen was due, I spent a few hours there cleaning, putting fresh sheets on the bed, and stocking the bathroom with paper goods and clean towels. Before I left, I filled some vases with roses and hydrangea blossoms from Margaret's garden. I remembered finding fresh flowers in the great room and bedroom when I first arrived to stay in the cabin. They had been a sweet and welcoming touch.

Ellen's plane was scheduled to arrive in late morning, so after we took care of our chores and ate breakfast, Tom drove us in Margaret's Jeep to the Atlanta airport. The flight was slightly delayed, and by the time it landed, I was practically bubbling over with excitement. Tom kept looking at me and grinning.

The passengers began to deplane and, at last, Ellen saw us and came running over. She and I hugged each other for a long moment before I introduced her to Tom. He made a comical show of examining both of us and trying to decide which of us was me and which was Ellen. Then, he picked up her carry-on, and we laughed and joked all the way to the Jeep.

But, I was worried about her. Under cover of our laughter, she seemed sad and very tired. She was too pale and there were dark circles under her lovely green eyes. I hoped, this visit, brief as it was, would do her good.

When we arrived at Margaret's cabin, I asked her if she wanted to rest, or if I should come inside with her.

"Oh, Suzi, please come in with me. I have so much to tell you, and I need your advice. I don't think I can rest easy until we've talked."

I looked at Tom, and he got the message. "Okay, ladies. You have a good talk and I'll go get ahead of some of the paperwork I'm behind on. But, Ellen, Suzanna and I are takin' you out to our favorite restaurant tonight, Billy's BBQ. Suzanna will tell y'all about it. There's lunch fixin's in the fridge, but don't eat too much. You'll see why later."

He brought Ellen's suitcase inside and looked around approvingly. "You did a great job in here, Suzanna. I'll just put this in the bedroom, and get out of your hair. Expect me to pick you up for dinner at about six o'clock, okay?"

Ellen nodded and I looked up at him, thanking him with my eyes. "Have a good time with your paperwork."

He laughed, and leaned down to kiss me good-bye.

As soon as the door closed, Ellen reached for me. We hugged each other for a long time, both of us shedding tears. We always missed each other when we were apart, and being apart was happening more and more often over the past few years. Our daily texts and occasional phone calls were important to us, but there was so much we had to leave unsaid in those brief communications.

I sat down in the great room to wait while Ellen used the bathroom. When she rejoined me, she brought the box of tissues from the bathroom with her.

"Do you want anything to eat or drink, Ellen? Tom wasn't kidding. There's plenty of food in the fridge, and an assortment of drinks, from water, sweet tea, and soda, to beer and white wine."

"Nothing to eat just yet, though I think I'll get a bottle of water. How about you?"

"Yes, thanks. Then let's hear whatever it is you're dying to tell me. You've got me really curious!"

She came back with water for both of us. "Okay, but now that I'm here, I don't really know where to start."

"How about at the beginning?"

"Yeah, but I'm not sure exactly when that was. All I know is this: things haven't been right with Jon and me for a very long time. I kept putting it down to my being away so much, and tried to make it up to him when I was home. He seemed to welcome that at first, but for the past two years or so, he's been less and less responsive. It wasn't that he was angry with me, or at least that's the way it seemed. It was more that he was indifferent. Like I could do whatever I wanted and it didn't matter to him anymore."

"Oh, Ellen. I'm so sorry."

"That's why I proposed that romantic holiday we were supposed to have taken this summer. He seemed willing but again, not enthusiastic. He wasn't meeting me halfway.

"I don't know why I wasn't more suspicious of him. There were times when he seemed nervous, even guilty, but I always made excuses for him. Huh, as it turns out, his little fling with our client was not his first. He's been having way more fun than I've been having."

"What do you mean? What kind of fun?"

"I hired a private detective to investigate his actions over the past few years, and he turned up dozens of weekend trysts and one-night stands, both in hotels and in my home! I can't believe he'd be so callous as to bring his bed-mates into my house! Into my bedroom!"

She paused for a moment. "Suzi, do you remember when my mom and Nicholas moved to Europe?"

"Of course, Ell. I remember how lonely you were for them."

"My father designed and built that house for our family. Just Dad, Mom, and me! Then, of course, Nicholas came along much later. When Mom and Nicholas left for Europe, I moved into the master bedroom. And even before Jon and I married, it became our bedroom. As far as I am concerned, that bedroom is off limits to anyone not related to me by blood or marriage! How dare he?"

"You mentioned a prenuptial agreement."

"Yes. I'm afraid he'll try to break it. I'm willing to pay him handsomely to go away quietly, but I'd be devastated if he winds up with any part of my house or my firm!"

She was sobbing again, angry tears. I moved over to her and pulled her into an embrace.

Eventually, she stopped crying and began to mop her face. I moved slightly away, but within reach.

"But, here's the kicker. Turns out that not all of his bed-mates were women. He says he's bi-sexual. I'm having a really hard time getting my mind around that. At first, I couldn't believe it at all, but then, I realized that that is probably the major reason why our marriage has gone sour. Apparently, I'm not attractive to him anymore. He craves much more sexual variety than I can give him!"

She was quiet a moment. I was surprised at Jon's revelation, but not really shocked. More people were experimenting openly with their sexual identities now that it seemed safer to do so. I feared that sense of safety was a mirage, however. There were still many places, even in our own country, where it was not safe to be gay, or bi-sexual, or anywhere on the LGBTQ spectrum.

Ellen laughed, but without humor. "Funny, last year, when I was in Russia, I met a man, a Russian diplomat. We felt an immediate attraction, and while he wanted to have an affair with me, I just couldn't do it. I wasn't ready. Though things were far from ideal with Jon, I still had hope that we could revive our marriage. I wanted to think we could make love with real passion once again. Plus, I was only in Russia for a little over a month. I didn't think I could agree to an affair, and then just go home. What if I fell in love with this Russian man? What kind of future could we have?"

She looked away, sighing. "Oh, well, what's done is done, I guess. But, in view of what happened with Jon, maybe it's too bad I didn't indulge in a mini-affair after all. The idea of the passion that 'might have been,' is making me a little less weepy over Jon's betrayal, despite what you've just seen. Those tears were from anger, not so much from loss!"

Shaking her head, she paused to take a deep breath. "But, I'm here now, and I want to put all this behind me for a few days. I imagine you've got lots of plans for this weekend, right? I'm dying to be distracted!"

I nodded. "Yes, Tom has a list of places to show you and things to do. But, we'll make it easy on you and not keep you out late. Don't be offended, but you look like you could use a good rest."

"I'm not at all offended. I know exactly how I look! And thanks so much for this chance to get away. This place is great. I'm so thankful for the generosity of the owner of this cabin. Margaret, is it?"

"Yeah. She's coming home next week to help us carry off our wedding. Sheila has done the bulk of the planning, dragging me along in her wake. It's my job to say 'Yes, Sheila' or 'No, Sheila' to whatever she proposes. So far, things are going great. I'm so lucky. Not only does she have great taste, but she knows what Tom would like, and that's not too much fuss. She also knows who to call to make everything just perfect. I'm putty in her hands."

"I'm surprised. Didn't you want to plan your own wedding?"

"With my track record, I thought it would be better to put it in someone else's hands."

"But, you didn't plan the first one either!"

"True. But I'm with people here that I trust. Looking back, with 20-20 hindsight, there were so many things about Jay's courtship, the wedding ceremony, and the honeymoon, not to mention our short married life, that made me uncomfortable. I just never spoke up for myself. With Sheila in charge, it's not like that. She gets my opinion and, bless her, my permission, before she arranges any detail."

☾

We ate a light lunch at the kitchen table and shared a beer. I told her about Tom's and my close encounter with the Blue Ridge justice system, about the money raised at the 5-K Run/ Walk, and the Foundation we were setting up in Colleen's name.

"Wow, Suzi-que. What an ordeal. It must have been terrible to be under all that suspicion. Poor, sad Colleen. I'm so glad all that's in the past!" She pulled me into a hug, and we shed a few tears of relief.

A minute later, we mopped our eyes again, and sat grinning at each other. It was thrilling to have her here. We knew and understood each other so well. Not even Tom knew me as well as Ellen did. Not yet, anyway.

"And now, you and Tom are becoming local

celebrities. I love the foundation idea. I'm not sure *I* would be that generous. On admittedly short acquaintance, your Tom seems to be a fine man, though I'm probably not the best judge of male rectitude right now. But, seriously, I do envy you. You're so happy, you're almost glowing!"

"Tom *is* special. I love him more than I can say."

"Lucky girl. It looks mutual to me. But I have a delicate question for you. It's not politically correct, but I'm curious, and in a way, it pertains to your future happiness."

"What is it?"

"This is the South. Of course, you know that, but I wonder how well you know attitudes towards Native Americans here. From what I've heard, relations have not been all that cordial. And that makes me nervous for you."

"Okay. That isn't politically correct, but I understand why you might be wondering. As far as I can see, Tom is well liked and respected here for several very good reasons. In the first place, he's a local man who's made good. He's not only a role model for Cherokee kids, he's someone white kids can admire. He won honors as a student athlete, both in high school and college. When he went into business in real estate, he joined and became actively involved in the Chamber of Commerce, the Rotary Club, and several other community organizations. He's become very successful in his career, and he's a smart investor. He's been able to help several people financially, and he's generous in other ways, too."

"Really?"

"Yes." I nodded. "The thing is, he's genuine.

He doesn't lie to people, and he doesn't let anyone down who is depending on him. There may be people who think less of him because he's Cherokee, but they must be a small minority. I haven't seen anybody be disrespectful either to him or to me."

"That's a relief. I hope you realize I only asked because I love you."

"Yes, I do. And I answered because I love you, too."

☾

We finished our lunch, and after we washed our dishes, I took her outside. The spectacular mountain view thrilled me each time I saw it, and Ellen was appropriately appreciative of it. We toured the rose borders, and admired the hydrangeas, and then I showed her Margaret's herb garden and the journal that had taught me not only to love herbs, but to take a chance on growing my own tomatoes, as well. The vines were large now and covered with flowers and I was already harvesting bushels of grape tomatoes. Tom had promised me that within another few days, the first beefsteak tomatoes would begin to ripen. I was almost embarrassed to be so excited, but Ellen just laughed.

"Who knew you'd turn out to be such a country girl? Taking care of Tom's animals? Gardening? Who'd have thought my sophisticated Manhattan-dwelling almost-sister would want to move to rural Georgia? By the way, what do you plan to do with your condo?"

"That's a very good question. Tom and I are trying to decide where to go on our honeymoon. Maybe I can persuade him to come first to the big, bad city to help me decide what to do. He knows real estate, though of course, not Manhattan real estate. But he might have some good ideas. No guarantee he'll agree to go though, unless I beg him. I don't want to have to do that."

"You'll have to tread carefully. You don't want to scare him!"

"Don't laugh. He's right at home in Atlanta, and that's a city!"

"Yeah, but Atlanta's not the Big Apple, sweetie."

"Okay, you're right. So, anyway, the answer is, I have no idea. The tenant you recommended seems to be happy there, or at least, he hasn't complained. Do you ever see him?"

"No, but I still have friends at his company. Maybe I can ask somebody to feel him out. If he wanted to buy it from you, would you be willing to sell it?"

"Sure. I can't see needing it anytime soon. I might as well sell it if I can get a good price."

"Hah! It's Manhattan. Everything gets a good price."

"I hope he can afford it, then. If, of course, he wants it."

We wandered back inside and settled down in the great room. Soon, Ellen began to drowse. I let her stretch out on the couch, while I moved to an armchair. We had always been comfortable with each other. She needed a nap, and I was fine with that.

I pulled out my cell phone to check my emails and found a text from Tom. I texted him back: *She's napping, & I luv u 2. c u @ 6.*

# CHAPTER 28

*(*

ELLEN SLEPT UNTIL ALMOST FOUR-THIRTY.

"Hey, sleepyhead. Did you have a good nap?"

"Wow. I didn't see that coming. But, yes. I feel much better."

"You have an hour and a half before Tom picks us up for dinner. Do you want to shower and change?"

"Yeah, good idea."

She stretched and headed for the bedroom. Soon I heard her putting clothing into dresser drawers, and humming tunelessly as she decided what to wear.

I tapped on the bedroom door.

"Come in, Suzi. I'm just about to hit the shower."

I opened the door just far enough to stick my head through. "I just wanted to tell you not to fuss. Billy's BBQ is not the kind of place you'd wear a ball gown to. Jeans and a nice top will do. While you're getting ready, I'm going to go sit in the porch swing. Come outside when you're done, okay?"

"I won't be long."

When she joined me on the porch, I marveled again at how much we resembled each other. She had followed my advice and was dressed in dark blue jeans and a blue and beige striped sleeveless top. She wore low-heeled, strappy sandals in a medium tan and a darker tan bag was slung across her body. She was carrying a beige sweater for later. Her makeup was subtle and her hair was tied back into a low ponytail. My clothes were similar, though I was wearing a short, casual skirt instead of jeans, and my outfit was less expensive. Designer clothes were beyond my current budget.

"Ell, you look great. Did you get that pocketbook in Mexico? It's beautiful, and it's handmade, right?"

"Thank you, ma'am. Yes, there's a little shop in Mexico City, not too far from my hospital project. The man who owns it sells the most gorgeous pocketbooks, belts, wallets, key chains, and everything is handmade by him, his son, and other artisans who still live in his village. I visit the shop whenever I'm in Mexico City. He's very humble, but he's a genius with leather."

She sat down in one of the rocking chairs and looked around. Hydrangeas were blooming near the front porch in shades of pink, blue, and lavender. The soft, warm breeze through the trees that sheltered the cabin, and the soft buzzing of bees and other insects, busy in the late afternoon sunshine, were the only sounds.

"I'm beginning to see why you wanted to spend the summer here in this cabin. It feels so comfortable and welcoming."

"I think that's Margaret's influence. I'm

convinced her spirit lives here whether she's here in person or not. So far, it's a very benign spirit, but I'm a little worried. She's cutting her visit with her daughter and new baby granddaughter short to come home next week to help with our wedding."

"Why, exactly, are you worried?"

"She's Tom's surrogate mother and taught him just about everything he knows about manners and being a good person. She taught him how to garden and cook, and he's like this celebrity chef! Everything he makes is *so* delicious. I'm intimidated by all Margaret's skills and talents. I just hope she'll like me. Tom will be very unhappy if we don't get along."

"Can I give you some advice?"

"Okay. What?"

"Stop worrying. She knows Tom loves you, and she loves him. She won't treat you badly because that would make Tom unhappy. Besides, from everything you've told me about her, she doesn't sound like that kind of person. I think you're worrying needlessly."

"Thank you, Swami. Did you get that off your Ouija Board or from your Magic 8 Ball?"

"Very funny. Oh, look. Here comes Tom. Wow! Is that the sports car you told me about?"

"Uh huh. Tonight, you get to sit in the front seat, and I'll sit in the back. There's just enough room if I sit sideways."

"Oh, boy. You're too kind!"

"Not so much. Next time, *you* get the back seat! Tonight, we're giving you a chance to enjoy the scenery. It was getting dark when Tom took me to Billy's BBQ the first time, back in April. I couldn't see anything then, and the views are pretty nice."

@

Billy, Jr. met us at the restaurant's door. He gave Tom a bear hug and kissed me on the cheek. Then he noticed Ellen and did a double take.

"Suzanna, is this your twin sister? I didn't know you had a twin."

"We're as close as sisters, but actually, we're not related. Billy, this is Ellen Grant. She was my college roommate, and is now a famous international architect."

"Well, Ms. Grant, we're honored to have you visitin' us. Will you be stayin' long?"

"Please, call me Ellen. It's good to meet you, Billy. Tom's told me a little bit about you and your Dad and the amazing food you serve here. But, to answer your question, I can stay only for a few days just now. But, I'm planning to attend Suzanna and Tom's wedding. I'll be sure to come again then."

"Good. Please come right this way. Tom's table is waiting."

"Thanks, Billy." Tom grinned. "Ellen, he's not kiddin'. They always keep a table in reserve for me. Makes it very convenient. No waitin'."

"Really?" She slipped into the seat Billy was holding out for her and turned to look at him. "That's unusual. Why do you do that?"

"We started it a few years ago. The restaurant was strugglin', and Tom, here, lent my Dad some money to upgrade. Ever since, we've kept a table ready for him if he calls us by six p.m. to let us know he's comin'. If we don't hear from him by then, we let ordinary folks sit here." Billy smiled. "Well, I've got to keep movin'. Dad and I hope you'll enjoy yourselves tonight." He nodded to us and turned away to greet other diners.

"How generous of you, Tom." I could tell Ellen was impressed.

"Blue Ridge needed a really good barbeque restaurant. Billy, Jr. and I have been friends for years, and I knew how good his Dad's barbeque tasted. The restaurant just needed a little sprucin' up and some better equipment. As you can see, it was a very successful investment. This place is really popular with the locals and durin' tourist season, like now, it's hard to get a table. The food is that good, and there's a lot of it! By the way, did Suzanna tell you about the no-menu part?"

"Yes. I thought that was strange."

"Well, it's a good thing she warned you. I forgot to do that the first time I brought her here. She was so mad when I ordered for us both without consultin' her! She was mad at me anyway for teasin' her, but I couldn't help it. She was so much fun to cross swords with, and she gave me back as good as she got. I began to fall in love with her that evenin'. After spendin' the next day with her, I was pretty sure I wanted her in my life, but there was Colleen. I didn't know what to do."

He looked at me in a way that inflamed my cheeks. "When she left to go back to New York, I felt like there was this great big empty hole where my heart was supposed to be. I wasn't sure I'd get to see much of her again, even though she was goin' to 'rent' Margaret's cabin and I'd promised to help research her grandmother's family. After all, that was business. And then, too, there was Colleen."

Desire was arcing between us, probably visibly. I was sure Ellen was aware of it.

"Well, I heard a lot about you after Suzi came home. My antennae went up right away. She hadn't been that interested in a man since her divorce. I'm very happy you two found each other."

"I was thrilled that she was able to come back down here so soon. I'm even grateful to her old company. If they hadn't given her a good severance package, she probably would've cancelled her stay here this summer. Then, I would've had to go to New York to court her. I'm not a big fan of city life, but I would have done just about anythin' to see her again."

"And yet," Ellen said, "you waited until after Suzi came back down here to break it off with Colleen."

"Yep. I guess that makes me a terrible coward, but I needed to know whether Suzannah was really interested in me, or whether I'd just made up this fantasy in my own head. I got my answer while we were visitin' the Cemetery in Epworth, and I couldn't wait to tell Colleen we were through. I tried to tell her that day, but she wouldn't hear of it. I feel awful that it got so ugly. I keep thinkin' I should have realized she was disturbed, but like I told Suzanna, I just saw the pretty girl she *seemed* to be, and never looked beneath the surface. I've learned a lot about building a true and lasting relationship since then, thanks to Suzanna."

He was holding my hand under the table. Now, he squeezed it and placed it high on his thigh. We had to behave in public, but I was wishing we were doing amazing things to each other at home in bed. Just then, the food came.

Ellen stared at her plate. "I can't eat all *that!*"

Tom and I smiled at each other. "Just do the best you can, Ell, or Tom will tell you what happens to the leftovers around here. Trust me, you don't want to know!"

Tonight, there was barbequed pork butt, sliced and served with caramelized onions; wild rice; a grilled medley of peppers, mushrooms, and zucchini; and Billy's famous cornbread and butter.

A few minutes later, Billy, Jr. reappeared at our table. Predictably, he asked how she liked the food.

She rolled her eyes and grinned. "This is the best barbeque I've ever tasted. I think I'm in heaven."

Smart woman. She had just made herself forever welcome at Billy's BBQ.

#### ☾

After dinner, Tom drove us through downtown Blue Ridge. Ellen asked about the railroad tracks that split Main Street into East and West, and admired the antique train.

"I really like the looks of this town. I've never seen a split Main Street before. That's unique. Suzi has already told me about The Elms, and about shopping in a couple of the boutiques. Oh, look!" She pointed. "That Japanese restaurant looks like it's doing a good business. I guess it's not all barbeque in Blue Ridge."

"Right. Tom, tell her about the French, Italian, and Mexican restaurants here."

"No need, babe. She's got eyes. What we do have is a couple of good places to get authentic Southern food. A lot of places have restaurants that advertise Southern food, but it's usually a pale imitation of the real thing. We actually have the real thing here in Blue Ridge!"

From my uncomfortable sideways perch in the back seat, I could see Ellen lean back against the head rest and close her eyes. It was only eight-thirty, but I knew she was feeling the soporific effects of the mountain air, not to mention her enormous dinner.

"Tom, I think Ellen's pretty tired. Why don't we take her back so she can get a good night's sleep?"

He glanced over at her and nodded. "Sure. We'll be there in less than twenty minutes."

"Thanks, Tom. Suzi-que, you're a mind reader."

Tom turned his car into Margaret's driveway in seventeen minutes flat. I got out and gratefully stretched my legs. Ellen leaned down to thank Tom, and then hugged me. I walked her to the door.

"Ell, I won't come in. Just have a good night's sleep."

She embraced me again. "By the way, there's a big package waiting for you in the front seat." She was grinning.

"What are you talking about?"

"You'll see!" She waved at Tom, and went

inside.

Puzzled, I glanced at Tom as I got into the car. Sure enough, I saw immediately what she meant. A massive erection was straining his jeans, and threatened to break open his zipper.

"Oh, my!" I gasped in delighted anticipation.

He gave me a warning look, and backed down Margaret's driveway. "You'd better not touch. If you do, I'll probably explode! And then, I'll wreck the car and kill us both. You can touch all you want, please, when we get home."

"Okay, but hurry!"

He pulled the car back onto the road, and we drove home in a food euphoria, fueled by desire. We were barely inside the door before he picked me up and pinned me against it. In less time that it takes to tell it, I unzipped his fly and whipped off his shirt, while he rearranged my clothing for easy access. Our kisses turned fiery as we hungrily sought sweet release.

Afterwards, holding me tightly, he rested his cheek on the top of my head, and impatiently waited until we could regain our breath. Then, he picked me up again and carried me to our bedroom. Soon, the rest of his clothes littered the floor along with mine, and even neat, organized Tom was willing to leave them there.

Later, as we were about to go to sleep, Tom leaned over to kiss me again. "So, how is she? Does she seem okay to you?"

I snuggled into his arms and rested my head on his shoulder. "Yeah, but she's got a lot on her mind. She's worried Jon will try to break their pre-nup agreement, and she doesn't want to lose any part of her father's firm, not to mention the house her Dad designed and built for his family. Jon was living there with her, of course, but she couldn't bear it if he somehow managed to take it or the firm away from her."

"I'm sure she can afford good lawyers. Did you know Jon very well?"

"No. I was in their wedding party as Ellen's Matron of Honor, but I didn't see very much of him before they were married, and not at all since then. She met him in grad school and they lived together for a couple of years before they married. He's also an architect, but he doesn't have half her talent.

"Tom, it's hard to believe he could be stupid enough to sleep around! But it goes way beyond stupid! Ellen told me that he's been seeing men as well as women, and claims to be bi-sexual."

"Oh, wow. She must be havin' a hard time with that, not that it's so uncommon. So, of course, that's a major reason why they're done. But there could be other factors involved, too, like jealousy. Maybe he thought she'd be content to stay home and be a small-town architect. Or, it could be that he just didn't think her career would take off like it did."

"They seemed so much in love when they got married. I'm so disappointed that it hasn't worked out."

He was winding a tress of my hair around his fingers. "I know you are, but if her situation makes you worry about us, don't. I'll never cheat on you. Why on earth would I? You're not the only one who feels the electricity between us, but that's not all. You're everythin' I'll ever need or want."

We clung to each other. His kiss was a promise, and I met it with my own.

Later still, I fell asleep with my head still on Tom's shoulder, cradled in his strong arms.

# CHAPTER 29

NEXT MORNING, AFTER WE TOOK care of our animals, I called Ellen to see if she wanted to join us for breakfast.

"Hey, Suzi, thanks for a wonderful evening. I had a really good time, and a fantastic night's sleep."

"I'm glad. I called you because Tom's cooking a country breakfast, and it's not to be missed. If you're ready, I'll come get you."

"Great! Believe it or not, I'm famished!"

I put three place settings on the island, and kissed Tom before I left. He was making his delicious, fluffy biscuits to go with cheese, spinach, and herb omelets. I was pretty famished myself.

I hummed to myself as I drove to Margaret's. The route was as familiar to me now as my commute to work in Manhattan had been, and the scenery was far better.

Ellen was waiting on the porch when I pulled into the driveway. She ran down and flung herself into the Jeep.

"Good morning, Suzi-que. You look like sunshine itself."

I looked down at my yellow tank top and laughed. "Thank you, ma'am."

"I can't believe I'm here in this beautiful, tranquil place after all the turmoil in my life lately. And to be here with you and to meet Tom, that's amazing. So, tell me, did you two have fun last night? The sexual tension at dinner last night was obvious."

"Guilty as charged. We did get pretty wild, and don't assume it was all missionary position."

"Stop! Too much information! Keep all the details to yourself!"

"Oh, you're so funny."

We were both laughing so hard, I had to pull over. "Ell, stop making me laugh!"

"Me? It's just as much your fault!" We wiped away our tears of laughter and I started the Jeep again. We pulled into the driveway just as Tom opened the front door.

"Hurry up, ladies. Your food's gettin' cold."

We sat down at the island and picked up our forks. Ellen, not used to lavish presentations of food at home, gaped at the array. Fresh fruit cups, simple Cheddar cheese, spinach, and fresh herb omelets, apple-cured bacon, and freshly made biscuits served with creamery butter and assorted jellies and jams, were on the menu this morning, all beautifully plated and garnished with sprigs of mint from Tom's herb garden. There was also freshly squeezed orange juice, and piping hot coffee.

"Oh, Tom, this is amazing and looks absolutely delicious. Did Margaret, or you, make these jams and jellies?" She took a biscuit and slathered on blackberry jam. "Mmmmm, I think I've died and gone to heaven." She swallowed and dug into her omelet.

Tom laughed. "You guessed it, most of 'em were preserved by Margaret, but I'm responsible for the strawberry and blackberry jams." Ellen stared at him, awestruck.

After a few minutes, she laid down her fork. "Wow! That was incredible. Suzi told me she had wondered if you were some sort of celebrity chef. Maybe you are?"

Tom laughed again, slightly embarrassed. He held up his hands, and shook his head. "No, but I do like to cook, especially for beautiful and appreciative ladies such as yourselves."

"And gallant too? Anyway, Tom, I want to thank you and Suzi for taking me to Billy's last night. It was magnificent! But I have a question for you. Suzi kept wondering why you were always trying to feed her. Is she too skinny?"

"Oh, no. You're not goin' to trap me that way! Oh, noooo! She's perfect, just the way she is. So are you, as a matter of fact, but I'll stick with Suzanna, if you don't mind."

Ellen looked Tom in the eye. "Tom, I couldn't be happier for you both. She *is* a keeper! I know her secrets, and I can still say that!"

"What? She has secrets?"

I was shaking my head in denial. "No way, Tom. She knows no secrets of any concern to you!"

"Huh. Don't know if I should believe you!" He grinned and squeezed my hand. "But, I guess I'll have to. I know better than to think I could pry any real secrets out of either one of you!

"But, if I can change the subject for a minute, Ellen, I thought we'd take you on the scenic railroad you saw last night in Blue Ridge. It runs from there up to Copperhill, Tennessee, and we'll have time for lunch there. Then, when the railroad brings us back, maybe you'd like to walk around Blue Ridge a little. Do some serious shoppin' in our boutiques. How does that sound? We'll have dinner here at our house tonight."

"Thanks, Tom. That sounds great!"

"Then, tomorrow, we could take you on a scenic drive to some other parts of the county, and take a picnic lunch to a nice place we learned about last spring. It's on the Toccoa River, close to Dial, where Suzanna's grandmother was born. We've been to the picnic spot quite a few times. We sometimes fish in the river and the scenery is nice."

"It all sounds perfect! Is there any chance I could do some hiking while I'm here?"

"Sure. There's a trailhead at the edge of our property. The trail's well maintained and there are loops of two, three, and five miles. You can do that Monday mornin' before you have to fly home."

"That's perfect. If Suzi doesn't mind picking me up early, I can hike while you guys take care of your animals. All right, Suzi-que?"

"Sure. I'll go with you if you want me to."

"Oh, thanks, but that's not necessary. I need to do some thinking, and there's nothing like hiking to focus my mind."

I was slightly disappointed that I was not invited to join her, but I understood her point.

❧

The weekend flew by. By Monday morning, even though I picked her up before six o'clock, Ellen was looking refreshed, and much happier.

I took her to the trailhead, and showed her how it was marked. The two-mile loop was an easy hike, with only a few hills and very little underbrush to push through. The three- and five-mile loops were extensions of the shorter one, though there were a few trickier spots on the five-mile loop. I handed her a stout stick, in case she encountered an animal. We had never seen anything other than deer and birds, but there was always the chance of a black bear or a snake.

Reluctantly, I left her and returned to Tom's house to help him with the chores. When we were done, he drove the Jeep to the trailhead to pick Ellen up. Not enough time had passed for her to have finished the five-mile loop, but he wanted to be waiting for her when she returned.

I went inside to wash up and start preparing breakfast. We were going to have waffles and fruit this morning, and Tom felt I was competent enough to handle the electric waffle iron.

I showered and changed and made the batter for the waffles. I washed the blueberries, sliced the strawberries, and watched the time pass. Wondering what was keeping them, I called Tom on his cell.

I began to worry when his voicemail picked up. Before I could call Ellen's cell, my phone rang.

"Suzi, I've got a situation here. Tom's been hurt.

Not badly, he's okay, really, and I'm going to drive him back."

"What? What's happened to him? Is he really okay?"

"I'll tell you when we get there. We're getting into the Jeep now, so we'll be there in just a few minutes."

She disconnected. Frightened, and impatient for their arrival, I still remembered to unplug the waffle maker, and put the batter and fruit into the fridge. Then, I ran outside to wait for them.

Five long minutes passed until I saw the Jeep pull into our driveway. I ran to the car before the engine stopped.

Tom was leaning against the passenger window. I eased the door open, and bracing a hand against his shoulder, helped him sit up straighter. He was awake, but seemed dazed. He was pressing a bloody scarf to his wound, and when I pulled it away, I saw that he had a gash near his hairline. The bleeding seemed to have slowed somewhat, but the area was swelling, and looked painfully bruised.

"Ellen, I'm going to call Sheila at the hospital. She can arrange for Tom to be seen as soon as we can get there. But, *what happened*?"

She came around the Jeep to stand beside me.

"Suzi, he took a pretty sharp blow to the head. He was unconscious for a few seconds, but came around almost immediately. He's woozy now, but before you call Sheila, I want to tell you what happened."

"Ellen, I don't understand? I…"

Tom's voice was low and shaky. "Suzanna, let

Ellen talk. Then you can call Sheila. I'm okay, just a little disoriented."

"Okay... Ellen, what happened?"

"First, I want to thank you so much for arranging for me to stay in Margaret's cabin. It was great! But, remember that Russian diplomat I told you about? Well, I had no idea that he would turn up on her doorstep, but he flew into Atlanta yesterday, picked up a pre-arranged rental car, and drove up here. He arrived late last night. Please forgive me for not calling you immediately, but we lost all track of time. I never intended to use Margaret's cabin for a tryst, or to deceive you."

"How did he know where you were? Wait, he's here now?"

"No. He's gone back to Washington where he's attending talks between Russia and our government. I think he may have found me through some sort of surveillance. But anyway, here's the thing. He met me this morning in the woods to say one last good-bye. We'd already said our good-byes last night, or rather, early this morning, but I had told him I was going hiking and approximately where I was going to be.

"When Tom came to get me this morning, he saw me in my friend's arms. We were kissing, but I guess, Tom must have thought I was being attacked. He called my name and began to run toward us. I could hear his boots pounding on the path, and my friend and I turned just in time to see Tom trip on an exposed root. When he fell, he hit his head on a sharp tree stump, and he blacked out for a bit. You can see the gash. I used my scarf to mop up the blood."

I was stunned by this turn of events, but anxious to get Tom to the hospital. "Okay, Ellen. Thanks for doing that. I'm sorry to cut you short, but I need to call Sheila now. We'll talk again before you have to leave for the airport."

❦

I dropped Ellen at Margaret's and drove Tom straight to the hospital in Blue Ridge. Sheila, an ER doctor, and several nurses met us at the entrance to the Emergency Room. While the doctor and nurses took charge of Tom, Sheila hugged me tightly and led me to the Admittance Office. I took care of the paperwork as quickly as possible, and we went back to the ER.

Tom had already had stitches for the gash, and the doctor was finishing his examination when we found them. I could see that there was quite a bit of swelling at the site of the gash, but thankfully, the bleeding had stopped.

Tom was relieved to see me. "Suzanna, darlin'. Let's go home. All these folks are fussin' over me way too much. I just got a little bump on the head."

"I heard that, Tom." Jim Granger, Tom's family doctor, appeared. "Let me see if that bump is little or not."

I remembered meeting him at the 5K Run/ Walk Fundraiser. He checked Tom's stitches, the swelling and bruising, and looked at his chart. Jim motioned me to the other side of the curtain.

"Suzanna, Tom's going to be all right, but he's got quite a nasty bump. I'm worried about a concussion, so I'm going to send him downstairs now for X-rays and an MRI. If he did sustain a concussion, and I'm almost sure he did, he'll be spending the night here in the hospital. There's always the danger of complications, and we're much better equipped to handle that possibility here than you would be at home. They'll have a room ready for him when he's done downstairs, and I'll arrange for you to stay with him. He's going to have a headache for a few days." He pressed my hand. "Don't worry too much. I'll see you later."

"Thanks, Jim." He walked quickly away and I went back to Tom's side. We held hands until the orderly came to wheel his gurney into the elevator.

I was not allowed to go downstairs with him, so I went outside to call Ellen to update her on Tom's condition. Her flight was not until late afternoon, but there was no way I could drive her to the Atlanta airport today.

"Oh, Suzi. I can't find the words to tell you how sorry I am that this happened."

"Ell, I still can't believe all this. Are you having an affair with that diplomat? Does he have a name?"

"Well, yes, to your first question. Now that Jon is pretty much history, I saw no reason to put him off any longer. I certainly didn't plan this. I had no idea that he was in the U.S., let alone in Washington. As to your second question, yes, he does have a name. I call him Vladi, short for Vladimir, but I can't really tell you more about him right now. I need to see where, if anywhere at all, our relationship might go. It's brand new, but it's certainly gone beyond friendship now."

"I really don't know what to say. Except, please be careful. This seems awfully quick. Are you sure you're ready for *any* new relationship, and especially one with a Russian man? I'm assuming you don't know very much about him yet, right? I don't want you to get your heart broken."

"Don't worry. I'll be fine. I can take care of myself. In fact, don't give me another thought today. I'll call for a car to take me to the airport, and charge it to the firm. Just give my love and thanks to Tom when he's feeling better. Suzi, this visit with you and Tom has been awesome. I can't thank you enough. I'll call you when I get home. And, Suzi, I love you."

"Tom and I loved showing you around. Come back anytime. And, Ellen, I love you too."

# CHAPTER 30

❦

SHEILA WAS WAITING FOR ME when I came back inside the ER.

"I was able to speak with the technician who took Tom's X-rays. He thinks Tom will heal just fine, but Jim, Doctor Granger, I mean, will give us more information when he's seen the results of the tests. Try not to worry."

"He said I can stay with Tom in his room."

"Great! That's usually a privilege only for immediate family, but you're as close to immediate family as Tom's got, right now."

"What about his grandfather?"

"I don't think there's any reason to worry his grandfather at this point. Gramps has had some health issues lately, and the last thing he needs is to fret over Tom."

She gave me a big hug, and went to find out which room was going to be Tom's.

I paced around the waiting room, and watched the clock, unable, at first, even to sit. Eventually, I sank into an orange plastic chair, and picked up a magazine. I tried to focus on it, hoping it would distract me, but found myself flipping pages without seeing them.

Finally, Jim, Dr. Granger, came in. Sheila was with him and he was laughing at something she had said. I relaxed a bit. If they were laughing, Tom must be all right.

The doctor motioned for us to sit. "Suzanna, Tom got quite a thump on the head. He definitely has a concussion, and we'll keep him overnight, just to make sure he has no complications. As I said before, we're equipped to manage them here more easily than you could at home."

"Thank you, Jim. My brother had a concussion once, so I'm aware of what can happen. Can I see him? Is he in pain?"

"Sheila will take you to his room in a couple of minutes. He'll have a headache tomorrow and probably for the next few days, but the pain medication in his IV drip is taking the edge off for now. Your job tonight is to watch out for problems such as double vision, dizziness, and vomiting. Try to keep him quiet and let him sleep if he wants to."

I nodded.

"I'll stop in to see him tomorrow before you leave to take him home. At that time, I'll give you a few pain pills and a list of instructions. Try not to worry, he should be feeling much better in a week or two."

He nodded to me, waved at Sheila, and left the ER. Sheila hugged me again. "Tom's goin' to be fine. He's got a really hard head." Taking my arm, she led me out of the ER and into an elevator.

It rose to the third floor, and opened onto a busy nurse's station. "If you need somethin', this is where you can ask for it, and there's a call button attached to Tom's bed for emergencies. His room is the third one on the left."

I kissed her cheek, and hurried down the hall.

When I pushed the door open, Tom was sitting on the edge of his bed with his back to the door. I had a moment of panic when I saw his bandage and the IV drip.

"Tom?" I spoke softly, trying not to startle him.

"Suzanna, darlin'!"

I ran around the bed and into his arms. Our passionate kisses were fierce. After a long moment, he held me away so he could see my face.

He smiled his sweet smile and, for a few seconds, closed his eyes in relief. "I'm so glad you're here."

I smiled back at him and gently touched his bruised cheek. "Where else would I be?"

I looked around for a chair. I seemed to remember that visitors were not allowed to sit on a patient's bed. There was a large green recliner in one corner of the room that looked too big to move. Near the door, however, there was a mate to the orange plastic chairs in the ER waiting room. I pulled it as close to the bed as I could, and picked up Tom's free hand.

"How are you feeling?"

"Sort of numb, but I don't think that's goin' to last. They tell me I have a concussion. Funny, I played football and other sports all through high school and college and never had one."

He tugged on my hands for more kisses. I stood up to comply, but after a few minutes I pulled away a bit to rest my back. Leaning forward like that was putting a strain on it.

"You're not leavin', are you?"

"No, of course not." I reached forward to cup his face in my hands. "In fact, you're not going to be able to get rid of me. It's my job to keep you quiet and comfortable until Jim examines you tomorrow morning. After he signs the release papers, we can go back home."

I leaned back again.

"They won't let me have anythin' to eat or drink, but you must be starvin', Suzanna, darlin'. I bet Sheila would get you somethin' to eat."

"Tom, I don't want to bother her. She's working. I can go down to the cafeteria myself."

"I know she'd be happy to do it, but okay, we won't bother her."

Meanwhile, Sheila was tiptoeing into the room. She came around the bed so Tom could see her. "Bother who?"

"You!"

"Me? What do you need?"

"Nuthin', now that Suzanna's here, but she hasn't eaten anythin' yet today."

I gave Tom a look. "Didn't you just say we wouldn't bother her?"

"Yeah, but she's here now. She doesn't mind."

"I hope not."

"Stop talkin' about me as if I'm not standin' right here! Of course, I'll get you somethin' to eat, Suzanna. I'm about to take a break, so I can go right now. Is there anythin' you particularly want? Not that this is a gourmet restaurant, but we've got basic food and it's mostly okay. There's burgers and fries, ham and cheese, turkey and Swiss, both tuna and chicken salad sandwiches, green salads, yogurt with fruit, and baked goods."

"Hey, how about me?"

"Sorry, I can't get anythin' for you today, Tom. You can take it up with your nurse."

I threw Tom a sympathetic look. "Well, I guess I'll have a chicken salad sandwich and that yogurt sounds nice."

"You got it. My treat. No! Put your money away. It's my treat!"

"Thank you, Sheila. We owe you."

Tom pretended to pout. "Hey, I'm not gettin' any food. What do I owe her?"

I put my hands on my hips in mock indignation. "Your undying devotion, Tom! And I'll take that too, okay?"

"You guys!" Sheila was trying not to laugh too hard. "I'll be back in about fifteen minutes."

Tom pulled me down to sit with him on the edge of his bed and looked deep into my eyes. "You already have my undyin' devotion."

I leaned over to kiss him and there was no more talking until Sheila came back with my food. I forgot to notice whether my back was still aching.

"Okay, you guys. Break it up. Suzanna, here's your food, and Tom, I brought you a couple of magazines and a book from the hospital's patient book cart. It's non-fiction, about some guy who was an astronaut. I thought you might like it."

"Thanks, Sheila. If Suzanna will read it to me, it might make the time go faster. I think I'm supposed to stay awake for a while."

"Only if you feel like it. It's a myth that you have to stay awake. It's better if you can sleep. Listen, I'm goin' off duty in four hours. If you need somethin' before I go, ask one of the nurses to page me. Okay? Otherwise I'll drop by your house tomorrow on my way to work to see how you're doin', Tom. Follow instructions, okay? Love you guys. See you soon."

༺

The chicken salad sandwich was, as Sheila warned, not gourmet, but it was edible. I enjoyed the yogurt much more. Besides blueberries and banana slices, there was some granola, all layered with the yogurt like a parfait. I felt sorry for Tom, who watched my every bite while pretending to be starving. I offered to go into the tiny bathroom so he would not have to watch me eat, but he refused to let me out of his sight.

"Are you really hungry?"

"Nah, I'm not hungry at all, but I could use a sip of water. The nurses haven't let me drink anythin' yet. They fed me some ice chips at one point, so maybe there's a couple drops of melted ice in that cup." He pointed to a plastic cup on the bedside tray we had moved out of the way. "Would you hand it to me?"

I checked the cup before I gave it to him. There was only a tiny sip of water left.

"I didn't know you were such a good actor. I'll have to watch out for that."

"You don't have to worry too much. I only do stuff like that for laughs."

We chuckled softly, but the chuckles built into full-throated laughter.

A nurse came in with an instrument trolley

to take Tom's temperature, check his pulse, and update his chart. She caught us still laughing, and gave Tom a disapproving look.

"Try not to laugh. You need to keep quiet. Also, you must get into the bed, not sit on the side of it."

"Yes, ma'am." He swung his legs around while she waited to tuck the bed sheets over them. She also raised the head of the bed so he was not laying completely flat.

She turned to me and frowned. "You need to keep him quiet. No laughing."

"I'll try, but I can't make any promises. He's a funny man."

She made a harrumphing noise and pushed her trolley out the door. She probably wished she could have slammed it.

Tom grinned. "Well! I guess we've been put in our places!" And we dissolved into laughter again.

❦

The time passed slowly. I read several magazine articles to him, and started on the book. We got through about four chapters before my voice gave out.

Around dinner time, a different nurse brought a note from Sheila telling us that she had arranged for Tom's neighbor to take care of the animals this evening, and planned to do that herself tomorrow morning with her friend, Joe's, help. To my relief, they promised to continue until Tom was cleared to do physical work again.

The nurses came in to check on Tom about

once every four hours, and in between, I squeezed into bed with him. He was restless with me sitting in the chair, and was much calmer when he was holding me close with his free arm. I kept an eye on the time, and made sure I was sitting in the bedside chair when his nurse came in.

Around eleven o'clock in the evening, Tom dropped into a heavy sleep. I eased out of his bed and after doing a few stretching exercises, I sat in the bedside chair to watch him.

I had helped him into the bathroom earlier, as he was light-headed and unsteady on his feet. So far, that had been his only problem. I hoped, after sleeping so soundly now, he would be less dizzy when he woke up.

Mostly, I just watched him. I loved his looks, his body, his mind, his personality, his... everything. I could no longer imagine wanting anything other than to be with him for the rest of my life.

Eventually, the window beside his bed began to show the first signs of light. Tom stirred, opened his eyes, and reached out his arm to me. I opened the window blinds before climbing back into bed with him, and together we watched the sun rise on a new day. Cradled against Tom's body, I hoped we would have no more mishaps or other problems, at least until we were safely married.

# CHAPTER 31

❦

WHEN THE SUN WAS SHINING brightly, Tom sat up and tentatively swung his legs over the side of the bed. He felt no more dizziness, and though I stayed at his side helping him push his IV pole, he walked into the bathroom under his own power.

At eight o'clock, his nurse came in to check his vitals, but brought no food, much to his disappointment.

"Don't worry. I put yesterday's waffle batter into the refrigerator before I drove you here. I'll make us some when we get home. In the meantime, relax and try to doze until Jim comes in to examine you."

"Okay, boss." He grinned at me. "I'll just dream about a whole stack of those waffles."

An hour later, Jim came in. After he checked Tom's chart and his bandage, he smiled. "I'm pleased with Tom's progress so far, Suzanna. Bring him to my office in two days for a check-up. He's coming along fine now, and I expect he'll continue to improve. Here are the pain pills I mentioned. You're in charge of dispensing them. For the first couple of days, give him two at a time when, or if, he feels his headache returning. After that, give him only one at a time if he needs it, and there will be no more pills when these are gone." He handed me a list of do's and don'ts.

Jim signed the discharge papers, and then, we were free to go home.

I found the Jeep in the visitor's parking lot, where someone on the hospital staff had parked it when we arrived at the hospital. Tom was waiting in a wheelchair at the curb outside the front entrance. I stopped in front of him, and an orderly helped him up and buckled him into the front passenger seat.

"Tom, how are you feeling?

"Now that I'm up and dressed, my head's beginning to ache, and I'm slightly dizzy again, But the good news is that I'm still not nauseous. In fact, I'm starvin' to death, Suzanna, darlin'! When do we eat?"

"Patience, Tom. I have to get you home first."

I drove slowly, with Tom clutching my thigh. He was a nervous passenger at the best of times, and this hardly qualified as that. We finally arrived, and Tom thankfully got out of the car. I ran around to lead him into the house, and after helping him undress, I sent him straight to bed. I promised to join him as soon as I showered and made breakfast. He was already snoring softly before I left the room.

I made coffee and the promised waffles, topped with yesterday's fruit, and served them with a side of scrambled eggs. I hated to wake him, but he needed nourishment as well as sleep. We ate together, sitting up in bed. When we finished, I left our tray in the kitchen and slid naked into our bed. Snuggled against each other, we fell into a dreamless sleep.

When I woke later, and glanced at the clock, I realized I had slept more than seven hours. Tom was awake and, propped on one elbow, was gazing at me. He grinned.

"Finally! I was about ready to blow into your ear. That's how Mike always woke me up. It tickles, and it's impossible to stay asleep when someone's doin' that! Get up, woman, I need to shower, and I need help. What if I drop the soap?" He growled, and tried to grab me. I scooted away and stood.

"No sex, Tom. Not for another day at least."

"Aw, Suzanna, darlin'. There's more than one way to play. I'll show you after my shower."

And he did.

❧

Tom was feeling much better by the time we arrived in Dr. Granger's office for his follow-up visit. Jim was pleased with his progress and removed a few of the restrictions on his activities. There still could be no heavy lifting, and he was not to do his usual outdoor chores for at least another three or four days, but unless his headaches returned, he could go back to his real estate work by the following Monday.

Reading down the list, we discovered Tom was cleared for "light" sex. We looked at each other and grinned, we were already doing that.

❦

Tom's cell phone was ringing as we pulled into his driveway. It was Margaret, with the news that she would be flying home on August 16, a little later than originally planned. Could we please pick her up at the Atlanta airport in the Jeep?

"Margaret, that's terrific. What time is your flight due in? And I need the flight number, too. Email me, please. We'll make sure your cabin is ready and the fridge stocked. I've missed you, and I know Suzanna is lookin' forward to meetin' you. Yes, I'll tell her. See you soon."

"Well, I guess you heard. We better get our weddin' preparations finalized before she gets here, or she'll want to do every last thing herself. She'd do a great job, but I want her to be our guest, not stuck in the kitchen, or on the telephone, the whole time."

"I'm a little nervous about meeting her. She's so important to you, and I want to make a good impression."

"Don't you worry about that. She told me to tell you she can't wait to meet you." He reached over to capture my hand. "Stop frownin'. She's goin' to love you. How could she help it?"

I was far from sure of that, but I swallowed my fears. I hoped and prayed that everything we had planned would be perfect, but I resolved, with Sheila's help, to double and triple check with all the people we had hired. We needed to make sure everyone had the correct date and time, and go over our wishes again with the caterer, florist, DJ, Justice of the Peace, and photographer, all before

Margaret arrived.

During another phone call, she reminded us that she was baking our wedding cake. It would be chocolate, of course, with stiff, white royal icing. She suggested decorating it with dark red and delicate pink icing rosebuds, with leaves in pale green icing. On its pedestal surrounding the cake, she wanted to use pink and red rose petals from her garden.

Tom had put his phone on speaker, so I could hear her description. I agreed immediately. It sounded so pretty, and having already sampled some of her cooking and baking, I was sure it would be delicious.

Tom was in charge of renting a suit. We were debating whether he should wear a tuxedo. I thought a tux might be too formal for an outdoor wedding with a bride who had been married before, and was not going to be wearing a traditional white gown. Tom wanted to do things right though, and he thought wearing a "monkey suit" was the right thing to do.

"Look, Suzanna. I'll ask Margaret's opinion. If she says to go with the tux, will you be okay with that?"

"Of course. Just make sure it's what *you* want."

He pulled me into his arms. "I already have what I want."

# CHAPTER 32

❦

BY AUGUST 16, TOM WAS fully recovered and back on his usual schedule of activities. Margaret's plane was due to arrive at eleven a.m., and Tom and I picked her up at the Atlanta airport in her Jeep. The plane was slightly late, and by the time it landed, I was having a hard time sitting still. Tom did his best to calm me, but I was too nervous to relax.

At last, the plane landed and passengers began to trickle into the gate area. We stood as close as possible to the door, so she would see us immediately, though it would have made little difference if we were at the back of the crowd. Tom towered over most of the people waiting to welcome their friends and family.

At least thirty people exited the plane before Tom stepped forward, pulling me with him. He dropped my hand to hug a tiny, stylishly dressed woman carrying a gigantic zippered tote. His exuberant bear hug left her feet dangling in mid-air, but she seemed not to mind. She was too busy hugging and kissing him, and then telling him to put her down so she could meet me.

Tom obeyed and grabbed my hand again. Margaret looked me up and down, while I stood transfixed, not knowing what to say. I could feel my face beginning to warm.

"Mrs. Buckley, I've been looking..."

"No, dear. I'm Margaret." She looked up at Tom. "Yes, she'll do." She hugged me, took my arm, and pulled me with her toward the down escalator. "I'm so glad to finally meet you. Now, tell me all about what you two have been up to. You should know, you can't keep anything a secret in this town. I've had calls from at least seven people telling me about what happened to Colleen, and Tom cracking his head. I've never known him to trip and fall in the forest. I want to know everything that's happened from your perspective."

"Now?"

"Well, I guess I can wait until we're in the Jeep."

Tom retrieved her bags from the luggage carousel, and went to bring the Jeep around. From the depths of her tote, a cell phone rang. She dragged it out, and looked at the screen. "Oh, excuse me, dear. That's my sister Gladys calling. She has an uncanny ability to call me at the most inopportune times."

She punched the answer button. "Hi, Gladys. Yes, the plane just landed. The flight was fine." Pause. "Tom looks great." Pause. "Suzanna's beautiful. I'll bring her to meet you soon. I've got to go now. Tom's getting the Jeep. I'll call you later."

Tom arrived and I helped him load Margaret's bags into the back of the Jeep. In minutes, we were headed back to Blue Ridge, Margaret sitting in the front passenger seat, me in the rear.

Margaret kept up a monologue the whole way. She had had a wonderful visit with her daughter, the baby's delivery was easy, and the little girl was thriving. The baby's name was Margaret Josephine, in honor of both her grandmothers. She thought that was an awfully old-fashioned name for a baby born these days, but her daughter had insisted. Margaret had loved being with her daughter, but she knew it was time to come home. Too many nannies spoil the baby. My, how she had missed Blue Ridge, her friends, her own bed, and especially Tom. She could hardly wait to get to know me better.

Tom flashed me a grin over his shoulder. "Well, Margaret. If you'd let Suzanna get a word in edgewise, you could get started right away."

"Oh, my, Suzanna. I'm so sorry. I'm just so glad to be coming home, I can't contain my excitement. Tell me, how did you get on with my herb garden? Was it too hard? Tom told me you were not too thrilled at the prospect."

"I was scared, at the beginning, that I'd kill all your plants. I was sure I couldn't do it. But, Tom offered to consult, and your journal was so helpful. I learned so much from it that I began to feel more confident. I even bought two tomato plants. They're doing great. They've been covered with flowers, and I've already harvested what seems like hundreds of grape tomatoes. The beefsteaks are doing well too, and I've already had several big ones. They are delicious. What a difference from store-bought tomatoes!"

"And how are the herbs doing? And the roses?"

"The herbs are beautiful, and the roses have been blooming gorgeously all summer. I knew very little about gardening, and especially about herb gardening. Your journal has helped me in so many ways. I'm even cooking more confidently now too, thanks to Tom's help and your recipes and hints on how to use the herbs. And, I can't thank you enough for letting me live in your cabin. I love it. If it weren't for Tom, I never would have left it, until you came home, of course."

"Did your friend enjoy her stay?"

"Yes. She loved your cabin too. We had a great time. She's been traveling too much and working too hard lately, and the change of scene was good for her. You'll find a note of thanks from her waiting for you in the bedroom."

Tom pulled the Jeep into Margaret's driveway and handed her the keys. "Thanks for the use of the Jeep. It really came in handy. Now that you're home, we'll have to get another vehicle. Suzanna can choose whatever she wants."

This was news to me, but I smiled in anticipation. We had gotten used to having the Jeep as well as Tom's sports car. It would be very difficult to have only one vehicle, especially when Tom was away in Atlanta.

We let Margaret go into her cabin alone, while Tom and I unloaded her luggage. She came back out a few minutes later.

"Come on in with those bags. Just put them in the bedroom and I'll deal with them later. Suzanna, thank you so much for putting flowers in the bedroom, and for taking such good care of the cabin. Everything looks wonderfully clean and tidy. After you've helped Tom with the bags, please join me in the garden. I want to see how everything is."

We brought in her luggage, and then, worried she would find something wrong, I stepped down off the deck into the garden. Margaret was crouched over her herbs, touching each one with tender fingers.

She looked up as I approached. "Suzanna, you've done a magnificent job. Every herb is healthy and thriving. Thank you so much for your time and energy."

"I didn't do it alone. There were times when Sheila and your neighbor, Betty, had to fill in for me when I couldn't get here. And, Tom helped me, too. He's made me feel more confident in my abilities." I paused and took a deep breath. "He's told me so much about you. I know how much you've done for him. I wonder if he'd be the sensitive and loving man he is today without your influence."

"It was in his genes. His grandfather is also a fine man. But thank you. You've given me a lovely compliment." She stood, and put her arms around me. She barely came to my shoulder, and I had to bend down to hug her back. "Suzanna, I think you and I will get along just fine."

"I do, too."

Tom, who had been waiting for us on the deck, came down into the garden.

"Margaret, I'm goin' to have to take Suzanna away now, but you'll have lots of time to get to know each other. Your lunch and dinner are in the fridge, and we brought in a few staples. Enough to get you started, at least. Call us if you need anythin' else today. No need to go shoppin' until you've rested a bit. That's a long flight."

"Thanks, Tom. Go on, you two. I'll be fine. I want you to come to supper tomorrow evening. We've got to talk about the wedding cake I'm going to bake, and I want to hear about all your plans."

"Yes, ma'am." Tom swept us into a three-way hug, and we drove his sports car, which we had left in front of her house before we drove Margaret's Jeep to Atlanta, back home.

"How does she look to you, Tom? Does she look the same?"

"She looks older. I hadn't really noticed her agin' before. Of course, I was seein' her almost every day, so I probably wouldn't have noticed that yet. But, in every other way, she seems just the same."

He paused, and glanced over at me. "Do you like her? Of course, you've only just met her. I'll ask you again after we've been married for a while."

"Married for a while. I like the sound of that."

"Me too." He pulled into his driveway, and opened my door to help me out of the car.

"Welcome home, almost-Mrs. Wolf." He kissed me and hugged me tightly.

# CHAPTER 33

❧

SOMEHOW, WE MADE IT THROUGH the last two weeks before our wedding without any major disagreements or problems. It was a frantically busy time with unexpected last-minute details, and if Sheila and Margaret had not been there to give advice and help, we would have been in trouble.

We had invited about forty people, including Ellen, Sheila and Joe, Margaret, Tom's grandfather, our lawyers, Frankie and his wife, the two Billy's, several other friends of Tom's, and my brother, Ron, and his family, to a private, late morning ceremony in Margaret's garden, with a catered lunch to follow. Later that day, we were going to host a cake and champagne reception for about 150 guests in the same hall that had been the scene of the ill-fated square dance I had attended with Dan. When I hesitated, Tom promised me he would be on his best behavior this time. I believed him. He was still embarrassed about his actions that evening.

❧

A week before the ceremony was to take place,

Tom got a panicked phone call from Sheila just as we finished our breakfast. He put the phone on speaker.

"Hey, Sheila, what's up?"

"Tom, when was the last time you visited your grandfather?"

"Oh. Well, I guess I haven't gone over there in a while. Why do you ask?"

"He's been sick. In fact, he's still runnin' a low-grade temperature and I don't like the way he's strugglin' for breath. I've been bringin' him soup, and tryin' to keep him clean, but it's very hard for me to get over there every day and to stay with him longer than an hour or so. He needs someone right there, full-time, to care for him."

"Sheila, I'm so sorry. I've been selfish. But, what can I do? I can't be there as often as he needs either, and I don't want to ask Suzanna to help, though I know she would." He gripped my hand.

"You're right. She would, but the timin' is terrible for all of us. I want to get your permission to hire a live-in caretaker."

"Who can you get at such short notice? And, a better question, who would he tolerate?"

"There's a woman he used to see. She was married, so their relationship was platonic, or at least, I assume so. Anyway, her husband is dead now and her children are grown and livin' away from here, so I think she might agree to it. It would be a good thing for her financially and it's possible she still has feelin's for him. He still talks about her once in a while."

"Really? I had no idea of this relationship!"

I stood up and began to clear away our breakfast

dishes.

"He's old, Tom, but he's not dead yet!"

"Okay, okay. Will you speak to her?"

"Yes. I'm goin' to do it today. I just wanted to get your okay."

"What if she says no?"

"I don't think she will, but if she does, there's a nursin' agency we can contact. It would be much more expensive, of course."

"Yes, but don't worry about that. I can take care of the fees."

"Hopefully, you won't have to pay what an agency would charge. I'll let you know what she says. But, Tom, you need to get over there to visit him. Do it now, today, if you can, and bring Suzanna. I've just come from there. He wants to see you both."

"Okay. We'll go today."

He disconnected, and looked over at me. "Suzanna. I guess you heard all that."

"I heard. I'm so glad nothing's wrong with Matt. But, I'm sorry to hear your grandfather's not doing well." I rinsed the last dish, put it in the dishwasher, and dried my hands.

"I feel so bad. I've been neglectin' him, and I had no idea that he's been sick. You probably heard that she wants me to go over there today, and to take you with me. Are you up for that? The situation sounds pretty serious."

"Of course, Tom. Do you want to go now?" I came around the island to stand next to him.

He grabbed my hands and pulled me into his arms. "Yes, Suzanna, darlin'. Thank you for being you."

"Who else would I be, silly?" I knew what he meant, though, and my heart swelled with love. "I'll just be a minute. I need to put shoes on and grab my pocketbook. Why don't you wait for me in the Jeep?" We had a new-to-us, gently-used Jeep of our own, now.

❧

Five minutes later, we were driving on a gravel road I had not yet seen. "You haven't talked about your grandfather very much. Is that because you don't get along very well?"

"Probably. Our relationship is complicated. He wants me to be someone I'm not, and I can't get him to understand why I can't be that person."

"Sheila mentioned once that he wants you to remember the old ways, and you are uncomfortable with that. Is that part of it?"

"Yep. And he wants me to be more like Mike. Independent. Angry. A seeker after truth. Someone who puts himself out there as a leader, but not just that, as a crusader for justice for the Cherokee nation." He shook his head. "I'm not that guy."

"That's quite a burden to lay on someone's shoulders, especially a grandson. If he feels you haven't lived up to some idealized firebrand, do you feel that way too? Surely you're not ashamed of who you are!"

"Wow! How did we get into this conversation?"

"Tom, this is important. Please stop the car."

He looked at me, and shook his head, but he found a place to pull over and brought the car to a halt. He sat with his hands gripping the steering wheel, his head turned away from me, his long, dark hair a curtain that hid his face. If he was gazing out his side window, I knew he would be seeing something other than the landscape framed there.

"Tom, listen. There is no way any one person could live up to all those expectations. And, by the way, are you sure your grandfather really wants you to be all that? I know you looked up to your brother as a hero, and yes, he did some heroic deeds. But that was what he was trained for, and it's possible he wouldn't have chosen that path if he had been given a choice.

"You, on the other hand, did have choices. You were guided, at least in part, by Margaret Buckley, but you weren't compelled by her. You were an excellent student and a star athlete in both high school and college. You could have chosen any number of careers and moved far away, but you chose to stay here, near your grandfather and Mike's widow and son, and become the fine man I fell in love with. You *are* a leader, but instead of leading with arrogance or bluster, you lead with kindness, integrity, empathy, and generosity."

He turned his head and looked at me. There were tears in his eyes. "Is that really how you see me?"

"Yes."

"I love you, Suzanna." He ran the back of his hand over his eyes and crushed me in his arms.

"I know." I hugged him back.

"How did you get to be so wise? Hopefully, it's in your genes." He smiled his sweet smile at me, and gently caressed my cheek. "Our kids will all be geniuses."

I laughed. "Come on, Tom. Let's go. I'm excited to meet your grandfather, at last. By the way, you've never told me his name."

He put the car in gear and pulled back onto the road. "His name in English is Charlie Runnin' Deer. He was a moccasin maker, renowned in these parts. But he couldn't make a livin' doin' only that, so he worked on the line in the Levi Jeans plant in Blue Ridge. He retired from there when the plant closed. He has arthritis in his hands now, but he still makes moccasins. It takes him much longer to finish a pair than it used to, but they're still in great demand."

"So, your mother was his daughter. Do you remember your grandmother?"

"No, she died before I was born."

"And, he's been alone all this time?"

"I thought so. I didn't know until today that he'd been in love with another woman for years. She's a widow now, but even if she's interested in the job, who knows if Gramps will accept her help. Whatever happens, when we come back from our honeymoon, we'll have to go visit him more often than I've been doin'."

"That sounds good."

He pulled into a small yard and stopped the car. "Well, we're here."

I looked out the window at the tiny cabin. "Is this where you lived when you were a child?"

"Yep. Not as fancy as my present house, but this is where I grew up. No electricity, no air conditioning or heat, no runnin' water, no indoor bathroom, but it was ours. I was never ashamed of it." We got out of the car. There were wildflowers blooming in the dooryard among the un-mown grasses.

"No reason you should be, Tom. Lots of people have less. Let's go inside. I need to order some moccasins, and I'm told a very good maker lives here."

"Suzanna, darlin'…" Tom kissed my forehead and crushed me again in a long embrace. At last, he took my hand and led me to the door.

"Gramps, it's Tom. I'm comin' in. I've brought you a visitor, Suzanna, the woman I've told you about."

There was a shuffling sound, and the door opened slightly. "Tom, come on in."

A large elderly man, stooped, but still handsome, stood by the door. He tottered slightly, and it looked as though he might fall. Tom grabbed his arm, and helped him back into his chair. There was a table near it, covered with pieces of leather, tools, and tiny beads, carefully sorted by color.

Tom lit an oil lamp and cleared a spot on the table to put it down. His grandfather was staring at me. His voice, when he spoke was low and breathy. "Tom, cover her hair so I can see her features."

Tom took off his baseball cap and set in on my head with its bill facing backward. He gathered my long red hair in his hands and gently pulled it behind my back.

"She has her grandmother's features, but not her colorin'."

I was startled. "Mr. Running Deer, did you

know my grandmother?"

"Call me Charlie. Yep, I knew her." He stopped, closed his eyes, and nodded slowly. "I knew her. I thought I was in love with her." He stopped again, and looked at Tom. "Tom showed me your picture of her when she was young. He also told me your story about the men on horseback who came to her farm to trade with her father."

I sat transfixed, straining to hear his halting speech.

"I was the leader of that party, the one who stared at your grandmother. I lied to your great-grandfather when I said she looked like my sister. She did not look like my sister. My sister was ugly. Your grandmother was beautiful."

Could this be true? "Did you know her well? Did you talk with her?"

"No. We didn't talk much with white people. We traded with 'em, sometimes worked for 'em, but we weren't invited to talk to young white girls."

"Oh. Charlie, I'm so sorry."

"That was just the way it was. It's a little better now, but there are still plenty of poor, uneducated Cherokee, especially the little kids on the Boundary and the old ones, who have very little contact with whites."

"I don't understand. If you didn't really know her, why did you think you were in love with her?"

"I saw her grow up. I used to watch out for her, though always from the proper distance. She was special. I wanted to marry her, but I knew that was only a dream. Did you know she taught school for a year before she married?"

"No! What did she teach?"

"What they used to call the three Rs: readin', 'ritin', and 'rithmetic. It was a one-room schoolhouse. There was another teacher for the older kids, and your grandmother was in charge of the younger ones. She used to take 'em outside on warm days. Sometimes I stopped in the woods to watch her, if I was huntin' or trappin' nearby."

"You said she only taught school for one year?"

"Yep. That summer, the Methodist preacher's son, who was a few years older than me, came to visit him. The preacher was old by then, and he wasn't preachin' anymore, but he still did weddin's and funerals. Your grandmother's people were Methodist, and I guess she met him at church."

"Was the preacher's son my grandfather?"

"Yep, and not long after that, they married and moved away. I never saw her again, but her image has stayed in my heart. I am proud that she remembered me."

"Charlie, thank you for telling me this. She claimed to be one-eighth Cherokee, but I don't know if she was right. Tom and I have been trying to find out more about her family, but we haven't been very successful. Do you know whether she had Cherokee ancestors?"

Charlie stared at me in silence. I reached for Tom's hand.

"Gramps, are you tired? Do you want to lie down? Can we fix some food for you?"

"No, I am not tired, and I don't need nuthin' to eat. I'm rememberin'."

He sat without speaking for several more

minutes. Finally, he nodded. "There was a story I heard. My great-grandfather told it to his son, and the story was passed on in that way. This is the way it was told to me.

"There was a young white man who loved a Cherokee maiden. She was promised to the Chieftain's son, but he was killed by the soldiers who came to round up the People. The soldiers killed men, women, and children alike. They burned and looted our villages, destroyed our farms, and tore down our schools and businesses. They forced some of the People to leave our lands, and made 'em travel far away to the west on the Trail of Tears.

"The young white man wanted to save his lover and her family from this end, but her village was destroyed and they were gone. He wandered in the forest for days hopin' to find her until, finally, her little sister found him and brought him back to the hidden place where her family had sheltered.

"They nursed him and saved his life. In time, they allowed their daughter to marry him. Though he was shunned by his white family, he and his wife were happy together, and had many children."

"Charlie, do you know their names?"

"The young white man was called Jacob Smith and his Cherokee wife was called Rose. That was her English name. She was named for the wild white rose that blooms in the forest. Accordin' to the story I heard, they had one daughter whose name was Rose Smith. All the other children were sons."

Tom and I looked at each other in amazement.

"Charlie, that was my grandmother's name, and it's mine too. I was always called Suzanna Smith-Walker to avoid confusion with my grandmother, but my first name is Rose, and so was my mother's."

"Gramps, I think that means Suzanna is descended from that first Cherokee Rose."

Charlie nodded.

Tom looked at me with amazement. "The answer was here all the time. You *are* part Cherokee. Yes, only a small part, but you wanted to know if you had the right to honor a Cherokee ancestor of your own. It looks like you do." He squeezed my hands, and folded me gently into his arms.

"Gramps, thank you." Tom kissed my temple and dropped his arms, but held onto one of my hands. "I know you've been disappointed in me. I'm not Mike, and I can't be like him. And, I can't be the leader of our people you'd like me to be. I can only be who I am, but I can promise you this, I will stay in touch with our tribal leaders, learn and remember the 'old ways' you cherish, and teach 'em to our children."

"Tom, that is good. It is enough."

Tom helped his grandfather with a few household chores and personal needs. Mostly, I stayed out of the way, only helping when I felt it was proper for me to do so. Finally, we were ready to leave.

I approached Charlie and took one of his hands in mine. "Thank you, Charlie. You have given me a precious gift today. If you are able, will you come to our wedding ceremony?"

He looked deeply into my eyes and squeezed my hand. "I will try. In case I cannot, I will give you my blessin' now."

Tom came closer and took his other hand. Charlie spoke, looking from me to Tom and back again. "Suzanna, Tom, I grant you my blessin'. I see for you a long, happy life together, with many children. You will have sorrows and disappointments as all people do, but you will overcome 'em and prosper."

I blinked back tears. "Charlie, thank you. I know my grandmother would be glad."

# CHAPTER 34

ℭ

THE DAY BEFORE OUR WEDDING, I waited excitedly to hear from my brother, Ron, that he and his wife, Cindy, and their two boys had landed safely in Atlanta. They waited in the airport for Ellen, whose flight from New York came in shortly after theirs, and then they shared a rental car, arriving in Blue Ridge just before noon. They were staying in the same hotel, and after they checked in and freshened up, Tom and I met them for lunch at The Elms. It was so good to have my little family here for our wedding.

After the children's dessert came, Ron and I stepped away for a few minutes alone. He looked much the same as when I had seen him last, now several years ago. At 34, he still had most of his hair, but I could see the beginnings of a paunch. He was living the good life. I made a mental note to ask Cindy about his diet and exercise regimen, if there was one, before I spoke with him directly about it.

"What do you think of Tom?"

"Well, on very short acquaintance, he seems great. He's certainly big and strong. I hope he'll be good to you. He promised me he would be."

"You don't have to worry. He's the best man I know besides you. I love him, so much more than I can say."

When Tom and I met Ron and his family at the restaurant, the two men had held back for a moment, sizing each other up. Then, to my relief, they stepped forward to shake hands, and that had quickly morphed into a bear hug. I had been holding my breath, and let it out when they began pounding each other's backs.

"Ron, somehow, when I was in Manhattan, it seemed it was a long way to Houston. It's still a long way from Georgia, but we need to make a pact to visit each other much more often. Okay?"

He hugged me and kissed me on the cheek. "Yep, sister dear. I promise!"

❦

Ellen, Sheila, Margaret, and I went to Billy's BBQ for my "bachelorette" dinner last night. When the evening was over, I went home with Margaret and spent the night with her in her cabin. We had become close since she returned from California, and I was happy to spend my last night as a single woman sharing a double bed with Tom's surrogate mother.

The weather cooperated. Our wedding day was sunny, but not too hot. Early that morning, Sheila arrived to help Margaret fix us a light breakfast. She pulled me aside for a moment. "Suzanna, Gramps is feelin' so much better, he's plannin' to come to your weddin' today. In fact, he seems to be doin' great. I came in unannounced yesterday to bring him some soup I'd made, and found him and his new companion huggin' each other. I don't know what else they've been gettin' up to, but the change in him is amazin'."

"He seems happy, then?"

"Yep. They were sittin' together holdin' hands when I left."

"Wow! I'm so glad, Sheila. At least for now, Tom and I can go away without having to worry about him so much."

We took turns in the shower, and clustered around the big mirror on the dresser to apply makeup and fix our hair. At last, we stepped into our shoes and Margaret and Sheila put on their dresses. They were in different print fabrics and styles, but the colors in both dresses coordinated with mine.

When they were ready, they took my gown from the closet and slipped it over my head. I had a panicked moment as it fell over my shoulders, wondering if it would still fit after our decadent evening at Billy's. To my relief, it did.

While Sheila zipped the zipper, Margaret fussed with the rosebud wreath in my hair. They had a hard time accomplishing these tasks because we were laughing so hard. When they stepped away, satisfied at last, I led them onto the back deck, and with the gorgeous mountain view in the background, took a selfie of the three of us.

Ellen arrived next, followed by the florist, the caterer, the photographer, the DJ, and their various helpers. The Justice of the Peace appeared a few minutes later.

We four women sat on the deck and watched as one side of the backyard was transformed into a wedding chapel, complete with a lectern, a flower-covered archway, white plastic folding chairs set up in rows with a white runner down the middle aisle, and speakers for the music. Across the lawn, a large, white tent went up, filled with buffet-style food service on one whole side of the tent. Opposite that, long tables were covered with white tablecloths and set with silver-rimmed white china, crystal glassware, and silverware patterned with rosebuds. Above each place setting, a single pink rosebud lay. White folding chairs for our forty guests encircled the tables.

At ten-thirty, Sheila, who had volunteered to be our lookout, shooed me inside. The groom had arrived with his best man, the Wall Street guru whom I was looking forward to meeting; his grandfather with his new companion; and our ring bearer, a very excited Matt.

Ellen came inside with me, and we embraced. We were crying a little, and trying not to smear our mascara. "I hope you understand about not being my Matron of Honor this time." I said. "I couldn't choose between you, Sheila, and Margaret, but I'll be living in very close proximity to them, and you did this once already…"

"Suzi, of course I understand. You are absolutely doing the right thing, and I'm so happy for you. You and Tom are amazing together. Next time I visit, you'll probably be pregnant. Are you sure that's what you want? I know that's what Tom wants."

"I'm absolutely sure. I can't wait to have Tom's

children. We even have names picked out."

"You're kidding!"

"No. If we have a boy first, his name will be William, for my father, and Charles, for Tom's grandfather. Our first girl will be Margaret, for Tom's Margaret, and Jeanine, for my mother. We'll call them Will and Maggie."

"You two are amazing! I wish your grandmother was still alive to witness your happiness today."

"Me too…" In contrast to my first wedding day, I was relaxed, and so happy that I felt almost giddy. I did wish my Grandma Rose was here to help me celebrate, but as always, I felt her presence and love. She was watching over me, and that was enough.

☾

Tom and his best man escorted Tom's grandfather, his companion, and my brother's family, to seats in the first row of chairs, and took their places at the lectern. Then, almost before I realized it, the music began to swell. The florist handed us our bouquets, and first Ellen, then Margaret, and then Sheila, holding Matt's hand, stepped down from the deck and slowly moved up the white runner toward the lectern.

At last, it was my turn. As I appeared on the deck, Tom's serious face was transformed by his sweetest smile. Ron, waiting for me at the foot of the deck steps, took my arm and escorted me up the runner toward Tom, so handsome in his tuxedo.

Ron stopped several feet from the lectern,

kissed me on the cheek, and stepped back. I continued on, my shoes hurting me. I ignored them, until, three steps from Tom, I tripped. He had been standing immobile, but now he moved quickly. He gripped my upper arms to steady me. Predictably, they began to tingle.

I felt my face turn hot with embarrassment. His eyes lit up with mischievous laughter, and grinning, he turned to the crowd. "Well, folks, this is how it all began. She tripped on the steps to my porch on the first day we met."

Everyone laughed. I laughed too, shaking my head and shrugging elaborately. "If I'd had any sense at all, I never would have bought these silly shoes. But they're so gorgeous..."

There was more laughter, and we waited until it stilled. Then, I put my hand in his, and we faced the Justice as she began the service. When it was time to recite our vows, Matt, who had managed, so far, to stand quietly beside his Uncle Tom, reached into his pocket, exactly the way we had rehearsed, and handed Tom two rings. Tom picked him up and we each hugged and kissed him, before putting him down so he could run to his mother. Tom handed me the ring intended for him, and we turned to face each other, holding each other's left hands.

We began in unison: "I," we each said our names, me first, then Tom, "pledge to you this day my everlasting love. I promise to help you in every way I can to be happy and fulfilled, to keep you secure in the knowledge that, whatever might happen, I will never forsake you, and to help you bring up our children in a safe and happy home. With this pledge, I give you a token of my love. This ring, that I place on your finger today, is a symbol of the eternal circle of life, and my promise that my love for you will endure forever."

Tom slipped my ring onto my finger, and I placed his ring on his. The electricity between us, always present, but usually masked when we were in public, sparked and sizzled.

When the Justice intoned "I now pronounce you husband and wife," I looked up at my husband with all the love in my heart. I saw my answer in his eyes.

We clung together, our lips seeking and finding succor even before the Justice said, "You may now kiss the bride."

❧

Our photographer captured that moment, and so many more: the handsome groom and the lovely bride with eyes only for each other as they walked hand in hand back down the white runner and paused only to embrace Tom's grandfather and my brother and his family, the small ring bearer hugging his Uncle and his new Aunt around their legs, the bride being mobbed by the three women she loved best, the groom being congratulated by his best man and envious friends, the bride and groom cutting the beautiful rose covered wedding cake and feeding it to each other without mishap, the toasts by the matrons of honor and the groom's best man, the family and friends gathered under the tent for the wedding luncheon, and finally, the bride and groom in their going-away-on-their-honeymoon outfits, she wearing a sundress in the same pale aqua as her wedding dress, and more sensible shoes, and he wearing shorts, T-shirt, and sandals. His T-shirt read "Just Married to Her, with an arrow," a present from his best man, Ian O'Connor.

We were flying to New York, and then to Aruba, but not until after the cake and champagne reception at the dance hall. We arrived to the sound of music played by our DJ, who had moved his equipment from Margaret's backyard to the hall. He introduced us to our guests with great fanfare and we danced the first dance alone together. Then Tom danced in succession with Margaret, Sheila, and Ellen, while I danced first with Ron, then Ian, and finally with a beaming Matt.

Holding Matt between us, we danced one last dance. Tom took the microphone from the DJ and toasted our friends and neighbors. We toasted each other and kissed to applause, hoots, and whistles. "Get a room" somebody yelled.

"That's just what we're goin' to do," Tom yelled back. "We'll see y'all again in two weeks!"

I tossed my bouquet to Sheila, and we made our escape. Ellen was waiting in the limo we were sharing with her for the ride to the Atlanta airport. Our luggage was in the trunk, and we were ready to go.

"Well, Mrs. Wolf. That was fantastic. I had a great time, which is good, because that's the last weddin' I'll ever have." He kissed me while Ellen made a show of averting her eyes. "Yikes, get a room!"

❦

When we landed in New York, we said a reluctant good-bye to Ellen, who was going back to her upstate home. Tom and I were only staying in New York for a few days, so I could show him my Manhattan and finalize the sale of my condo to Bill, the young architect who had been my tenant.

While we were in the City, we walked the High Line from south to north, visited both the Metropolitan Museum of Art and the Museum of Natural History, had lunch at my favorite pizza place, and attended a Broadway show. When we checked out of our hotel, Tom conceded that Manhattan might not be as awful as he had thought, but he drew the line at moving there. I was fine with that.

Our ten days in Aruba were completely indulgent. We spent most of the time in bed. We became quite familiar with the room service menu, because whenever we ventured out to the beach or pool, if we looked too deeply into each other's eyes, we had to make a mad dash back to our room. It was easier just to stay there. My body was humming all the time, my hormones on high alert for Tom's slightest touch.

Of course, I knew we would fall back to earth again after we arrived home, but I had never been happier, and Tom demonstrated his joy in a thousand ways.

❦

When our plane touched down in Atlanta,

Margaret was there with her Jeep to pick us up. Laughing, she wisely insisted we sit together in the back seat.

She chuckled. "You two are shameless. You have sex written all over you. I'm not going to be the one to make you sit apart!" She started the engine and put it in gear. "You still have a couple of days before you go back to work, Tom. You might as well make the most of them. I promise not to peek if you get feisty back there."

Margaret was right. We were clinging together in a desperate embrace even before she drove out of the airport. It had been at least eight hours since we last made love!

She took us directly home, and waited as we unloaded our luggage. "Have fun, kids. I won't bother you until next week." And with that, she drove away.

Leaving the bags in the driveway, Tom grabbed my hand and pulled me to the door. As soon as he unlocked it and pushed it open, he scooped me up into his arms and carried me across the threshold. "Welcome home, Mrs. Wolf."

"Tom, have I told you yet today how much I love you?"

"No, but you can show me as soon as I bring in our luggage. Okay?"

"Okay." And, a few minutes later, I did.

# SEVERAL YEARS LATER

&

"MOMMY? MOMMY!" THE SCREEN DOOR slammed, and four-year-old Will ran into the kitchen, trailed by his three-year-old sister, Maggie. "Daddy's home, and he's got a great big box!"

"Really? Did he say what's in it?"

"No! He wouldn't tell me." Will's face crumpled for a second, then brightened. "Don'tcha wanna see what he's got?"

"I wanna see!" Maggie copied Will in almost everything.

I smiled as I dried my hands on the tea towel draped over the oven door handle. "Okay, let's go see whether Daddy needs some help." I reached down to pick up Maggie, whose thumb was in her mouth. I gently pulled it out and kissed her lips. She grinned.

I was just finishing my eighth month of pregnancy. It was goin' be twins this time. I knew I probably should not be picking up Maggie, but I was doing a lot of things I probably should not be doing. I was big and unwieldy, and unable to sit still for very long. In my defense, there was plenty to do, and I liked to keep busy. Our housekeeper came in three times a week now, but still... there was plenty to do.

Carrying Maggie, and with Will pulling my other hand, I waddled outside onto the front porch. Tom was headed toward the barn, and sure enough, he was carrying a large box. As soon as he saw us, he put it down and came to gather us into a big hug, his lips lingering on mine. "Suzanna, you shouldn't be carryin' Maggie. Let me take her."

Maggie put up her chubby little arms and he lifted her high over his head. She shrieked and giggled until Will said, "Hey, no fair. Isn't it my turn yet?"

Tom set Maggie down and lifted Will. "You're gettin' too big for this. We'll have to invent a new game."

I never tired of watching Tom with our children. He was an expert at inventing games, playing with them and their cousin Matt whenever he could spare the time. Matt was five years older than Will, but he loved his little cousins and adored Tom. It was lonely being an only child, and Tom and I made sure that Matt and his mother, Sheila, were included in our family activities as often as possible.

"So, Tom, what's in the box?"

"It's a surprise for somebody who's goin' to have a birthday soon. Do we know anyone who's goin' to celebrate a birthday next week?"

Will was jumping up and down. "Me! Me!"

Tom made a show of looking around to see who

was shouting. "Oh, Will. Is it you?"

"Yes, Daddy! I'm goin' to be five!"

"You're goin' to be five? That's a pretty big number. But you know, if I tell you what's in the box now, you won't be surprised on your birthday. Don't worry, you'll find out what it is then. Okay, so I'm goin' to put that box in the barn, and then I'm comin' inside. Why don't y'all wait for me in there?"

I led the kids back into the house and perched on a barstool next to the kitchen island. I was feeling tired, and standing was as uncomfortable as sitting too long.

The children waited by the front door, as patiently as they could, for Tom to come back.

When he reappeared, he kissed me again. "How are you feeling?"

"Pregnant. Really, really pregnant." I looked up at him. "But I'm feeling pretty good, all things considered."

He leaned down to kiss me thoroughly, reluctantly pulled back, and gently caressed my cheek. He looked around at the children, impatiently waiting for his attention.

"Okay, I'm goin' to go take off my shoes and put on my boots. Anybody want to come help me?"

They followed him like ducklings into our bedroom. I smiled when I heard his deep voice and their answering treble laughter.

When they emerged, we all trooped out to the barn to feed our animals. Our supper waited in the oven.

A few weeks ago, when helping him with the chores became too much for me, he brought a patio chair into the barn for me and insisted that I sit in it. From my seat, I could see what everybody was doing without participating physically. Next to me, there was a child-sized chair for Maggie. She was too little to help much, though she did have specific jobs, mostly cleaning tack. Will was allowed to help Tom brush and groom the horses, but Tom did all the heavy lifting and the mucking out.

To make the chores more appealing to the children, Tom and I had devised a guessing game with questions about our animals' food, habits, riding tack, grooming equipment, and anything else we could think of. It was for Will's and Maggie's benefit, but Tom and I had the most fun. The horses nickered and "danced" in response to our laughter.

Next, Tom fed and watered the goats, then the pigs, and finally, the chickens. His human audience was as loud as the animal one. When he finished, we went back to the house and washed up for supper.

Tom settled me into a dining room armchair, and took over serving our meal. Maggie was next to me in her booster seat, and Will sat across from me, next to Tom. Though I had learned a great deal about cooking from Margaret and Tom, he was a much better cook than I was. He had an intuitive ability to know which ingredients would taste well together and was always trying new dishes of his own devising. Neither I, nor our kids, were picky eaters, so we were Tom's willing, and usually appreciative, guinea pigs.

❦

After dinner, Tom walked me over to the couch, handed me my book, and sat beside me. He kissed me and held me tightly for a moment.

"Don't move until I call you. I'll bathe the kids and get 'em into their PJs, and then you and I can read to 'em." He kissed me again, then smoothed my hair back from my forehead, and tucked an errant strand behind my ear. He gently rubbed my belly, then sat gazing at me for a long moment, his love reflected in his eyes. These days, he was reluctant to let me out of his sight when he was at home. I smiled at him and shooed him away.

We usually got the children ready for bed together, but my increasing bulk and tiredness kept me from helping as much as I wanted to. I was looking forward to my scheduled delivery date in two weeks.

These little ones were doing well, but Maggie's birth had been difficult, and I had lost two babies, each one at the beginning of the second trimester, before this successful pregnancy. My obstetrician wanted to take the twins by C-section before I went into labor. He also warned us to consider very carefully whether I should risk future pregnancies.

Tom and I had discussed this at length. He offered to have a vasectomy, but we knew of a couple who became pregnant despite the husband's procedure. We finally decided to have the doctor tie my tubes during the C-section, when performing a tubal ligation was a relatively safe and convenient operation.

Lately, Margaret visited us almost every day for a few hours, so I could rest. As soon as we needed her, she was prepared to move to our house to take care of Will and Maggie. She planned to stay for about three weeks, and longer, if we needed her. We had already prepared our guest room for her, and two weeks ago, she had packed a small suitcase with clothing for several days, and left it in "her" room.

❦

"Suzanna, we need you. These sleepyheads are insistin' they need to hear you read a story to 'em."

I lumbered to my feet and waddled into Will's bedroom. Tom was sitting on the bed with Maggie in his lap. I eased myself into the padded rocking chair next to the bed, and reached for *Goodnight Moon*. It was the children's favorite, and either Tom or I had to read it to them every night.

I smiled at them, and began to read.

❦

Later, after the children had fallen asleep, Tom and I sat on the couch, just holding each other. I had been cramping a little since supper, but I thought it was only Braxton-Hicks contractions, false labor. Suddenly, my water broke, and the cramps turned into pain.

Tom, steady as always, called Margaret first. She promised to be there in five minutes, though we knew we probably could expect her in less time. She was a safe driver. She knew these mountain roads well, but she liked speed.

Next, he called Sheila. She was on shift at the hospital tonight, and promised to get everything ready for our arrival.

Tom scooped me up in his arms, and carried me out to our Jeep. He hurried back to the house to wait for Margaret and two minutes later, she roared in. Tom hugged her briefly, and ran back to join me.

"Margaret says, good luck, and she loves you." He grabbed my hand and squeezed it before pulling out onto the road. "Are you okay?"

"I will be, though right now, I don't think I can talk." A small moan escaped me, and Tom clutched my knee.

"You don't have to talk. I'll just get you to the hospital as soon as I can."

"I love you, Tom."

"I guess you do. You'd have to love me an awful lot to go through all these pregnancies. I can't even express what you mean to me. You're the bravest person I know. 'I love you' doesn't come close to coverin' it."

"It will do for now!" I moaned again, louder this time.

Eventually we arrived. Though it was only about a fifteen-minute drive from Tom's house to the hospital, it seemed like an eternity.

Sheila, my doctor, and several nurses were waiting for me, and whisked me into a prep room. Minutes later, Tom joined me, and walked with me, clutching my hand, as Sheila and an orderly wheeled my gurney toward the operating room.

Tom and Sheila had to leave me at the door. She squeezed my hand and blew me a kiss. Tom brushed my lips with his and promised to be with me as soon as possible. I knew he and Sheila would wait together.

That was my last thought, as strong hands lifted me onto the operating table. Everything was white, then black.

### ❧

My eyelids were heavy. I knew Tom was near. I could hear his voice. I reached for him, but discovered I was alone in the bed. Where was I? Then I remembered.

I must have made some sort of noise. "She's awake, I think." Tom grabbed my hand. "Suzanna!" His lips brushed mine. "Have I told you yet today how much I love you?"

I finally managed to open my eyes partway, and tried to focus on Tom. I shook my head. My voice was rusty. "Tom, my babies?"

"They're fine. We have another beautiful little girl and handsome boy. They're in an incubator for now, because they're still pretty small, and they need to grow a bit before they can come home."

"And Will... Maggie?"

"They're fine too. I spoke with Margaret this mornin'. She's feedin' 'em their breakfast right now."

"It's morning? Have you been here all night?"

"Yep, and yep, of course. I wasn't goin' anywhere with you in here!"

"Tom?"

"Yep?"

"You called Ron and Ellen?"

"Yep. They both send their love and congratulations."

"Okay, then. Tom?"

"Yes, darlin'?"

"Kiss me. Properly."

He groaned, and leaning closer, captured my mouth in exactly the way I wanted him to.

❦

Later that day, after my nurse helped me wash and walked me down to the nursery to see my babies, Tom came back with Margaret, Will, and Maggie. He took them first to the nursery to see the children's new sister and brother.

Next, he brought them to see me.

Margaret kissed my cheek and squeezed my hand. "I know it's hard in a hospital, but try to get some good rest. I'll see you at home tomorrow, and don't worry about Will and Maggie. We're getting along just fine." She squeezed my hand again and left the room.

Will and Maggie were wide-eyed. "Did you know we have a new brother and sister?" Will shook his head. "I didn't want another sister, but I'm sure glad to get a brother. He can't play with me yet, though. He's too little."

"Maggie," I asked. "Are you happy to have a little sister?" She nodded, her thumb creeping back into her mouth.

"Come on, kids." Tom smiled at me. "Say good-bye to Mommy now. She'll be home tomorrow and you can talk some more to her then, okay?" They waved and blew good-bye kisses. He turned them over to Margaret, who was going to take them on a picnic before driving them back home.

"Alone at last. How are you feelin'?"

"Relieved that the babies are actually here, and okay. I'm still amazed that we got through almost the whole pregnancy. I kept expecting the worst." I was trying hard not to break down in tears, but Tom knew better. He sat on the edge of my bed and carefully gathered me into his arms. Rocking me gently, we both shed tears, a mixture of grief for the babies we had lost and overwhelming love for the babies we had. We were incredibly lucky, and we knew it.

Finally, he kissed me with his usual passion, answered with my own, and we slowly replaced our tears with laughter.

"Okay, we needed that. But, I really meant, how are you feeling physically?"

"Oh. Well, awkward sums it up best. I'm not happy with the IV, my stomach is full of stitches, and I'm especially not happy to leave our babies in the hospital tomorrow. I can't believe they would send me home without them, but I have to trust that they know best."

"When the pediatrician examines 'em tomorrow, he may be able to tell us how long they need to stay here. But, we'll come visit 'em every day. In the meantime, let's talk about names."

"I thought we had agreed on Jacob Ian and Ellen Rose."

"Yep, I just wanted to make sure. Someone will probably visit you today with birth certificate forms."

"I'm ready."

"Oh, yeah? Me too!" And he kissed me again, and again…

☾

A week later, we brought the babies home. Jacob was over his jaundice, and they had each gained more than a pound.

For the next several weeks, it was busy in our house. Twin newborns are at least triple the work of one, and it took us a while to work out a reasonable schedule. I needed sleep and quiet to keep my milk flowing, which put most of the burden on Margaret, Sheila, and Tom. They were terrific, as I knew they would be, and I got moral support from Ellen, who was back in Mexico City, and Ron, who was, of course, in Houston.

Going somewhere, anywhere, with four children, two of whom were tiny babies, was a huge undertaking. Eventually, we got the hang of it, but as the little ones grew, it became both easier and more difficult. Almost everyone we encountered wanted to exclaim over the twins, and ask questions about them. It might have been worse if they had been identical, but there was no hiding the fact that they were twins.

☾

During the quiet times, I counted my blessings. Thanks, partly, to our unwanted notoriety, Tom's real estate business was booming. After Will was born, Tom had opened an office downtown in Blue Ridge. It was too distracting to run his business out of our home with a baby in the house.

Now, he had other realtors working for him, and he was planning to expand his reach by opening offices in other counties. The Governor had offered to appoint him to a permanent commission, but Tom decided not to accept it while our children were so young.

The Colleen Jenkins Scholarship Foundation was booming as well. In lieu of wedding presents, we had asked for donations to the new fund. We were amazed at the amount of money that was donated at that time, and contributions, some quite large, had continued to arrive.

Each year, we hosted a big party to help raise awareness of the need for qualified mental health practitioners, and to solicit donations to help educate them. Before our first gala, Tom and I were asked to appear on the local TV station to talk about the foundation, and that led to other opportunities to publicize it. The editor of the Blue Ridge newspaper asked me to write a column about it, which had been picked up by other papers.

This year's gala would be our sixth. It was, as always, timed to closely follow Blue Ridge High School's graduation ceremony, when we announced each year's scholarship winner. As they had for the past two years, both the scholarship presentation and the gala were going to be covered by both local and state media, including the regional affiliate of ABC-TV.

To my surprise, I had recently received a standing offer from our local TV station to do weekly feature stories whenever I wanted to start. I was both excited and daunted by the thought of what it would entail. Tom loved the idea, though, and slowly, I was beginning to believe I might really enjoy the work.

I realized how lucky I was. I had a loving husband whom I adored, and four beautiful, healthy children. I had my brother Ron and his family, and Margaret, Sheila, and Ellen as my friends, the three women I loved most in the world. And, as Tom's wife, I had the friendship of everyone who knew and loved him, a number that seemed, at times, to be legion.

Besides those blessings, I had something worthwhile to do beyond keeping Tom, and our children, healthy and happy. I loved running our Foundation, and the prospect of doing stories for and about our community, even though that would be sometime in the future, were the missing elements that provided the balance I had been afraid I might never find.

I believed Grandma Rose would be proud of us and what we were doing. I felt her love, still, all around me.

*❦*

Will's birthday party was postponed for a few weeks because of the twins' arrival. He was disappointed at having to wait so long, but he seemed to understand and accept the necessity of it.

Margaret and our housekeeper helped Tom and I keep the ten invited children from running amok. True to form, Tom was the adored ring leader and kept all the little boys enthralled. Will played the role of miniature host to perfection. He thanked all his friends for coming, and for the generous gifts they had brought. When the party was over, he stood at the door handing out party favors and waving good-bye.

Earlier that day, Will finally found out the contents of the box Tom had put into the barn. It was a blue bicycle with training wheels. Will was thrilled.

As soon as the cake and ice cream was gone, and the last child had been picked up, Tom escorted me into our bedroom and insisted I take a nap. He lingered a few moments with me, but when my eyes began to close, he tiptoed out.

*

Sometime later, Tom blew gently into my ear. I woke up from my nap with his hands gently cradling my face and his lips devouring mine. When, at last, he pulled back, he picked up a small, elegantly wrapped box from the night table, and handed it to me.

"What's this? It's not my birthday."

"That's okay. It's for you, anyway. Go on. Open it." His sweet smile lit his face.

Inside, on a delicate chain, was a gold and diamond pendant in the shape of a standing wolf, ears pricked forward, tail aloft.

"Oh, Tom. It's exquisite." I gazed up into his eyes with all the love in my heart. "I'll wear it always."

He took it from my hands, and fastened the clasp around my neck.

"I love you, Tom."

He pulled me into his arms, his lips closing passionately on mine. The electricity between us sizzled and, just as they had done throughout six generations, ever since Jacob Smith kissed his Cherokee Rose for the first time, the sparks of our love re-ignited a flame destined to burn forever.

# Acknowledgements

M Y HUSBAND AND I VISITED, and fell in love with, the town of Blue Ridge, county seat of Fannin County, Georgia, and the nearby hamlet of Dial. My heartthrob character, Tom, is right: Fannin County and other parts of northern Georgia are great tourist destinations with colorful history, beautiful scenery, excellent camping, fishing, and water sports, great accommodations and restaurants, and some of the friendliest and most helpful people I've ever met. Many thanks to **Danny Mashburn** of Blue Ridge's historic Baugh House, **Vanessa Pittman** and other librarians of the Blue Ridge Public Library, **Jane Newton** of the County Tax Assessor's Office, and **Lynn** of the Blue Ridge Chamber of Commerce, all of whom gave me genealogy help and advice, and suggestions for further research. Also, thanks to **Jimmy** of the **Dial General Store and Luncheonette**, who told us about the picnic area mentioned in this book.

Special thanks to **Linda Galloway Fitch**, friend and editor to **Dale Dyer**, Blue Ridge's and Fannin County's beloved historian, who treated us to a delicious dinner at a local restaurant, took us back to Dale's home, and patiently answered my many questions about Fannin County and Blue

Ridge. Their gift of friendship and hospitality to perfect strangers was heartwarming and very much appreciated.

To **Marcia Attard, Lucille Cazzetto, Dixie Dugan, Doreen Van Gjin, Randye Korte, Hetty** and **Zach Davies**, my sister **Judy Scott**, my daughters **Rachel McNaughton** and **Lisa Khavkin**, and my many supportive friends in the **Baby Boomers Book Club,** the **Florida Book Club,** and the **Birchwood at Spring Lake Book Club**, I can't thank you enough.

Without my family, immediate and extended, I would be nothing. Thank you for everything you are and do. I am so proud of all of you.

As always, **Larry Speciner** is my first reader, my knight in shining armor, my forever love, and somehow has managed to put up with me for *years*. "Thanks" is not a big enough word.

# OTHER BOOKS BY P.F. SPENCER

*The Other Side of the Door,*
*Doors of the Heart, Book 1*

# AUTHOR BIO

Author of *The Other Side of the Door, Doors of the Heart, Book 1,* P.F. Spencer has a BA in Environmental Journalism and published numerous freelance articles and features before exchanging science-based non-fiction for romantic fiction. She and her husband live in New York and Florida. This is her second *Doors of the Heart* novel.